SQUALL LINE

The Inland Seas Series - Book 1

GWYN MCNAMEE

Squall Line
by Gwyn McNamee © 2019

Cover Design: Michelle Johnson at Blue Sky Designs
Cover Models: Jonny James and Tiffany Marie
Photographer: Wander Aguiar
Editing: Proofing With Style

❀ Created with Vellum

The tempest within is often more dangerous than the one outside. Stand strong through the storm, and you will find your way to calm waters.

Acknowledgments

Thank you to my husband and daughter for always supporting me. I know I get crazy when I'm finishing a book, and this one was no exception.

To my amazing beta readers (and my super alpha reader Christy), thank you for always being brutally honest and for taking the time to read my early drafts.

Jacquelyn Burton and Catherine Horn Gianelloni - your expertise on all things maritime has been invaluable. Thank you for helping me assure these stories are as accurate as possible.

I couldn't have finished without the love and support of all my friends and family.

ONE

War

———

The barrel of the shotgun wavers slightly but remains pointed squarely at my chest.

Blood surges through my veins and roars in my ears. My hands squeeze around the grip of my .45.

Pull a fucking gun on me? This won't end well for you...

Staring down the business end of a damn shotgun was not on my to-do list today...or any day, for that matter. But in this profession, it was inevitable.

I can't do this type of work and expect everything to go smoothly all the time. After five years on the waters, hijacking ships and stealing cargo, it was bound to happen. Someone was going to fight back with more than a few lamely thrown punches eventually.

Beating someone into submission is just part of the job. Using steel is too.

But this—she—is unexpected.

Cargo ships don't usually have firearms on them, which makes hijacking them a fuck of a lot easier.

This time should have been the same...yet the reality is right in front of me.

My stomach churns slightly at having to point my gun at

my would-be assailant. But the tiny, redheaded pixie, who looks as pure and innocent as a fresh Wisconsin snowfall, seems rather fucking intent on blowing a hole in my chest.

What's a woman like her doing on a cargo ship in the middle of Lake Michigan?

The shotgun dips slightly. She struggles to regain control and re-center the barrel. That thing must weigh seven or eight pounds—a lot for a small thing like her to handle—and she's been holding her aim for almost three minutes.

This standoff won't last much longer. Rion will notice my radio silence and come looking for me. Either the pixie will give up, or she's in for a *big* surprise when he makes an appearance.

The warm breeze drifting through the open door to the bridge whips her wavy hair around her pale face in crimson swirls. Her green eyes narrow, and she flicks the tip of her tongue around her cupid's bow lips.

Jesus. Fucking. Christ.

Under any other circumstances, I might take her against the wall of the bridge and screw her until the sun goes down. Too bad she's a giant pain in the ass and the one thing standing between me and what I need.

She squares her shoulders and raises the gun slightly. "I said, drop your fucking gun."

Despite the shaking in her body, her command is strong and unwavering.

Too bad it's all a fucking act. She's scared shitless. And she should be.

I smirk, and a red flush creeps up her throat and across her lightly freckled cheeks. Yet, she stands her ground.

She has balls. I'll give her that. But the blush of her pale skin proves she isn't immune to my charms. That should make this easier.

Scare her or seduce her. Either way, I'm getting what I came for.

A single step brings me closer to her, and the damn gun. At this range, I'd be fucking toast.

"Sweetheart, you and I both know, there is no way in hell I am going to lower my weapon."

Her giving me orders might be adorable if we weren't in such a time crunch. We'll have hell to pay if the Marconis don't get their shipment tonight, and the incoming storm front is already threatening the job. Choppy waters and swells will make the trip to Chicago a real bitch once we get what we came for. The last thing we need is some princess wanna-be Annie Oakley trying to stop us.

She presses her lips together and clenches her jaw so hard, the muscle at the side tics.

Red has some attitude, that's for sure.

The shotgun repositions, and she makes sure it's aimed directly at my face this time.

Trying to intimidate me, little girl?

Another step forward and I'm close enough to catch a faint whiff of something floral—lilacs, maybe—and I shift my shoulders back and puff out my chest to provide the maximum effect.

If my gun isn't enough to intimidate her, maybe my size and proximity will.

She stumbles back a step, shaking her head and sending her red locks floating around her face. "Don't you fucking move, asshole."

Another command? Cute.

But she also just showed I'm a hundred percent right. It's all an act.

False bravado.

I stop my advance, but my smirk widens to a full-blown smile despite my best efforts against it.

A crack in my armor is never good, which is why smiles don't come often for me. In this profession, it's essential to assert dominance, to let people know *you* are in charge and won't back down, that you are unbreakable. Smiling shows you are human, and being human means weakness.

Weakness can't exist here. Not with her.

But, since the moment I stepped onto the bridge and found her with that shotgun pointed right at me, I haven't been able to keep the corner of my mouth from twisting up with just about everything she says.

That's dangerous—for me and her.

"For such a pretty little thing, you sure curse like the big boys." Having her bent over the captain's chair screaming four-letter words into the air while I plow into her briefly crosses my mind.

Too bad. Such a waste of a tight body.

She scowls, her eyes focusing on the barrel of my gun, currently pointed directly at her surprisingly ample chest.

I'd rather not shoot her, but if it means getting what I came for, then I'll do what I have to. She needs to know who's in charge here, and, despite what she may think, it isn't her.

Over her shoulder, through the open door, Rion silently climbs the stairs to the bridge.

I school my expression. Poor thing has no clue she's about to lose that false sense of power in her hands.

Sorry, Red.

"I'm not telling you again, drop your..."

Her words trail off the moment the barrel of Rion's gun touches the back of her head. Standing six foot five, his two-hundred-seventy-pound frame dwarfs her maybe five foot one, one hundred pounds.

God, she's tiny.

Everyone looks small next to Rion—even me—but next to pixie, he looks more like something from the Marvel Universe.

He grins in my direction.

I take another step toward her as I holster my gun. The situation is under control now. I won't be needing it again. My hand wraps around the barrel of her shotgun, and I tug it from her hands and set it on the console next to us. The desire to fight flashes across her face, but she's smart and lets her hands fall to her sides.

"Sorry, sweetheart. Valiant effort, though."

She glares at me, clenching her small, empty hands.

There's something else I would love to have those fists clenched around. Maybe in another place, another time.

I understand her seething rage. We came onto the ship with clear malcontent, but as long as she and the rest of the crew cooperate, we'll be on our way quickly and she can go on with her life, forgetting we ever existed.

The insurance will cover the cargo we take, and, more than likely, the owner of the vessel will file false losses anyway so they'll end up ahead. That's the way it always goes. No one has any integrity anymore. But in the end, it's a win-win for everyone. We get what we need for *Il Padrone*, plus whatever's in the safe, and the owner gets some extra cash for a few hours of inconvenience and some added paperwork.

Rion yanks her arms behind her back.

"Oww!" She looks over her shoulder at him while he secures her wrists with a zip tie. "What the fuck?"

When her eyes return to me, they blaze with the fire of a thousand suns.

"Sorry," I turn to look for the logbook on the bookcase behind me, "but you've already proven you're too ballsy for your own good. If you tell me what I need to know, this will be a lot quicker and a lot less painful for you."

Making threats and being willing to follow through are necessary evils in this job. Each and every one of us will do whatever's necessary—some, more easily than others. That includes getting rid of anyone in our way, but I'm not totally heartless. These people are just employees doing their jobs, trying to make a living. They don't deserve to get hurt or to die…as long as they don't do anything stupid. Then…all bets are off. The job and the guys come first and always will.

My radio crackles to life, and Cutter's voice cuts through the static. "Secured the deck and holds. We have six hands on deck. Offload started."

Good.

Recon indicated there would be a crew of seven; that means there isn't anyone lurking beneath us, calling for rescue or waiting for a chance to pounce on us as we offload the cargo.

"Bridge secure," I reply. "We have one. No sign of the captain, though."

I glance back at her, hoping she'll fill me in on where the man in charge might be. He must be with the crew Cutter and Elijah rounded up.

Anger glints in her eyes, and she squares her shoulders. "I won't tell you anything. When I get free, you'll pay for this."

The bravado in her voice is fake. We both know it, but I'll let her cling to the comfort her act of defiance holds for a while. It makes people feel better to talk back, to think they have any say or ability to control what's happening around them—even when it's all in their heads.

Rion covers his mouth to hide his laughter, and I chuckle to myself.

She glowers at him over her shoulder then focuses on me.

This girl is a piece of work.

It isn't often we find a woman on a cargo vessel. I can only think of one, and she was nothing like pixie over there. Suffice it to say, women working on cargo ships generally don't look like swimsuit models.

The tiny redhead, on the other hand, is every man's wet dream. At least, any man who likes redheads, and, God knows, I have a weakness for those of the ginger persuasion. Which means keeping my guard up is even more important. I can't let my dick get in the way of what needs to happen to get out of here safely with what we need.

Her forest-green eyes bore into me, and I have a sneaking

suspicion she can see into my soul—a terrifying prospect for someone like me. Someone who depends on people's fear to succeed.

She's ready for a fight and is just looking for an opportunity to get the upper hand again. I may not *want* to use that gun, but I will if I have to. There's too much at stake. And Rion, Elijah, and Cutter will pull the trigger before there's even time to consider it. She needs to know we're a real threat.

An unusual tightness forms in my chest, but I ignore it in favor of returning my attention to the bookcase.

A blue logbook sits on the second shelf, exactly where it should be. I grab it and carry it across the bridge to the captain's chair in front of the console, the metal floor creaking with every step. I drop onto the seat, and plush leather cradles me. I prop my feet up on the console and open the book across my thighs.

"Get your damn feet off the console."

I glance over.

Those damn eyes drill me again as she looks between my boots and my face, like a mother annoyed her kid has his feet on the coffee table.

Why does she care so much where I put my damn feet?

"Where is the captain?" I tap my boots against the console intentionally, letting little bits of dirt and who the hell knows what else drop off them onto the clean surface.

Tipping her chin up, she snarls. "Fuck you."

Her non-answer almost brings another smile, but I'm finished with games.

Whoever manages the logbook has impeccable penmanship. The names of the six crewmen appear below that of the captain. "Captain G.A. Albright, where is he?"

No women on the crew list.

So, who the fuck is she?

"And who are you?"

She presses her lips together until they're white. I radio to Cutter. "Bring me a member of the crew."

Her shoulders tense, and the fear finally begins to show in her eyes despite her best efforts to appear unaffected.

She gets points for that, at least.

"Roger that, Cap. Two minutes."

I raise an eyebrow, waiting for some verbal response from her, but she remains silent. "Still have nothing to say? That's okay, I'll get what I need from someone else in about two minutes." I flash her my best panty-dropping smile. "I always get what I need, from someone."

She clenches her jaw, clearly picking up the innuendo in my comment.

Good. I was laying it on fairly thick.

Footsteps on the metal stairs alert me to Cutter's arrival. He doesn't bother sneaking up here the way Rion did. He nudges a zip tied and terrified man into the room. Sweat beads the crewman's weather-beaten forehead and temples, and his eyes immediately fall on me, then move to Rion, and then the feisty redhead.

This guy will be easy. I'll have my answer in no time.

Cutter nods at me then disappears back down the stairs to help get what we came for loaded onto the boat.

"Thank you for joining us." I drop my boots to the floor, rise to my full height, and toss the logbook onto the chair. "I'm hoping you can answer a few questions for me."

His gaze immediately flicks to the pixie, and I don't miss the subtle shake of her head.

Now, this is interesting.

Men rarely look to women for permission or direction, especially on the water. Most are misogynist pigs who believe women belong barefoot, naked, and pregnant in the kitchen. In reality, women are probably better than ninety percent of men at seventy-five percent of the things men try to do. Most

8

men are too macho to ever publicly admit they look to women for guidance. That is doubly true for seamen.

"Don't look at her, look at me." I step up to him, putting my face, and my chest, mere inches from his own. "Where is the captain?"

For a flicker of a second, his eyes land on her. I follow his gaze. She shakes her head at him.

He quickly recovers, looking at me and shaking his head, but it is too late—I saw it and he knows.

"I…uh…I don't know, sir."

I step between him and pixie and force her back until she hits the wall. Her face barely comes to the middle of my chest. I look down at her, and she tilts her head up, rebellion in her stance and eyes. A glance over my shoulder at the crewman tells me I've hit a nerve.

His tense body and skin shining with sweat scream he doesn't want me anywhere near her, but his tied hands and Rion towering over him prevent him from making whatever move he's clearly considering.

I turn to face him, step to her side, and put my right hand on the butt of my gun. "Who is she?" I point at her with my free hand.

His eyes beg me to stop, to leave, to move away from the woman.

Curious. Is he afraid of the pixie or protecting her?

I grasp a strand of her silky red hair, twirling it around my finger.

"Get your stinking hands off me!"

She tries to yank it from my hold by moving her head, but I tug until she yelps. The crewman lunges forward, but Rion grabs his zip tied arms, jerking him backward.

"Leave her alone!" He struggles against Rion's grip.

Crews who have worked together for a long time are tight, often willing to defend each other, even if it means endangering their own lives. Maybe that is all this is, maybe they are romantically involved, or maybe he just has a death wish. Whatever it is, this guy is just itching to get shot.

He's lucky none of us have twitchy trigger fingers.

"Tell me what I want to know and I will." I tug on her hair gently again and bring it up to sniff it.

Sweet. Flowery. Almost like lilacs in summer bloom.

She tries to jerk away again, but I tighten my grip and meet the eyes of the crewman.

He huffs out a breath, frantically searching her face for direction. She shakes her head no.

"I'm sorry, Grace. I have to…"

Grace.

Finally, I have a name for the woman who is as beautiful as she is a pain in my ass.

"Darren, don't." Her voice finally cracks and shows signs of her distress.

"I'm sorry." He turns to face me fully, takes a deep breath, and shakes his head. "She *is* the captain."

What?

I recoil slightly, accidentally pulling her hair with me.

"Ow!" She jerks and yelps, leaning toward me to take the strain off her red tresses. "Watch it!"

She's the fucking captain?

I look down at her, meeting her determined gaze. I clamp my jaw shut, trying to hide my shock. "Captain G.A. Albright? Well, well, well, isn't this interesting."

A female captain?

I should have suspected, but it's just so…unbelievable.

Dad would roll over in his grave if he heard about this. He always said "women aren't made for the water." And, given what I've experienced in almost three decades on the Lakes, I know exactly why he thought that. How this tiny woman ran an entire freighter is beyond me, since most seamen would never see someone like her as an authority figure, but my respect for her just went through the roof.

Clearing my throat, I release her hair and take a step back. My eyes meet an astonished Rion's, and I return to the captain's chair. "Captain Albright, care to tell me what the *A* stands for?"

She sneers at me, and I'm sure she would have spit if she were close enough to hit me. "Fuck. You."

Under normal circumstances, I would have come back with some witty retort—told her I would love to, because a lot of girls actually respond to that asshole shit—but, I hold my tongue.

I nod to Rion, and he ushers her forward until she's standing directly in front of me.

"Well, Captain, if you would be so kind as to unlock the safe over there," I point to the large safe in the corner of the bridge, "we will be on our way."

Anything in that safe is icing on the cake for this job, and there's no way we're leaving without opening it.

"Over my dead body." She hisses the words at me, throwing them with a fury I would never expect from such a tiny woman.

"That can be arranged." I pull my gun from the holster and lay it across my lap, barrel pointed directly at her.

If that doesn't get her attention, nothing will.

My radio, and our only lifeline to Preacher back at the warehouse, crackles to life. "Cap, we got a problem."

Shit.

If Preacher thinks we have a problem, we definitely have one. He isn't one to sound the alarm unless the house is really and truly on fire. The man rarely leaves his cave full of toys, and his concern over the approaching storm front interfering with our equipment almost forced us to call off this job, but the Marconis wouldn't take no for an answer. This cargo had to come off before the ship reached the Milwaukee port.

I glance up at the darkening sky. A storm is usually great cover for a hijacking, but this one looks to be nasty.

Fuck. What else can go wrong?

"What is it?" I look to Rion while I wait for Preacher to relay the bad news. Rion just shrugs.

The radio crackles. "Coast Guard is on its way. We're going to have unwanted company."

"Fuck!" I slam my feet to the ground and crowd Grace until she backs into Rion and can't retreat any further. "How did you call the fucking Coast Guard?"

Preacher's jamming device prevents ships from calling over the radio for backup while still allowing us to communicate on our dedicated channel. The tech is top-of-the-line. It hasn't failed in five damn years. No way it failed now.

So, how the hell did she manage it?

Her glare pierces me, with a smug tilt of her lips.

Holy shit. Red was buying fucking time.

If I weren't so angry, I might actually be impressed.

"Distress beacon. Before you even got up to the bridge. I hope you enjoy prison, dickface."

"Shit!" I scrub my hands down my face and groan.

We can usually work our way on board and get everyone away from the bridge before they realize it's a hijacking and can activate the beacon. This one is smart. She knew something was off despite our ruse.

One final glance at the safe we will never have time to open now is all I get before I kick the captain's chair and storm toward the door. "Bring them to the deck."

The metal stairs creak under me, and I slam my way down them to the main deck where the offload continues. Cowering crewmembers from the ship help deposit the cargo they're supposed to be delivering to Milwaukee onto *our* boat.

If I hadn't been otherwise occupied on the bridge and had to drag Rion and Cutter away, this would have been done already with the help of the hauler's crew.

Elijah approaches, his brow drawn down. "What's the plan?"

I glance back at Rion wrestling Grace and Darren down the stairs. "You and Cutter take the *Destiny* with the cargo and hightail it out of here. Head to the cove. This time of day, it will be foggy as hell and with the storm rolling in, you can disappear there and lie low until you can make it back to the warehouse. Rion and I will leave on the *Calista* and meet up with you later."

He nods and takes off, yelling something to Cutter as he heads toward the starboard side of the ship, where the *Destiny* is anchored.

Turning to our captives, I meet Rion's gaze. A question darkens his eyes.

He knows as well as I do, the second we leave the deck and get far enough away for the jammer to stop working, Grace will be on the radio, telling the Coast Guard exactly what we look like and which direction we left in.

Our plans have been well and truly fucked. Board, tie up the crew, unload, and get the fuck out. It's worked flawlessly for years. By the time the Coast Guard finds them, we are long gone and safe.

Damn woman fucked up everything.

My throat burns as acid rises from my stomach.

I have to do it.

"You..." I point to Darren. He jerks slightly, and Rion shoves him toward me. "You are going to be left with the rest of the crew. We will try to call them off, but if the Coast Guard comes, you'll tell them nothing. The distress beacon was a mistake. Everything is fine. You know *nothing*. Do you understand me?"

He doesn't respond, just glances at Grace.

Grace snort-laughs. "What's to keep him, or me for that matter, from telling them everything we know?" The edge in her voice hangs in the air.

She doesn't grasp what's happening here.

What has to happen.

The words I have to say sit like rocks in my throat.

It has to be done, War. So, do it.

I swallow past the regret and unease and turn to her. "Because we are taking you with us."

"No!" Her knees wobble slightly, and her pale skin turns even more ashen.

Darren cries out. "No, take me instead!"

Gallant. But no.

"You do nothing for me. She, on the other hand, is an insurance policy. If we get away and get the cargo where it needs to go without interference, I will release her, unharmed, within forty-eight hours. If, on the other hand, you don't shut your trap and the Coast Guard finds us, I will kill her before I ever surrender or let her go. Do you understand me?"

My words cut through him like knives. His shoulders sag, and he nods, his entire body shaking and his lip quivering.

When my eyes connect with Rion's, the shock and sympathy there darken his brown eyes. He knows what it means for me to do this.

Fuck.

Lie. Steal. Maim. Destroy.

Do whatever it takes.

Except this.

I'm breaking the *only* rule. I'm taking a fucking hostage.

TWO

Grace

F orget the fact this bastard is a good-for-nothing, cock-sucking pirate, he's also the kind of guy Mom warned me to run from. Tall, muscular, and tattooed. The man now holding me hostage is trouble with a capital *T*.

Trouble.

Of course, I had pictured more the slam-me-against-the-wall-and-fuck-me-so-hard-I-can't-walk-tomorrow trouble, and not the pull-a-gun-and-hijack-my-cargo trouble.

How did I let this happen? Am I too naïve?

This *is* my first time as solo acting captain. Maritime school can't truly prepare you for something like this, and it isn't exactly something we normally have to worry about in the Great Lakes. During school and my required time on the water, I always had Dad or someone else to help guide me and make sure I wasn't fucking things up. Having the degree, the captain's license, and the required training doesn't seem to mean much in a situation like this.

I shouldn't even be here.

I'm basically an accountant, for fuck's sake, a number cruncher who runs the office, not a *true* captain. If I had my way, I wouldn't have even gone to maritime school. Getting licensed was just to appease Dad, to give him the peace of mind that one of his children would be able to take over the family business.

If he hadn't dropped dead last week, and if we wouldn't go bankrupt without this haul because Dad managed to dig us into a financial hole, I would be sitting in my office, sipping a cappuccino and handling the books for the business, instead of being held captive by Captain Fucking Swashbuckler and wondering how I could have been stupid enough to let terrorists of the sea board Dad's ship.

Pirates.

Fucking pirates.

This man is no Blackbeard, Long John Silver, or Captain Jack Sparrow. There are no peg legs, eye patches, or parrots. And I sure as hell don't have treasure chests overflowing with gold doubloons deep in the ship's hull.

All they're getting are a bunch of pallets full of boxes of machine parts that need to get to Milwaukee.

Why the hell would they want that?

In certain markets, I guess they have their value, but pieces of metal are certainly not worth risking prison time to steal— or to take someone hostage, for that matter.

We should have been safe out here.

These are the Great Lakes, not the damn coast of Somalia.

I had no reason to suspect anything nefarious. It's not like they were flying the Jolly Roger when we saw them and they requested assistance. Smoke billowed from the engine; we had to stop. I couldn't, in good conscience, float on by, waving wave and pretending I hadn't seen them in distress. There isn't any way any of us could have known it was a setup.

Right?

Maybe a more experienced captain would have sensed something off though. I put the entire crew at risk, not to mention my livelihood. All because of my damn bleeding heart.

At least I realized something was amiss early enough to set off the beacon.

Was there more I could have done?

Standing here on the deck, with stiff plastic cutting into the skin on my wrists while I try to work my way out of the zip tie confinement, I guess it does me little good to wonder what I could have done differently. At this point, it's moot.

Get your head in the game, Grace.

They're going to take me. And once I'm off this ship and in their hands, who knows what they will do.

Rape? Murder?

It's probably all on the table with these thugs.

The beast of a man who held a gun to my head and tied me up looks especially menacing. If any of these guys will hurt me, it's probably him.

Then again, the guy who was just talking to Cap a minute ago appeared clean-cut, yet the way he carried himself seemed more like he was straight out of prison, and the other guy, the man with the reflective aviator shades, has that calm confidence people with no conscience and no soul exude. And not being able to see his eyes only makes him more ominous. So maybe he's the real danger here.

Who am I kidding?

The *real danger* is the guy they call Cap.

He had the nerve to hijack *my* ship, threaten me with a gun, and *flirt* with me at the same time.

Asshole.

I twist my wrists and shift my hands, trying to loosen the bindings.

"Hey! Stop that! You'll only hurt yourself more if you keep trying." The big guy's hands swat at my wrists, halting my lame attempt at escape.

I would kick him in the nuts if I could get my foot that high.

How is it even possible for a human being to be this large?

I strain my neck to look up at him, and he scowls at me. "Keep your eyes forward, princess."

Darren elbows me in the ribs.

"What?" I whisper, hoping to avoid detection by our babysitter, but the big guy whips his head around and glowers at us.

"You two, shut the fuck up!"

I toss Darren a warning look. The last thing I need is him setting off one of these guys and someone getting shot. Thus far, we've avoided bloodshed, and I'd like to keep it that way.

Dad will haunt me for eternity if I let someone get hurt on his ship.

Please forgive me, Daddy…

Cap emerges from the hold, all swagger and hard, mean looks. He motions the big guy over to him at the rail. We get another cautionary look from the guy who looks like the Hulk before he moves over to join Cap.

Darren doesn't waste any time. "You can't let them take you."

"It's not like I can stop them."

Every self-defense class in the world tells you not to let a kidnapper move you. Fight tooth and nail, because your chances for survival go down dramatically if you are moved from the location of your abduction.

But do I have a choice?

They need to get away fast, that much is clear.

Would they really hurt me? Kill me? Kill the crew?

If I fight, would they let me go, think it wasn't worth the hassle?

I doubt it. I'm their insurance policy.

"I have to, Darren. If I don't go, who knows what they'll do. I can't risk them hurting you and the rest of the crew, and I don't think they will hurt me if I play along. They say they will let me go if you do what they told you."

He scoffs and anger flashes in his eyes. "And you believe them?"

Fair.

Can you really trust the word of a pirate? Or the instincts of an accountant with zero experience dealing with criminals and almost zero captaining ships?

Anything I do is probably the wrong choice.

Let them take me—insane. Defy the people with the guns and power threatening to kill you and your crew—even more insane.

"Just do what they ask. Get the Coast Guard off their backs if they come. We have insurance for the cargo; it's not worth our lives."

Darren grumbles low and shakes his head. "Your life will be in their hands. That's *not* okay."

A lot of it is basic macho male protective instinct, but I've never been one to need protecting. I can *mostly* take care of myself…when there aren't burly pirates threatening me with guns.

If that giant hadn't snuck up on me from behind, I might have managed to get Mr. Tall, Dark, and Angry under control up there on the bridge.

Yeah, right, Grace. You were practically peeing in your pants and almost blew chunks twice.

"Grace, I *won't* let them take you." His words, said in anger or maybe frustration, or both, aren't even close to whispered.

The Hulk whips around and bares his teeth. In five colossal steps, he's in front of Darren, his enormous barrel chest at Darren's face level. "I told you to shut the fuck up."

My chief mate, the man whose job it is to watch my back, sucks in a deep breath and squares his shoulders. "You're not fucking taking her."

The swing comes so fast, Darren doesn't stand a chance. The Hulk's colossal fist collides with his jaw. Darren rocks back but somehow manages to remain on his feet. He shakes his head to try to clear it, and the Hulk pulls his arm back again.

"Stop!" Cap grabs the Hulk's arm, preventing him from striking Darren again.

Thank God.

Another hit like that might have killed him.

The Hulk turns and leers at Cap, but the man just glares right back. Some unspoken order passes between them, and the Hulk drops his arm and stalks away from us and toward the starboard side of the ship where one of their boats is waiting.

A brief flash of relief crosses Cap's face, then he stomps over to the rail after him.

Darren groans next to me.

"Are you okay?"

He nods slowly, clearly still rocked from the shot he just took. "Shh."

He's right.

The last thing we want to do is draw any more attention to ourselves or bring any further violence.

I keep my eye on Cap, and he leans over the rail, his strong profile pinched in contemplation, looking down at something on the water. When he turns to face us, his eyes, grayer than the approaching storm clouds, meet mine, and the hint of compassion and amusement I saw there earlier has completely vanished.

All that's left is stone-cold fury.

Shit. I may have misjudged him.

He's *definitely* the one to worry about on this team of thugs.

He points to Darren. "Take him and put him with the rest of the crew. I'll take care of her."

Take care of me? What the hell is that supposed to mean? Where the fuck are this psycho and his giant taking me?

He advances toward me, eating up the distance between us on the deck in quick, purposeful strides. I take an instinctive step back, but he continues forward and moves behind me. His hand wraps around my forearm, and he pushes me forward across the deck toward where he just stood at the rail.

"What the hell are you doing?" I pull against his hold, trying to break free, but his hand coiled around my arm like a vice doesn't budge.

I don't know why I bother to ask. He's made his intentions clear. He will use me as a bargaining chip, and that means taking me.

I'm an idiot.

Dad would kill me if he knew I was letting myself be taken hostage. He ultimately had no intention of letting me run this ship when he retired. He thought Leo would come around once he finished his time in the Army and want in on the family business. Maybe there was a good reason for Dad to doubt my ability given how my first time captaining alone has gone.

But what was I supposed to do?

Mom is useless when it comes to anything besides being a homemaker, and Leo's deployment won't be over for another six months. Dad never expected to need a successor so early. He never planned for anything catastrophic.

His death left us dangling on a precipice. It was either I take over and complete his contracts, or lose everything—the ship, our house, our livelihood. I couldn't just sit at home in Traverse City and pretend it wasn't happening. I had to complete the shipment.

I didn't have a choice then. And I don't have a choice now. As captain, it's my job to protect the crew. That means going with these guys.

It's only for forty-eight hours. I can survive forty-eight hours.

We stop at the rail, and I lean forward, looking down toward the churning lake.

A sleek speedboat to jet us out of here quickly or a large

vessel stocked with the cargo they just stole doesn't sit in the water.

The fifty-four-foot Cruiser Yacht rolling majestically in the waves takes my breath away.

Holy shit!

That's a two-million-dollar boat.

How did guys like this get a yacht like that?

Stole it, no doubt.

Rushed footsteps approach from behind. I turn slightly and see the Hulk charging across the deck. He climbs over the rail, descends rapidly on the ladder, and leaps onto the deck of the yacht.

Surprisingly agile for his size.

Cap hasn't said a word to me since he announced his intent to take me. His silence could mean any number of things—none of them good.

A shudder rolls through my body.

This is bad. Really bad.

He grips my wrists and instinctively, I pull away. He yanks me back until my body presses against his, my hands in a very precarious position.

When I first saw him climb aboard—before the guns came out and I realized we were in trouble—I had imagined getting my hands on his junk, but not quite like this.

"Hold still." His breath flutters along my neck, and I shiver despite the warm, humid air brought in by the impending storm.

Something slides between my palms, and the bindings around my wrists pop free. I glance over my shoulder and see him returning a switchblade to his pocket.

Guns and blades—this is looking better and better for me.

I shake my arms out and rub at the stinging skin on my wrists.

His eyes meet mine, and a flicker of something resembling

warmth, or maybe even sympathy, appears before he drops his guard back in place.

"Go." He points to the ladder.

I shouldn't do this.

I shouldn't go without putting up more of a fight.

That's what a smart woman would do.

But I can't physically compete with these guys. I'll have to appeal to something else.

I pause at the rail and turn back to my soon-to-be captor. "If you let me go, I'll tell the Coast Guard it was all a misunderstanding. I'll give you whatever is in the safe."

It's not much, but it may appease him.

His hand tightens around my upper arm. "You *are* going to call the Coast Guard and tell them the beacon was activated in error and everything is fine. If you try to alert them in any way, you and your entire crew will end up at the bottom of the lake. Once they are satisfied help isn't needed, you'll climb down this ladder and get on that damn boat."

Bile rises up my throat, and goose bumps break out across my skin with his threat.

I don't have a choice.

He pulls out a radio, adjusts the channel, and holds it out to me.

I take it and glance at the screen. Channel 16. He really is making me call off the Coast Guard. My eyes drift over the gun at Cap's waist, over the guns visible on the two men herding the crew together…

Just do it, Grace. It's your only option.

I press the call button. "Coast Guard, come in."

"Coast Guard Sector Lake Michigan, copy."

"Uh, this is Grace Albright, Captain of the *Neptune's Daughter.* I activated the EPIRB, but there is no emergency. All is fine."

"Yes, ma'am. We received the EPIRB signal and already

have vessels heading your way. Please confirm there is no active emergency and you are not in need of any assistance."

I suck in a deep breath and stare at the radio. This is my only chance to change my mind, to not go along with this crazy plan. But I can't risk my crew.

"That's correct. There is *no* emergency, and we are *not* in need of assistance. Please cancel any response."

With this storm system coming in, the Coast Guard will welcome the end of the call. They'll have other things to deal with.

"Affirmative. Glad everything is all right, ma'am. Let us know if you have any trouble."

With the call completed, there's nothing else I can do to delay the inevitable. Not if I want to ensure the safety of my crew. I hand the radio back to Cap and turn to the rail.

His hand meets my lower back. "Go."

I follow his order and swing over the rail, climbing slowly down the ladder toward the yacht and the churning water of Lake Michigan.

Strong hands grab my waist and yank me from the ladder. My feet land on the polished wood deck. I twist around and glare at the big guy. "I could have gotten down myself."

The last thing I want is to encourage any of these assholes to touch me.

He growls low and flexes the humongous mitts he calls hands. "Not fast enough."

Cap follows down the ladder, drops onto the deck, and motions for the Hulk to head to the controls before turning to me. "Down."

He points to the door to the cabin and, after taking one last longing look at *Neptune's Daughter*, I climb below with my captor close at my heels.

Warm, rich colors and leather greet me below.

This place is nicer than my apartment. Nothing like having a luxurious prison.

And this place is a prison. There's no doubt. One set of stairs leading to the deck. One way out. A way that will undoubtedly be guarded by these two. The small windows along the top of both walls won't provide an escape route either. Even if I were half my size, I couldn't fit through one, and the only thing out there is endless water for miles. There's nowhere to go.

He motions for me to take a seat on one of the leather couches running along the walls and strides to the kitchen. A cabinet door opens, and he yanks out a bottle of Maker's Mark. Two glasses join it on the counter.

What the hell?

I sure hope he doesn't intend to bring a drink up to his buddy driving the damn boat. That's all I need, a drunk driver taking me to my doom.

The engine rumbles to life, and I fly sideways as we shoot away from the *Neptune's Daughter*. I brace myself on the couch, and Cap grabs the side of the counter in the kitchen to steady himself.

He pours two fingers in each glass and returns to stand in front of me. His dark eyes meet mine. "I think we both need one of these."

I stare at the dark amber liquid. "I somehow doubt taking booze from one's kidnapper is a good idea."

An ironic laugh fills the cabin, and he shakes the glass at me.

You don't need to drink it. Just take it to appease him.

I accept the glass with a shaky hand, and he drops down onto the couch across from me.

He leans forward, running his free hand back through his hair. "Probably not, but who the fuck knows? It's not like I've done this before."

"Done what?"

His gaze meets mine. "Taken a hostage on a job. I don't take hostages. Hostages are more trouble than they're worth."

Is that supposed to scare me or relax me?

On one hand, someone who doesn't normally take hostages is probably not as scary as I initially thought. It means there's hope they won't hurt me, or worse, and I'll actually be released, maybe even sooner than anticipated. On the other, someone who doesn't normally take hostages may be more likely to make mistakes—and mistakes can be deadly.

More trouble than they're worth…

That means I need to *stay* worth something to them. As soon as I'm not, they can—and will—get rid of me, and maybe not in the way they've promised.

Rather than voice my concern over his hostage-taking virginity, I fuck common sense and take a sip of the proffered drink. The warm burn of whiskey is welcome. Dad always had a glass of the good stuff in his hand in the evening, and while I'm not really a drinker, I always took a sip of his before I headed to my place for the night.

Maybe thinking about Dad is a bad idea. The telltale burn of building tears begins, and I wipe at my eyes quickly to eliminate the evidence.

Don't show any fear.

He focuses his hard gaze on me. "We won't hurt you if you cooperate."

Guess I failed at that.

"I promise, we will let you go as soon as we know we're safe and we've delivered the cargo."

The sincerity in his voice almost dispels my fears. I almost want to believe him, but then I remember the flashes of ice in his stare when he was angry earlier, and the stone-cold terror his crew elicited with just their presences.

This man is a wicked combination, and I can't afford to let my guard down.

He drains his glass and drops it on the side table before standing and disappearing above deck without a glance back in my direction.

Leaving me alone here seems like an amateur move and a potentially deadly mistake for him. There are, no doubt, a dozen different weapons down here. The kitchen knives alone could do some serious damage.

Either he trusts me, or he's showing his virginity in hostage-taking again.

W e cruise at breakneck speeds for what feels like hours without Cap returning.

A thorough search of the main cabin proved fruitless. No means of escape. The only door, which must lead to the bedroom, is locked, and even if it weren't, that's the last place I want to be.

I've eyed the knives in the kitchen area several times, but what would I do with one? These guys are huge, and even if I managed to take down one of them, there's another, and they're both armed.

And even if, by some act of God, I managed to get away, that only puts the crew at risk.

The other two goons who left on the other boat could turn around and go right back to the *Neptune's Daughter* and slaughter everyone. My best bet is to play along until we get to land. Somewhere I might have a real chance of getting away and finding help.

We're going south based on the direction we headed away from the *Neptune's Daughter*, but on the open water, there isn't much to help you gauge location without your instruments, the sun, and the stars. Down here, I can't see much from the tiny port windows, and dark storm clouds have blocked out most of the sky.

When this storm hits, things will get a lot worse.

The boat slows and comes to a stop.

Goose bumps spread across my flesh.

Waiting is the worst, especially when you have no idea what you're waiting *for.*

The familiar sound of the anchor being lowered into the water clanks along the hull.

I peer out the small window, but the only thing visible is open water. The same is true through the window on the other side of the boat.

That doesn't make sense.

Shouldn't we be trying to get somewhere with some cover before the storm?

An argument between Cap and the Hulk floats in through the open port window. I climb onto my knees and lean toward the opening, desperate to gather any information.

"What the fuck are we going to do? We're fucking dead if we don't get the shipment to *Il Padrone* by tomorrow." The Hulk's booming voice carries on the wind.

I cringe at the hostility and panic there. That can't be good. They're working for someone. Someone who sounds really fucking dangerous.

Who the hell is Il Padrone? *What does he want with damn machine parts?*

"You think I don't know that? I know exactly the predicament we are in." Cap's voice is calmer but still holds the same edge of concern as his friend's.

"We're going to have company in less than five minutes. What the hell do we do?"

Company? The Coast Guard?

Hope blossoms in my chest. Maybe there's a chance of getting out of this alive and unscathed.

At least for me.

Something about the panic in their voices tells me they're serious about their lives being in danger because of this. More so than just prison for piracy.

"I have an idea…" Cap's voice lowers until I can't hear him anymore.

Boots thunder across the deck above me, and I struggle to return to my innocent-looking sitting position before Cap appears at the stairs to the cabin.

He descends quickly, and his eyes find mine. "The Coast Guard is almost here. We need to get rid of them."

This is my chance.

His hands move to the hem of his T-shirt, and he yanks it over his head and tosses it on the floor. He pops open the button of his jeans, and he lowers the zipper as he approaches me.

"Whoa!" I scramble back against the corner of the couch. "What the hell are you doing? You said you wouldn't hurt me."

He halts his advance, and his eyes widen slightly. He holds his hands out in apology, or is it surrender? "Shit, no, that's not what...shit. I need your help."

"Why the fuck should I help you?"

"If they come down here and think we're fooling around, they won't suspect anything. If you alert them of what's happening, things could end very badly."

He doesn't answer my question or add "for you and your crew." Maybe he isn't referring to me at all, but the threat that seems to exist against him and his men, but, either way, I'm not helping him.

Alerting the Coast Guard the moment they set foot on this boat is the obvious move...

But the man standing in front of me said they would harm the crew if I don't play along and make sure they all get to safety. Even if I were rescued now, there are still at least two more men who were on board with the pirates who left in another boat with the cargo

My stomach clenches.

There's obviously some threat to these guys, someone with more power who's pulling the strings. That might mean they don't want to be doing this.

I have to believe they aren't really a threat to me as long as I play along. I'll be safe and so will the crew as long as they get away with what they need and get it delivered.

But this man is *definitely* a threat to me in a whole other way. The sharp lines of his chest, abs, and those damn V things on his hips that drive women mindless are making it impossible for me to keep my head on straight. All the ink covering his body muddles together, and I can't focus on a single area.

I should be paying better attention. Memorizing his tattoos so I can go to the police with a good description, but my brain won't let me focus. All I can see is the crew flying overboard into the lake...

If I help him, if I cooperate, they won't hurt me. They won't hurt the crew. He *said* they wouldn't as long as we play their game.

They will let me go eventually.

Who the hell knows why I'm so sure of that, but I am. Maybe it's that damn naïvety again.

I stand and step up to him. Warmth radiates from his hard body mere inches from mine. "Fine, I'll help you to protect myself and the crew, but don't try anything. And you better release me the fucking second we are free of the Coast Guard."

A look of relief overtakes his face. "I promise, as soon as we are safe, I'll even drop you off wherever you want to go."

Maybe this won't even last the forty-eight hours. Maybe, by helping, I can end this even sooner.

He turns and heads toward the bedroom in the back of the cabin. He pulls a key from his back pocket and unlocks the door. It opens into an elegant bedroom.

He kicks off his boots, climbs onto the bed, drops his head on the pillows, and watches me expectantly. "I promise I won't do anything."

Damn right you won't.

This man may be insanely sexy, but he's also the enemy.

Danger, Grace. Danger.

I remove my shoes and toss them onto a pile with his. I survey him, and my stomach rolls slightly. With his hands tucked behind his head like that, his biceps bulge in a disgustingly hot way.

Cool your jets, girl. This is not a seduction. He kidnapped you.

Regardless of how I got here, the reality is, there's no way the Coast Guard will buy we're fooling around if I'm fully clothed.

My hands shake trying to pull off my shirt. Tears pool in my eyes. My chest tightens.

I can't believe I'm doing this...but my life, the crew's lives...that's all that matters.

He jerks up, bracing himself on his elbows. "What the hell are you doing?" The panic in his voice helps allay some of my fears.

He wasn't expecting me to undress.

"You really think they'll believe us if I'm not at least partially naked?" I kneel on the bed, and he watches me with hooded eyes as I work my way over him until I'm straddling his hips.

He drops back onto the pillow, and his eyes search mine. He slowly moves his hands up to my hips, almost as if he is asking for permission.

An engine roars at the side of the boat, and a speaker crackles. "This is the Coast Guard. Prepare to be boarded."

The pounding of footsteps on the deck sounds above us. My heartrate spikes, and muffled voices grow louder.

They'll be here any minute.

I drop down onto my elbows, bracing myself over him, my hair falling in red curtains around his face. His breathing shallows, and the sweet smell of bourbon surrounds me, mingling with the familiar earthy scent of the lake that clings to him the way it does everyone who spends so much time on the water.

Under any other circumstances, I would be devouring him without a thought of the consequences. Mother's warnings be damned.

But now, my heart races for another reason altogether.

This man holds my life, and those of my crew, in his hands.

Someone clears their throat near the open bedroom door, and I jerk up, turn my head toward the sound, and cover my chest.

A contrite-looking Coast Guard officer averts his eyes. "I'm sorry, ma'am, sir, can you please step out here so we can talk?"

I wait for Cap to respond, but he appears momentarily struck mute. I nod. "Yes, of course."

The officer closes the door slightly to give us some privacy, and I quickly slide off him and then the bed and pull my shirt on. He climbs off after me, zipping and re-buttoning his jeans.

Should I be relieved or insulted he wasn't hard?

Neither, you should be worried about how fucking insane you are for even asking that question.

THREE

War

I'm a sick fuck.

The only thing that kept me from getting hard while she straddled me was the fear and adrenaline racing through my system. Being attracted to one's captive is probably not a great sign for success or sanity. And taking a hostage at all has always been at the top of the *Do Not Do* list.

Hostages equal unwanted complications. I just never expected this to be one of them.

I follow her from the bedroom while re-buttoning my jeans.

God, let us get through this without tipping them off.

Our lives literally depend on it.

The Marconis will come for us unless we can get the shipment to them tonight, like we originally planned. Even asking for a day's extension is gambling with our lives, but we don't really have a choice. We can't go tonight. Not with the delays, the storm, and only part of the shipment.

The forty-eight hours I gave the crew as a timeline for Grace's return gives us enough time to ride out the storm, come up with a game plan to handle the half-shipment situation, get what we *do* have to them in Chicago, and get back to the warehouse safely before any law enforcement ever gets alerted.

Hopefully.

Two Coast Guard officers meet us in the main cabin, and we follow them up to the deck. The sky has darkened from gray to almost black, and the temperature has dropped significantly since I came down below. The wind whips around us, bringing the smell of rain.

A storm is definitely coming. Spring in the Midwest often means magnificent storms that can pop up at any time and systems that can linger for days. This one would have served as the perfect cover for escaping from the *Neptune's Daughter* without anyone else being on the water. If Grace hadn't set off the emergency beacon, we would be almost home free by now and safe before it hit.

"My name is Officer Mark Walters. Your friend here tells me you're just out on a pleasure cruise today? Is that correct?"

I glance at Rion, who has changed into board shorts and a T-shirt. "Yeah, that's right."

The officer eyes me suspiciously. "And is this your boat?"

"Yes."

"Can I see the registration for the vessel and some ID from everyone, please?" His eyes roam over me and Grace, whose gaze darts over to mine long enough to see the panic and turmoil there.

All it would take is one word from her and we're toast.

I flash her a hard look and squeeze her hand in warning before I walk over to the control panel and grab my wallet and the boat registration from the compartment near the captain's seat. I hand my driver's license and the registration to the officer and hold my breath.

Rion goes to a duffel bag on the deck and grabs his ID, then hands it over.

Grace looks toward me anxiously before plastering a fake

smile on her face. "Um, officer, I don't have my ID with me. I forgot my purse at the house when we left."

I shove my shaking, sweaty hands into my pockets. If he sees how fucking nervous I am, we are screwed.

He gives her an annoyed look and grabs a pad and paper from his pocket. "Give me your name and date of birth, please."

She doesn't miss a beat. "Kimberly Tyler, July 22, 1989."

Whose information did she just give him?

For all I know, she's made something up, which is certain to alert their suspicions.

The other officer wanders toward the back of his boat and uses his radio to relay her information to someone at dispatch. Officer Walters hands Rion's ID to his partner to call it in, then returns to me.

He pauses and looks at me, narrowing his eyes. "Warwick Pike? You aren't Martin's son, are you?"

Are you kidding me? What are the fucking chances the Coast Guard officer knew Dad?

"Uh, yeah, I am."

He smiles and hands back my ID. His partner returns with Rion's and hands it to him.

"I haven't seen you since you were knee-high and going out with your dad. You probably don't remember me...I was sorry to hear about his passing."

I don't remember him. There were a lot of different Coast Guard officers on board with us over the years, but I return his smile and nod. "Thanks."

The less I say, the better. It's already awkward enough. No doubt Officer Walters knows the details of Dad's passing, just like everyone else seems to.

"Are you running the business?" He closes his notebook and slides it back into his pocket, apparently now more concerned about catching up than whatever investigation had prompted this stop.

Maybe this isn't an inconvenience after all, but a saving grace.

"Yep, sure am."

Sort of. While still technically owner and operator of Pike Fish, I've turned over the day-to-day operations to others. Needing to be on call for the Marconis makes it difficult to run a business successfully. I'd rather leave it in more capable hands than my own.

He grins at me, crossing his arms over his chest and rocking back slightly on his heels. "That's great. There are so few family-owned fishing businesses left in the area, would have hated to lose it."

"Thanks, sir. Can I ask why you stopped us today? Is there a problem?"

He waves his hand. "Oh, no, no problem. A cargo ship north of here turned on their emergency beacon, but then the captain radioed and indicated everything was fine. We were already on our way out there and saw your vessel. I wanted to stop to warn you of the incoming storm in case you didn't have your weather radio on. It looks to be a big, nasty one. They're saying the system may continue for several days, too. You folks ought to pull anchor and get to dry land ASAP."

A five-thousand-pound weight lifts from my chest.

We're in the clear, at least with the Coast Guard. *Il Padrone*, now he is another story. I don't know what the hell we will do about him, but one dilemma at a time.

"Thanks for the warning, Officer, I appreciate it. We will head in."

After a quick handshake, the Coast Guard retreats, and Rion returns to the controls with an icy glare in my direction on his way.

Grace's eyes never leave me.

Fuck.

That was too close. I grab her arm and usher her back

toward the cabin. She climbs down in front of me, and as soon as I'm down, I move behind the counter.

More whiskey is needed.

Definitely.

She probably needs another one, too. I pour us each another glass and hold one out over the bar for her.

I expect a little hesitancy, but she accepts the glass from me before plopping right back on the couch, never taking her eyes off me.

She's contemplating something. I can practically see the gears turning in her beautiful head.

This can't be good for me.

The woman is smart.

And smart is bad in this situation.

A dumb hostage is more likely to go along with orders. Someone like Grace…she will make things very difficult.

She didn't rat us out to the Coast Guard, though. That's something.

That run-in with them frayed my last nerve. I shouldn't be drinking. I need to keep a clear head, or as clear as is possible with Grace in my orbit and an axe hovering over my head from *Il Padrone*, but my hands won't stop shaking.

Booze, it is.

I toss it back, savoring the burn in my throat and warmth in my stomach.

A mild calm starts to settle over me when we finally start moving. We'll be safely at the warehouse soon. Then we can deal with the Marconi problem, and I can get rid of the ginger one sitting on the couch watching me.

She takes a sip of her drink, and I almost miss the tiny corner of her mouth quirking up behind the glass.

Shit.

Dread slithers up my spine.

I don't like that little tilt of the lips.

Not one bit.

She lowers her glass, licks her lips, and grins. "So, should I call you Warwick or Mr. Pike?"

Fuck. Fuck. Fuck.

Forget simply being able to identify us—that's always been a huge risk given our tattoos and appearances—this woman knows my fucking *name*. And that I own a commercial fishing company.

It will take two fucking seconds before the police are cuffing me if she rats us out when we release her.

We are well and truly fucked.

If we survive only being able to deliver half the shipment to *Il Padrone,* and *late* for that matter, this woman is a guillotine waiting to fall on my neck.

I pour another shot and toss it back before I lock eyes with her. "You won't call me anything."

The smile disappears from her lips, and her eyes widen slightly.

Fear.

Good.

She *should* be afraid. I can't let any physical attraction toward her or guilt over taking her hostage interfere with my show of authority. She can never doubt I'm in control and that I can end her life if I need to.

I may not want to, but I can…

Theoretically.

"Whose information did you give the Coast Guard?"

She swallows, and a shaky hand pushes her red locks back from her face. "Um, my best friend from high school. She doesn't have a record or anything, so nothing will come up."

Good. Smart.

"Is anyone expecting to hear from you?"

She shakes her head. "No. Well, at least not for a couple days. My mom will probably wonder if I don't call her from Milwaukee at some point. We were supposed to dock late tomorrow and unload the following day."

"Your mom? That's it? No boyfriend you should be getting home to?"

I don't miss her slight recoil at the question.

Sensitive subject?

"Nope. Just me."

"And how did *you* end up on a freighter in the middle of Lake Michigan, Grace? You don't strike me as a full-time captain."

About as far from it as I've ever seen.

"I'm not. I'm basically an accountant."

I bark out a laugh and shake my head.

Her face scrunches up. "What's so funny?"

"That explains a lot."

She clenches her jaw. "I *am* a captain…technically. I got my captain's license and bachelor's from Great Lakes Maritime, along with a minor in accounting. I just…" she holds her hands up, "haven't ever done this alone before. I spend most of my time at the office, running the business side of things, while my father captained the ship."

It's impressive she had the balls to pull a gun on me like that let alone captain a ship alone for the first time and earn the respect of the crew she clearly had.

"How did you end up onboard?"

Her eyes shimmer with unshed tears, and she swipes her fingers under them. "My dad had a heart attack and died recently. This haul was already scheduled, and…" she trails off and glances toward the window behind me. "We are almost bankrupt. We needed the money."

My chest tightens. I know that situation all too well.

Thunder rolls somewhere in the distance. I wander over to the closest port window and glance out.

"That squall line is coming fast. We really need to get to cover."

Rion is already pushing the *Calista*, but he's holding back

39

from what it can really do. I don't want to take any chances of getting stuck out here during a storm like this.

I start up the steps to the deck.

"Wait!"

I look back over my shoulder at her.

"Where are we going? What are you going to do with me? You said you'd let me go when you were safe."

I step back down to the cabin and cross my arms over my chest. "You know I can't tell you where we're going. And we aren't safe *yet*. I have two more men out there and cargo we need to deliver to someone before we're truly safe. As for what we are going to do with you…"

The silence drags out.

Intentionally.

Let her squirm. It will help her remember who is in charge.

"That depends entirely on how cooperative you are."

"Fuck you! You said you would let me go."

I glower and step toward her. She recoils back into the couch.

"Let's get one thing clear, Grace. I am not here to reassure you. You are my hostage. The only things I care about are making sure my men and I are safe and our cargo gets delivered. Once we are and the job is done, I will release you. I give you my word on that. But in the meantime, the priority is us, not you. Understand?"

A tiny nod is the only response she gives me.

"Good. Now stay here and stop asking questions you know I can't answer."

"Because if you did, you'd have to kill me?"

Her question goes straight to the heart of the matter, and straight to mine. I swallow through the guilt choking my throat. I push it away and lock eyes with her.

"Exactly."

FOUR

Grace

I startle awake and push myself up into a sitting position as my eyes adjust to the dimly lit room. Thunder rolls outside, rattling something glass somewhere across the room from me.

Where the hell am I?

The events of the day come rushing back.

The stranded boat.

The pirates.

Being taken.

How the hell did I fall asleep?

My head aches, and the taste of bourbon lingers in my mouth.

Shit.

The alcohol. The storm. The rolling waves.

I must be the dumbest captive in the history of being taken captive to let down my guard enough to actually fall asleep.

This definitely isn't the bedroom on the boat, and there's no roll of the water.

I'm on land now, which means I was out cold enough to be moved without waking.

Holy hell.

They could have done anything to me.

I know he said they wouldn't hurt me if I played along, but they could've beaten me. Raped me. Shot me. They could've tossed me overboard. And it would have happened easily because I was dumb.

A shudder of dread rolls through me. I rub the sleep from my eyes and flick on a lamp that sits on the nightstand.

Another *boom* of thunder rocks the room, rattling glass and metal. That one was close. A storm must be right over us... wherever we are.

The sound of rushing water draws my attention to the left side of the room where a sliver of light creeps under the crack of the closed door. A wall of old glass and steel windows line one side of the room, and a glass panel door is closed on the other.

This setup is strange. It almost feels industrial, like this wasn't meant to be a bedroom. But it is.

The large king-sized bed I'm in and the silky sheets and comforter draped across my lower half are incredibly welcoming despite the situation. They must've been for me to have slept so deeply. I've never really had issues sleeping, but one would think all the adrenaline would have kept me awake and alert.

I shouldn't have taken that drink. I'm so damn stupid.

Warwick plied me with whiskey. That combined with the rocking of the boat and the fact I've been going nonstop since Dad's death was the lethal combination to make me the perfect pliant hostage.

So dumb, Grace. Seriously.

Oh, my God...

I tug back the covers.

Whew. Still have my clothes on.

I slide my hand across the gray sheet next to me. Cold. It doesn't seem like anyone else was in bed with me.

42

Thank God.

And now that we're on land, maybe there's a way out of here...

The windows on the wall of glass across from me don't tell me much. The old, peeling paper covering the panes doesn't let in much light, and with no exterior windows, there's no telling what time it is.

I scan the room for a clock only to come up empty.

Crap.

How far into the forty-eight hours am I? And does it even matter?

He said he couldn't let me go until he and his men were safe and the cargo was delivered.

What if they can't do that within forty-eight hours?

More thunder, this time cracking so close, it makes me yelp.

Shit.

The water shuts off, and I hold my breath.

It has to be Warwick.

But then again, it could be any one of these goons, including the Hulk. For all I know, Warwick stashed me in the Hulk's room so he can keep an eye on me and break me in half if I try to escape.

My heart thuds against my ribs, and my blood rushes loudly in my ears, echoing the torrential rain hitting the roof above me.

What the hell do I do when he comes out of there?

I clench my fists and frantically survey the room for any sort of weapon.

Nothing of any use.

Dammit.

Just a bookshelf along one wall, stacked and overflowing with books, a small desk in the corner, and a dresser with a single picture on top. I can't quite make it out from over here, but it looks like a family photo of a mom and a dad and a small boy. It's so normal, so human...yet this room belongs to a man who steals, who threatens, who hurts people…

The door clicks open, and I hold my breath. Warwick steps out, and all the air whooshes out of me.

Coal-dark hair glistens in the lights from the bathroom and water droplets trickle down the angel etched on one side of his neck and the anchor on the other, over his massive exposed ink-covered chest and arms, and between his defined abs to disappear beneath the small white towel wrapped around his trim waist.

Holy hell.

The myriad of artwork covering his skin is breathtaking. Scrawled words…hauntingly beautiful figures and images more like you'd see in a museum instead of on a man like this. It would take hours to explore them all.

His gray eyes flick over to mine and widen slightly. "Sorry, I didn't mean to wake you."

He's apologizing?

I'm not quite sure what to make of that.

What badass pirate apologizes for waking up his captive?

I run my hands back through my disheveled hair.

Christ, I must look like a fucking mess. I sure as hell feel like one.

The heat in his gaze as it roams over me gives me pause. Maybe I don't look so bad.

Why the hell do I care, though?

I clear the sleep from my throat. "You didn't. I woke up a few minutes ago."

It may have been the storm that did it. The pounding rain and thunder booming every few minutes mean it's a real mess out there.

He presses his lips together in a thin line and gives me a curt nod before he crosses the room and gives me his back to dig into the drawers of the dresser.

Tattoos cover his skin there too. There's barely an inch where there isn't some black-and-white or color swirling into words or images. I shouldn't care so much what they say… what they mean. Yet, something tells me each and every letter and drop of ink on his body means something very special to him. That makes me all the more curious.

Strong muscles ripple and bulge with every one of his movements, and I have to force myself to look away rather than be caught staring if he turned around.

Totally inappropriate, Grace.

Instead of ogling him some more, I focus on the wall of old windows in the odd room. "How did I get off the boat? Where are we?"

And how do I get out of here?

He pauses and turns around to face me. His penetrating gaze rakes over me for a moment, though I'm not sure what he's looking for.

"You can't hold your liquor and passed out. I had to throw you over my shoulder and carry you in here. And where we are doesn't matter. If you try to escape, there's nowhere to go, and you'll only be sealing the death warrants for your crew. You're not going to be here for long."

Relief floods my system, and some of the tension in my shoulders relaxes. "Does that mean you're going to release me?"

He scoffs and scrubs his hands over his stubbled jaw and then back through his hair before he returns his attention to me. "Frankly, I don't know what I'm going to do yet. We only got half of what we needed, and we need to figure that out. But I have no intention of keeping you here longer than I need to."

Longer than I need to…

Those words don't exactly instill any great confidence I'll be heading home anytime soon. After our interaction on the yacht, I knew this was foreign territory for him—the whole "taking a hostage" thing—but I never ever expected him to be still winging it. He had to have come up with a plan while we were on our way here, wherever *here* is.

Whatever mess he got himself into, he had to have figured out a way out of it...

Right?

I bite my lip and wait for him to say something. Anything. He just watches me and waits. I squirm under his stare. The heat in his eyes isn't anything I've experienced in a very long time. And even then, it was under *much* different circumstances.

This man is an enigma. One with a clear dark side, yet there's softness in his gaze at times. A juxtaposition that throws my whole sense of right and wrong off in a way I don't want to analyze.

What I *do* know is...he raided my ship. And I need to know why.

"I don't understand what you wanted from the ship. There wasn't anything worth stealing on there. We were shipping machine parts. Nothing that would be of any use to you."

A deep, cynical chuckle rumbles from his lips, and he crosses his immense arms over his chest and leans back against the dresser. "If you really think what was in the box is what was on the manifests, then you are far more naïve than I thought, and I've been giving you far too much credit."

Thunder cracks, along with my temper.

"I'm not naïve." My snapped response comes out sharp and a little more forceful than I probably should have said it, considering this man is armed and could kill me at any second.

And while I don't see any sign of the gun he had earlier, not knowing where it might be is almost worse than having it pointed at me.

"You *are* naïve. I've been doing this for a long time, and I can tell you that maybe twenty percent of the time what I'm stealing is actually what should be in there."

But...

"How is that possible?" Probably a naïve question that only plays into what he already thinks of me, but I know the process that's required to ship cargo and get things loaded onto those ships. "Things are inspected. I don't understand how anybody could swap anything out."

He flashes me a devilish grin. Electricity crackles in the air of the room—either brought on by the storm or the way he's looking at me...I'm not sure which. The heat of a flush spreading up my neck and across my cheeks might as well be a "come and get me" flag. Not exactly the sign you want to be sending to the man who literally took you captive.

"There are a dozen ways to get things into a box and onto a ship. Drugs and other illicit cargo are either hidden in secret compartments or packed inside other items. Most of the time, the captain doesn't know, and even the shipping company doesn't know what gets loaded by exporters. You may have a manifest that tells you what's supposed to be in there, but it's damn easy to pay off someone if you need to send something you shouldn't be, pretty much anywhere in the world. The people we are dealing with have so much money, they don't even know what to do with it. And what we get them only makes them more."

Money equals power.

And what I overheard earlier made it clear there's someone with *more* power pulling the strings here.

"Is that why you're so afraid of him?"

He recoils slightly before his entire body goes stiff, and he straightens his back and shoulders.

Shit.

His eyes darken to an almost black, and a quiver of fear runs through me. This is the dangerous Warwick, the one who will stop at nothing to protect himself and his men, like he's warned me.

"I'm not afraid of them." The low, menacing tone chills

the air in the room. Thunder shakes the room.

Shit. I wish I could take the question back.

He didn't know I overheard his conversation with the Hulk, and his narrowed dark brows tell me he's now wondering where the question came from.

Pointing out a weakness to the man holding you hostage probably isn't wise.

"Sorry, I wasn't trying to imply—"

He pushes off the dresser and towers over me at his full, neck-craning height. "I don't care what you were trying to imply. You don't ask questions."

With a low growl, he whips around and pulls something from the drawer. He tugs on a T-shirt before he grabs a pair of boxers and a pair of jeans and stalks back to the bathroom. The door slamming shut behind him makes me jump and has my heart racing.

Shit. Shit. Shit.

"Don't antagonize your captor. Isn't that another one of those don't do it rules when you get taken hostage?" The question is asked to the empty room, and not shockingly, I get no reply.

I must have a fucking death wish. My mouth seems to open and words come out before I can even process them mentally. Part of it is a learned response growing up with Leo as an older brother. Constantly defending myself against him and his friends gave me thick skin and an attitude that's gotten me into trouble more than once. It's one of the reasons I stay away from people and would much rather spend my time holed up in my office crunching numbers.

Numbers don't argue. Numbers don't get offended by my comments or observations. Numbers can't look at me like I have a second head when I open my big, fat mouth.

Get up. Get the lay of the land.

The more I know about where we are and what's going on, the better a position I'll be in to decide what to do. This storm could be a blessing or a curse. It could make getting away easier or harder, depending on where we are.

I wipe my hands over my face and climb from the bed. The chilly air of the room raises goose bumps on my flesh, and I rub my bare arms and wander over to the corner with the desk and the bookshelf.

*Moby Dick. To Kill a Mockingbird. The Complete Works of Shakespeare. War and Peace. 1984. The Great Gatsby. Wuthering Heights. Catcher in the Rye...*and too many more to even read the names off the spines.

Not what I expected to find in the bedroom of a heartless pirate.

I'm surprised he can even read.

I turn to the desk, and my eyes land on a leather-bound book sitting on top with a pen wedged in the center, opening it to one of the pages. A glance back at the bathroom door assures me it's closed, and I make my way over to the desk, unable to fight my curiosity.

The cover is blank, simple brownish leather, but it's clearly well-used and worn. I flip to the page the pen is marking, and my heart stills.

We have to get out of this. I can't keep doing this anymore. Living my life every day wondering if it's going to be my last. He's going to kill me one of these days. Kill us all. As soon as we're of no use to him, we're gone. He's never going to let us go, no matter what the original deal was. He's never going to let us go. We know too much, and now we fucked this up.

"What the hell are you doing?"
Another crack of thunder rattles the windows.
Fuck.

I jerk away from the book and whip around to face him. His dark eyes burn into me, and I shift away from the desk and what is clearly his journal. Something he definitely didn't want me to see. Being caught snooping is pretty fucking dumb.

I'll add that to the list.

"I'm sorry. I was just—"

He bares his teeth and charges over to grab the journal. He shoves it in the back of his pants and pulls his shirt down over it. "If you know what's good for you, you'll stop asking questions and snooping around. Don't make me regret promising to let you go."

Cold fingers of dread wrap around my spine, and I nod mutely.

"Stay here. Don't touch anything. Don't try to sneak out. There's nowhere for you to go."

Fear tightens those fingers, and I shiver despite my best efforts to remain calm and in control. I can't sit here thinking about what's next—whether that's life or death. I'll go crazy considering the possibilities, wondering if I'll ever see Mom or Leo again…

I need a distraction.

My eyes drift over to the bookshelf, and I point to it with a shaky hand. "Can I at least grab something to read?"

Those hard eyes soften from almost black to a soft gray—a momentary flash of humanity on an otherwise cold and unfeeling mask of anger. He nods.

"Don't touch anything else." He storms out of the room and slams the door behind him.

The old glass vibrates in the doorframe as do all the windows on the side of the room.

Jesus Christ.

That man is fury, and danger, and everything wrong in this world.

Who would have thought that would be so damn attractive?

FIVE

War

For such a tiny thing, that girl sure has a big mouth on her.

Where the fuck does she get off asking me questions like that? Where did that even come from?

I stomp down the staircase to the warehouse floor. She must've overheard my conversation with Rion on the *Calista*. It's the only way she would have asked that.

How else would she know that our taking the cargo had anything to do with anyone else and that it wasn't just for our benefit?

Her nosy nature could be troublesome. And we already have enough trouble to go around.

Thunder rumbles outside, shaking the warehouse. Rain pelts the metal roof, sending rapid pings echoing through the vast space. This system is hammering us and hasn't let up since we arrived back at the warehouse late last night. It's only making what we need to do harder.

Rion stands leaning over the giant makeshift table in the middle of the warehouse floor we use to plan our missions. Milo lies at his feet, his big, wrinkly head resting on Rion's boot. He lifts it and assesses my approach before he rises to his stubby legs, shakes, and wanders toward me. Rion takes a drink from a bottle of beer and looks up at me.

"Where's the girl?"

I hitch my thumb over my shoulder to the loft office that now serves as my bedroom. "She's still up there."

Milo rubs against my leg, and I lean down and scratch between his ears. The damn dog is always so desperate for attention.

Rion glances at my room again. "She asleep?"

Ha. I wish.

I shake my head. "No, she's awake."

And already prying into things that aren't any of her business. But I won't tell Rion that. He's already worried she'll make trouble for us, even more than she already has. If he knew she was snooping around my room and listening in on the boat, things could get ugly fast.

She just doesn't seem to know what's good for her. She couldn't help herself from reading what I wrote. I need to lock my journal in the safe, where it can't be accessed anymore by the nosy redhead and keep my thoughts to myself.

Rion leans over the table and studies the papers spread out on top.

I step to the opposite side of the table, with Milo close at my heels. "What are you looking at?"

He nods to the charts laid out in front of him. "Preacher and I've been trying to reach *The Destiny*, but neither Cutter nor E are responding. I don't know if it's the storm or what, but something is interfering."

Shit.

And they have all the cargo. Well, not all of it. We didn't even get half of what we are supposed to and therein lies the major issue. Even if I could explain a delay to the Marconis... I sure as hell can't explain half a missing shipment of whatever is in those boxes.

They don't tell me, and I never ask. It's better not to know.

I squeeze my eyes shut and fight the need to smash something. "They should be here by now."

It's been over twelve hours since we left *Neptune's Daughter*, and even with the violence of the storm that hit, they should have been able to make it back by now.

Unless something went wrong…

We were lucky to make it back in one piece ourselves.

He nods his agreement. "I was thinking the same thing. I'm trying to determine where else they could have gone to shelter from the storm that may have delayed them so they aren't back by now. Preacher is back in his cave, trying to contact them and scanning the radios for anything from the Coast Guard or police we should be worried about."

Alarm flashes red in my vision. Anything could've happened. The Coast Guard could've picked them up. They could have capsized. We don't even know if they are alive.

I let out a long sigh. "Have you guys tried the SAT phones and the radio?"

He nods. "Yeah, and nothing is getting through."

The storm is a real bitch. So is the woman upstairs.

Though, to be fair, I haven't put her in the best of circumstances. Had we met somewhere else—in a different place, a different time, when I didn't hijack her ship and kidnap her—things might've been very different between us.

There's definitely an attraction. A spark of something more than disdain between us. I felt the way her eyes roamed over me when I boarded the ship, before she knew my intent. I saw the way she licked her lips, probably without even realizing it. And even after I took her, after she knew how dangerous I could be, the look in her eyes when she straddled me in the cabin of the *Calista,* and again upstairs, when I walked out of the bathroom, *was* unmistakable.

It doesn't matter. She's our enemy, for all intents and purposes, and I am hers.

But the way her pale skin flushes when she gets angry, the

way her every thought is visible in those green eyes, the way she isn't afraid to stand up to me even given the circumstances...

God knows it does something totally unexpected to me.

I'm fucking impressed with her despite how intrusive and annoying her questions and demands can be. This woman can't weigh more than one hundred pounds and was captaining a cargo ship—something most men would find intimidating.

But I can't let that interfere with what needs to happen.

Until I have that cargo safe and sound and delivered to the Marconis, I can't let her go. And the longer she's here, the more information she has on us and the more likely she will run straight to the police as soon as we release her, and we'll be caught.

Fuck.

This is precisely why I've always had the *no hostage* rule. There's no good way to handle a captive, and feeling helpless doesn't sit well with me.

Yet, here we are, at the mercy of Mother Nature and the Marconis' demands...and trying to wrangle the spitfire upstairs.

"I guess all we can do is wait, then."

Rion nods and takes another drink of his beer. "You want one?" He raises the bottle.

I shake my head and narrow my eyes at him. It's not even noon yet. "No, I'll need something stronger eventually, but not until I know what's going on. We may need to get out of here quickly. I want to have my wits about me."

"Good call, man. This will be my last one."

Which means he's already had others this early in the morning. It might worry me, but it doesn't matter how many he has. Rion's a fucking tank. I've seen him drink a six-pack in half an hour and not feel anything. It's one of the reasons he never advanced very far in the military.

When you drink like a fish and don't want to give that up, it tends to cause problems with your superiors. Rion's a beast, a hard worker, and loyal as hell, but he wasn't willing to give up his love of alcohol, even though he can hold it.

He would've ended up like Cutter. An unstoppable machine with the skill set that gives people nightmares.

Rion is one scary motherfucker in his own right, but if he could do what Cutter can, on top of his size and strength...

Hell.

I chuckle to myself.

"What's so funny?"

I sigh and drop down into the chair next to the table and lean back. Milo curls at my feet with a huff. "Nothing."

There is absolutely *nothing* funny about this situation. All this should have been over years ago. When I went to work for *Il Padrone*, it was out of pure desperation to save the business. *Il Padrone* saw a young kid with a certain skill set, willing to break the law and do just about anything to protect the family legacy and make some money. He took advantage of that. And while my moral flexibility has certainly come in handy, it doesn't mean I want to keep doing this the rest of my life.

"Fuck. Fuck. Fuck." The words echo through the cavernous warehouse, mingling with another roll of thunder and the driving rain. I slam my palms on the table then run them back through my hair.

Rion's eyes flick up to my bedroom. "You aren't worried that you left her alone up there?"

I snort. "What the hell is she going to do? That staircase is the only way down and we're sitting right here."

Although, I'm confident she will sneak around my room and look for anything useful. Seeing my journal in her hand, the way she was reading the words I scribbled before I climbed in the shower, angered me more than I thought it would.

No one has ever seen it. No one has ever read it. It's only

for me—a holdout Mom started when I was young and she told me I needed an outlet for my thoughts and my anger.

I never thought I'd still be doing it at twenty-six. I never thought I'd be doing *this* at any point though, and knowing Grace read those words, that she knows how much trouble we are really in, has me gritting my teeth and biting back another round of curses.

But I have the journal now, and there's nothing else up there for her to get into that can cause me any problems.

The SAT phone on the table rings, and Rion practically jumps to grab it. He glances at the screen. His brow drops and he scowls. "It's Arturo."

"Motherfucker."

Using that phone is a last resort only. Something we rarely pull out. Only a handful of people know the number, and that's intentional. If we want to be reached, we will be. Otherwise, we operate under the radar as much as possible. Of course, the Marconis have the number. They must always have a way to get ahold of their lapdogs.

Why does it have to be Arturo?

I'd much rather be dealing with the big man himself. *Il Padrone* is one tough motherfucker, but the number two in the Marconi family is another level of evil compared to his uncle.

He has his sights set on taking over the family business, sooner rather than later, and he's doing everything in his power to ensure he strengthens the hold the Marconis already have over Chicago.

He's the one who made the call and ordered us to take the shipment for them. I can't even remember the last time I spoke with *Il Padrone* personally. He made it clear Arturo spoke for him and that we were to do whatever he asked. Arturo's the one who has been doing most of the dirty work with his uncle seemingly preoccupied doing God knows what.

I'm not privy to what is going on. All I know is, Arturo is the one who's been calling the shots and making the threats lately. If anything were ever to happen to *Il Padrone*, I'm sure Arturo would insist our deal continues with the family and doesn't die with him.

Paying off this debt is becoming a giant black cloud. I despise being at the beck and call of the Marconis, but I know better than to argue. That would mean a death sentence, not only for me but for the rest of the guys as well.

I can't put them in that position, which is why I've bitten my tongue, sucked up my pride, and done what's been ordered the last five years even though I know Mom and Dad are looking down at me, devastated by what I've been up to.

But I had to do it to save the business. The only thing Dad left me was the boats and some mixed memories. I can't lose it…as stupid and sentimental as that may sound.

I clear my throat and rise to my feet to grab the phone from Rion. "Arturo, what can we do for you?"

He chuckles low. "You can start by bringing me my delivery. You should've been here by now."

Which is precisely why my gut is churning and my blood won't stop thumping in my ears.

I'm not even entirely sure how much we got or if the boys will get it back here safely. There's no way I can tell Arturo that.

I have to stall.

"I know, man, but we have some major weather up here that has us behind schedule."

Rion raises an eyebrow and watches me, undoubtedly wondering why I'm lying to one of the most powerful mobsters in the United States. A man who could literally crush my nuts in a second.

"A storm?" His skepticism grates through the phone.

"Yes, check on the radar. It's tearing up the lake. Maybe it's missing Chicago, but we had to take shelter for a while and do some repairs to damage to our boat."

Even through the momentary silence on the line, I can

practically see his dark eyes flashing with anger. "How long of a delay are we talking?"

My heart leaps at the opening. This actually buys us some time. "Well, the weather report is saying the storms could last well into tomorrow or the next day. My boats can handle a lot, but after the damage they sustained, it will take a day or two to even get them back to working order before we can head down that way."

"A day or two?" The words are icy cold.

I raise my eyebrow at Rion but he offers no help. "Yeah, a day or two."

Silence from the other end of the line has my fist clenching around the phone.

"You have twenty-four hours. If my shipment isn't here by then, you're going to have to answer for it."

The line goes dead, and I toss the phone onto the table. "Well, fuck!"

Rion and I drop down in the chairs opposite each other. He motions toward the abandoned phone. "Well, what are we going to do?"

It's just like Arturo to give veiled threats. He's not dumb enough to flat out say what he'll do with us. We know. Everyone knows, which is why nobody fucks with the Marconis. The only people worse are the Gashis. Even I wouldn't touch those crazy Albanian fuckers with a ten-foot pole.

"We wait until E and Cutter get back. We figure out how much of the shipment we lost, and we go from there."

It's all we can do at this point.

He sighs and drains the last of his beer. "I know I said I wasn't going to have another one…"

I wave a hand at him. "Bring me one, too."

We might as well drown our sorrows while we wait.

"What are you going to do about her?" He nods up toward my bedroom.

I release a heavy sigh. "Right now, I plan to stick to my word and release her as soon as this all gets taken care of."

"And what if it doesn't get taken care of? What if we need to use her? Or what if she threatens to expose us?"

Visions of her red hair splayed out across my pillowcase, the way her lips parted slightly as her soft, deep breaths puffed in and out during her sleep flash before my eyes. A deep ache forms in the center of my chest, and I rub at it.

"I'll do what needs to be done."

I always do.

SIX

Grace

Pounding footsteps echo down what can only be metal stairs, ringing in my ears even through the closed door.

Yep. He's pissed.

Rightly so, I guess. I shouldn't have questioned him. I shouldn't have brought up what I overheard. And I sure as hell shouldn't have read his diary.

But how could I not?

The man kidnapped me, and he's already more contradictory than the Catholic Church. One minute, his black eyes are emotionless and hard, and the next, they soften to an almost gray and he seems...lost.

He would have to be...to be doing this.

What a damn mess.

There's no way I'll be able to sleep again, so I snatch a book off the bookcase without bothering to even look at the title. Getting lost in anything would be better than thinking about and dealing with the situation here.

If I do, if I *really* think about it...I may totally lose my shit, and staying calm is the only way I'm getting out of this unscathed.

I'm smart enough to know that. I'm also smart enough not

to even try to escape until I figure out where we are and if it's even possible. I can't run without knowing the crew is safe. And I'm not even sure if I need to. He says he'll release me.

Do I really believe it?

Part of me does, or at least wants to.

Thunder rolls, shaking the row of windows against their frames even though they're on the inside of the building.

That's one nasty storm out there, and despite the circumstances, I'm glad I'm at least inside. I wouldn't want to be on the water during this. Although, by now, the *Neptune's Daughter* would be in Milwaukee and we'd be enjoying a day or two in the city while we wait for the cargo to be unloaded. Instead, I'm stuck in this room, in only God knows where, with these crazy men.

Don't think about it too much…

I drop back on the bed and lean against the headboard to open the book I grabbed. *Moby Dick.*

Ha.

I chuckle to myself. Sort of ironic.

The soft, old leather of the book cover glides under my fingertips. I flip it open.

Holy shit.

1851. First edition.

This book is worth a fortune.

What's a guy like him doing with a book like this?

I flip to the next page and freeze. A handwritten note, in a light, delicate scroll.

Don't read it, Grace. It's none of your business.

But I've never been good at containing my curiosity.

He did say I could look at the books…

That should include everything inside them, right?

It's enough justification for me.

War,
I know this was always one of your favorites. A
story of surviving the perils of the sea and
friendship. I hope you never lose your love of
the water.
Love, Mom

My eyes automatically drift to the photo on the dresser, and I push up from the bed and slowly walk over to it.

The smiling couple and little boy make my heart ache. It has to be Warwick and his parents—the same dark eyes on father and son.

How could a child who looks so sweet and innocent and happy like this turn into a bitter, angry criminal like him?

Seeing the picture, reading his mom's words, it all makes him so…normal.

So why is he doing this?

It doesn't make any sense, and I can't seem to wrap my head around the logic of someone turning to this life. Things have been hard for a lot of people. Hell, we're close to broke and will probably lose the ship because of this. We'll have to wait for an insurance payout, and any delay in payment will be too long.

But no one I know would ever resort to becoming a damn criminal. I certainly wouldn't.

Who the hell is this guy?

The other books on the shelf seem to call to me, like somehow the contents will tell me everything I want to know about Warwick Pike.

I kneel down in front of the bookshelf and scan the titles again. One stands out.

Dr. Jekyll and Mr. Hyde.

It slides easily from the shelf, and a slip of paper falls out.

Another note?

I pick up the yellowing paper and climb to my feet. This

one is folded, which makes reading it seem a little more intrusive than the last one.

You've already done it once. What's one more?

A deep breath gives me enough time to stop overthinking it, and I flip it open.

War,
I know you're struggling with the demons that live inside you. Just know that you are stronger than them. The good can always win. You just have to let it.
Love, Mom

My hand moves to another book on the shelf almost of its own volition, the words of Warwick's mother tugging at me. I have to know if they are in every book. I have to know what she says about the man who now holds my life in his hands.

To Kill a Mockingbird...

War,
Defending your beliefs in the face of criticism and threats of violence takes bravery you must find deep down, but bravery doesn't always mean violence. Sometimes, it requires standing up in a way that's even more difficult than a show of physical force. Assess each situation carefully and determine what type of bravery is called for. Your heart will always guide you in the right direction.
Love, Mom

Adventures of Huckleberry Finn...

War,
You've always reminded me so much of Huck—

restless and wild, always looking for adven-
ture, and unable or unwilling to fit into any
mold society tries to cram you into. Don't ever
lose that spirit. Those molds only constrain
you from being who you truly are and civiliza-
tion isn't always so civilized.
Love, Mom

She's not wrong about civilization and the world today. I've never bothered to conform to my role as a diminutive girl who should do what she's told. Dad always appreciated my attitude and drive, the way I wanted to know more, but it's definitely been a problem for some other people.

And it seems to set Warwick off when I question him. It may be in my best interest to keep my mouth shut, but that's not my nature, and I need to know what's going on if I have any chance to survive this.

Another title catches my attention, and I grab it from the shelf. *Heart of Darkness...*

Reading it in high school, I found the entire thing a bit absurd. Marlow's reactions to the things he was witnessing always felt so foreign, maybe because I was so sheltered by Mom and Dad and had such a loving and normal childhood.

War,
Like Marlow, you will be faced with times
where it feels as though there is no "good"
choice, no choice that feels completely right.
Moral ambiguity exists everywhere in this
world and will appear in your life. During
those times, remember that sometimes,
choosing the lesser of two evils is all you
can do.
Love, Mom

Choose the lesser of two evils…

Is that what he's doing now? Is taking me instead of killing or harming the crew the lesser of two evils in his world?

I drag my hand along the spines on the shelf—classic after classic, all probably containing notes from his mother.

Hmm…*Lord of the Flies…*

War,
You've never been one to follow the rules. Like the young boys in the novel, you will face the constant conflict between wanting to live peacefully by rules, doing what's right and good for the group, and the instinct to fulfill your own violent desires to control others and get what you want. This fight between order and chaos, good and evil, and law and anarchy will never die. Choose to follow your own path, but always remember some rules are meant to be broken and sometimes, the only one looking out for you is you.
Love, Mom

The only one looking out for you is you…

Maybe that's what Warwick is doing. He's working for someone, someone willing to kill for whatever they took off the ship. And he took me to ensure he got it to that someone. He was protecting himself, and probably his guys too.

Choosing what's good for the group, even though it may not feel right.

I want to believe that's true—that he never would have taken me if their lives weren't in danger—but the damn man is so infuriating, it's hard to get a read on him at all.

A loud crack of thunder shakes the building. The lights blink out, plunging the small room into pitch blackness. A scream slides up my throat and out into the air. I drop the book and shuffle through the darkness toward the bed.

I sit on the edge and cling to the comforter while I wait for my racing heart and breathing to return to normal.

It's just the storm.

Calm down.

Footsteps thunder up the stairs, and the door flies open. A beam of light falls on me, and I raise my hand to cover my eyes and blink against it. The beam lowers enough for my eyes to adjust.

Warwick.

The relief that floods my system at seeing him makes acid rise up my throat. I shouldn't be happy to see him. I should be thinking of a way to use this blackout to my advantage.

Maybe I can get away...

Shove him down the stairs? Run?

To where, Grace?

I have no idea where I am or what, if anything, is around us. We could be miles and miles from any semblance of civilization, and in fact, I'm pretty confident that's exactly the situation. Warwick is smart enough to know to keep from being caught, he needs a base of operations far away from prying eyes. Which means, even if I got away without Warwick or the Hulk catching me, I would likely just end up wandering in the middle of nowhere during a violent storm.

Staying may be the lesser of two evils.

Warwick steps into the room. "We lost power. It'll take a little while to get the generator up. But we have plenty of flashlights. Just sit tight."

"Like I have a choice."

I release a deep, shaky breath and nod, but instead of turning around and returning the way he came, he just stands there watching me, his dark eyes reflecting the bright light from the flashlight still trained in front of me.

He scrubs a hand over his face. "Shit. I just realize what time it is. You must be starving."

Now that he mentions it, my stomach rumbles in complaint, and I lay my palm flat against it. The disorienting lack of a clock in here made me forget how long it's been since I last ate.

How can I have any appetite in this situation?

But somehow, I do. And I need to eat to keep my strength up in case I do need to make a break for it.

I shrug and offer him a tentative half-smile. "I could eat."

He motions with his hand for me to follow him out of the room. I'm not sure what I expected to find outside his quarters —a pirate hangout with a bar and serving wenches, maybe— but when I step out, I'm at the top of the large metal staircase overlooking a vast expanse of darkness spread out below us.

Three or four bright spots of light illuminate scattered places around what appears to be a warehouse. The various flashlights and lanterns set up barely touch the space, though.

Curses come from a far dark corner, and the faint outline of a figure is visible, bent over something. It must be the generator.

Warwick descends the steps slowly, keeping the light trained backward so I can see my way. I'm sure he knows this place like the back of his hand, but I might as well be blind.

A litany of screaming and more cursing echoes up to me while I descend, and I pause. "Do you need to go help the Hulk?"

Warwick stops on the second to last step and looks at me over his shoulder. A tiny grin pulls at the corner of his lips. "He's a big boy. He can handle it. I wouldn't call him that to his face, though."

The tiny flash of amusement again tells me Warwick is very human. That's not something I want to be reminded of. I want to be able to hate him. I want to be able to be raging angry. I want to demand to be let go again, but I can't push him or try to escape. Not yet. Not until I know more. Like where the hell we are.

When my feet hit the concrete floor, they echo through the space. "What is this place?"

My limited view of the things immediately in the beam of Warwick's light or lit by the handful of other places doesn't help much, but it feels very industrial.

He doesn't look back this time. "Anyone ever tell you that you ask a lot of questions?"

I bite my bottom lip and wring my hands. The ache in my gut moves from hunger to something totally different. He doesn't know it, but it couldn't be more of a sore spot for me. "Yes."

The man doesn't respond, just stalks ahead into the darkness with the flashlight as our only guide. We approach an open door, and he finally turns back to look at me with one raised dark eyebrow. "Anyone ever tell you it's going to get you into a lot of trouble someday?"

I scowl at him. "Yeah, I've been told that once or twice."

Or a million times.

By Mom and sometimes Dad. By Leo. By friends. By teachers. By the handful of boyfriends I ever had.

"Ever think of taking that advice?"

Asshole.

This time, I don't answer. I just scowl harder at his back as he disappears into the dark room.

A scurrying sound comes from down a dark hallway to my right, and something short, fat, and furry rubs against my leg.

They have a dog?

I bend down and rub my hand over the head of a very large bulldog. "Hey, buddy."

"You coming?" Warwick's question floats out the door to me.

I rise to my feet, and the dog and I follow him into what can only be described as a sparse industrial-like kitchen.

69

A long, low stainless-steel prep table dominates the center of the room. Various cooking implements glint in the beam of the flashlight as he moves toward a cabinet along the wall.

A giant stove occupies the corner next to a large fridge. The place is pristine.

Someone is anal about cleanliness…or they never cook.

Warwick grabs something from what must be a pantry, then stops at a row of cabinets to grab two bowls. He sets them on the counter next to the fridge and grabs a carton of milk. After retrieving two spoons and dropping them into the bowls, he gathers everything up and sets it down on the metal table between us.

"Who is this?" I point down to the dog.

He glances down. "Milo."

My eyes drift to the box.

You've got to be kidding me…

A chuckle I can't hold back builds and bursts forth out into the room. He jerks and looks up at me.

I brush away the tears forming. "I'm sorry. It's just…"

He raises an eyebrow. "Well?"

I finally regain my breath. "Well, it's Cap'n Crunch."

My laughter echoes off all the metal in the room and rings in my ears. I take a couple deep breaths and try my damnedest to get my shit together.

The man who probably hasn't ever laughed a day in his life eyes me for a moment then shrugs. "Yeah, so?"

Oh, come on!

"You don't see the humor in that, considering the situation?"

Warwick lifts the box up and examines it before his eyes return to mine. "Not really."

He's lying.

He thinks it's funny, too. He's just too hardheaded and assholey to admit it.

The two of us, captains of our respective ships, our

respective crews. One of us kidnapper. One of us kidnapped. Sharing a bowl of Cap'n Crunch during a storm.

You can't make this shit up.

He grabs the box, rips open the top, and pours us each a bowl before filling both with milk. Apparently, he intends to continue with the ruse that I'm not funny.

Whatever.

I grab my bowl, and he digs into his with gusto while I tentatively take my first bite. It's probably been a decade since I've had Cap'n Crunch. Maybe longer. I honestly can't remember the last time.

Damn, is it good...

Warwick's dark eyes roam over me, sending goose bumps and chills skittering across my skin and starting a low, fluttering burn in my belly.

I don't like it. But it's there all the same.

It doesn't matter how angry I try to be...the man just has a way about him. Something that tells me he isn't at all what he seems. Something that prevents me from trying to run, aside from not knowing where we are or how to get home...

There's more there. More to know. A truth lingering beneath the surface he tries so damn hard to hide. Maybe the tattoos are designed to distract from people really seeing *him*. But it won't work on me.

I struggle down three more bites and set down my half-eaten bowl. With a deep breath, I summon all my courage.

I have to know.

"What's a guy like you doing with a library like that upstairs?"

His spoon stills halfway to his mouth. Instead of eating it, he lets it fall into his almost-empty bowl and then sets it on the counter. His clamped jaw tics. His eyes darken to an almost black.

"A guy like me? A guy who takes hostages and robs innocent people? Is that what you mean? A guy like me, who's supposed to rape and pillage his life away. A guy like me, who has the IQ of a goldfish and isn't supposed to do anything else but cause misery?"

Oh shit.

Maybe that was the wrong way to phrase the question or maybe I shouldn't have asked it at all. God knows he gave me a warning to keep my mouth shut, and I didn't listen.

But now I need to explain. I can't let the man who holds my life in his hands believe I think so little of him. That feels dangerous in the same way being close to him does. Hostages should respect the authority of their captors if they don't want to end up hurt, or worse. I haven't done that at all.

"Look, I didn't mean—"

He slams his fists down on the counter. "I don't give a flying fuck what you meant. It was a mistake to leave you up there. Stay out of my stuff. Stop asking questions. Or there will be consequences."

SEVEN

War

Before she has a chance to respond and ask any more infuriating questions, I stalk past her and Milo, out across the warehouse floor, past a stunned Rion, and shove out the side door.

The cool, driving rain pelts my skin.

Good. Let it.

I rush into the storm and stride toward the beach and the lighthouse in the distance.

Who the hell does she think she is?

If she knew what was good for her, she would keep her mouth shut. She's been warned over and over again. I don't need her reminding me of what a shit storm I've created, or that we are in very real danger from the goddamn Marconis. And I especially don't need her reminding me of *who* and *what* I really am.

I'm soaked almost instantly, the chilly drops stinging every inch of my exposed skin, but I don't care. It helps quell the rage roaring through my body.

Her.

The situation.

All of it.

It's just too much.

How the fuck did this happen?

I failed. It's that simple.

"Warwick!" Her soft voice floats through the air, and even over the sound of the thunder and raging storm, it makes me pause.

I stop and turn back.

Why the hell did she follow me? Can't she see how fucking pissed off I am?

Rion should have stopped her. Told her it was a bad idea to go after me, to go out in this storm.

It's like this woman has no idea what's good for her. And maybe I don't either because now she's standing here in the pouring rain, her red hair wet and plastered to the sides of her face and down over her shoulders already, and, Christ…

She's beautiful.

She's exactly the type of woman I would be chasing right now were things different, but instead, she's chasing me when all I want is to be alone.

"What the hell are you doing? Go back inside. I can't believe Rion even let you out here."

My words carry across the distance between us, and a bolt of lightning tears through the sky, further illuminating her enticing form.

She stops and crosses her arms over her chest, which only accentuates the soaking wet fabric clinging to her breasts.

"Oh, your brute in there tried to stop me, but I told him to fuck off and slipped out of his hands and out the door. He started to come after me but I think he thought better of it."

What the hell?

That's so unlike Rion. He wouldn't have just let her go. She wouldn't have, couldn't have, slipped from his grip. It had to have been intentional. Why, is another question. He probably didn't want to have to deal with her and knew she wasn't going anywhere—there's nothing around for miles and miles and miles—and he knew there was no way I would let her get far.

I'll deal with that fucker later. Right now, my only concern is why this girl followed me out here in the storm.

"You come out here to question me some more? To sling more insults?"

She sighs and wraps her arms around herself to fight the cold wind. It tugs at her wet clothing and tries desperately to lift her soaked hair. "I'm sorry. I didn't mean to be nosy. It's just in my nature, and I don't really understand what's going on here. I feel like if I did, we might be in a very different situation. Maybe I wouldn't be so scared, so unsure."

I wipe the water from my face only to have it instantly wet again. Thunder rolls all around us, and she trembles.

"This is neither the time nor the place to have any sort of conversation. And even in another place, even inside, what makes you think I would tell you anything?" My fists clench at my sides, and I grit my teeth together, trying to temper my desire to scream at her. "The more you know, the worse danger we are in. Do you not understand that?"

The frustration burns through me, making me take a step back. I can't be close to her. Not when I'm this angry. That never ends well for the person on the other side of my rage. And while I've never hit a woman, and wouldn't, I might do something else very stupid.

She closes the distance between us before I can scramble away and lowers her voice since she no longer has to shout over the storm. "I saw your books, Warwick. I saw the notes from your mother. I've heard the way you talk. You—"

"If you know what's good for you, you'll stop talking."

"No, I won't. You aren't some uneducated thug. I can't believe that somebody like you is doing something like this for no reason. I feel like you're..." Her head shakes from side to side, and she raises her hands, searching for her words.

A fraud?

It's certainly how I feel lately.

What kind of fucking captain am I when I get my guys into shit like this?

But I know that's not what she means. I can see it in her eyes, the way she looked at me when she mentioned the books and Mom's notes. She thinks they mean something…far more than the truth.

"Like I'm what? Really a good guy underneath? Not the type of person who would do something like this?" I huff out a deep sigh and narrow my eyes at her. "I'm not a good guy, Grace. So, get that out of your head right now. I'm exactly what you see. And if you paid attention to the notes my mom left me, you would've seen that."

The neatly scrawled words I've re-read a thousand times since she died fill my head. Mom always had a way with words, and an uncanny ability to read me as well as any book. She saw my struggles, what was happening that I tried so damn hard to bury deep inside. The things that eventually broke free with disastrous results.

I can't even remember the number of fights I was in…the number of people I hurt. The number of times I put that look of disappointment on her face before she died.

Men like me don't deserve to be looked at this way by women like Grace. I fucking kidnapped her, yet she's staring up at me like I'm something to be saved.

That can't be further from the truth.

Lightning splits the sky, illuminating her green eyes. Her bottom lip quivers. "I don't believe you're a bad guy. I want to. I should, with everything that's happened, but I just…don't."

Idiot.

I shake my head. "I don't know if I'm disgusted by your naïvety or if I feel sorry for you."

Rain continues to drive down on us, but the cold barely touches me. Even across the foot of space between us, her heat radiates. She steps forward and looks up at me, and her emerald eyes ask a million questions I'm sure her lips are wanting to voice. But she doesn't speak; she just watches me, searches my eyes, like she can somehow see the depths of my soul and determine whether her assessment about me is correct.

This. Right now. It's more dangerous than anything Arturo or *Il Padrone* could do.

"You need to go back inside and leave it alone, Grace. Leave me alone. You're not going to like how this ends."

"How what ends, Warwick?" Another tiny step has her breasts almost brushing against my chest, where my heart is about ready to beat straight out through my ribs. "Are you going to hurt me? Kill me?"

"Fuck!" I whirl away from her to stand at the water's edge. The waves churn up and slam against the rocky shore, echoing the turmoil swirling inside me.

This situation has gone from bad to so fucking bad so quickly, it's giving me whiplash. Taking a damn hostage is bad enough, dragging someone innocent into the life and death game with the Marconis. Now, is she really forcing me to do something I can never take back?

Could I kill her if I had to?

Yesterday, before I climbed onto that ship, I might've said yes. I might've believed I had it in me to kill somebody if I really needed to, in order to protect myself and the guys. I've done some other bad shit and come damn close to taking someone's life without even thinking about it. When the situation calls for violence, it's not something I've ever balked at. And there's no doubt Rion, Cutter, and Elijah, even Preacher, will do anything needed. It's one of the reasons I brought them on to my crew. I needed men who didn't worry about shit like what's legal, or what's right. Men who would help me keep Dad's business going and pay back the debt I owed to *Il Padrone*. Men who would always have my back and my complete trust, no matter what I asked them to do.

But Grace? She's something else altogether, and I'm not sure what that is, but it has me second-guessing my ability to pull the trigger if it were truly necessary.

The woman might be tiny, but she has a strength and a passion that belies her size. It's as infatuating as it is infuriating.

I sense her moving behind me and turn before she can close the distance.

"Go inside and stay there."

She shakes her head. "What are you going to do if I don't?"

Well, shit.

That's a good question. I guess she's calling my bluff.

"You don't want to push me, Grace. You won't like what you see."

If she were a man, she'd be laid out on the ground right now, with impressions of my fist all over her face. But one thing I could never do, never in a million years, is harm a woman intentionally. She knows it even though she doesn't know *me*.

I must have "pussy" written across my face.

And that makes doing this job all the harder.

If she can see it, then so can the Marconis. So can Rion. So can Cutter. So can E. So can Preacher. And I'm supposed to be their leader. Supposed to be the captain. They look to me for what to do. If I don't have the balls anymore, then we are in real fucking trouble.

"I want answers, Warwick. That's all I want."

Fuck. Fuck. Fuck.

Thunder rolls around us, and the rain falls in sheets.

"Stop calling me Warwick."

"That's your name, isn't it?"

I growl and step away to create more distance between us. "Yes, I just don't like hearing you say it."

That's not true. I like the way it falls from her lips way too much. That's why she has to fucking stop.

"What do you want me to call you?"

"Captain is fine."

She snorts and rolls her eyes. "Well, since I'm a captain too, we can share that moniker. Call me that instead of Grace."

"You're not a captain." The words are out of my mouth before I realize how insulting they will be to her. She recoils as if she's been slapped.

Real nice, War.

She squares her shoulders and huffs. "Well, what I was doing on that ship begs to differ."

I snort and stare her down. "Those men may have followed you because you're their boss. But you have no idea what you were doing on that ship. If you had more solo time on the water, if you had been prepared, we wouldn't have gotten the jump on you."

A dark laugh slips from her wet lips. "I know what I'm doing. I *was* trained. Just because it was my first time solo doesn't mean I'm a damn idiot. I managed to set off the emergency beacon and get a gun trained on you. I don't think I did too bad. I'm good at my job."

"I don't doubt that, but this isn't your job." *And I'm not your knight in shining armor, or someone to fix or save.* "Now, go inside."

She frowns and opens her mouth to undoubtedly ask more fucking questions.

Why can't she just stop?

My lips are on hers before I realize what I'm doing.

I just need her to shut the hell up.

I wrap my arms around her and pull her against me as I devour her, pushing all the anger and frustration over the situation into the kiss.

A tiny moan slips from her lips and into my mouth.

That sound breaks through the veil of whatever it is that

possessed me to do it in the first place. I tear my lips away and step back from her, my chest heaving and my breath coming out in hard pants, visible in the chilly air.

Through the pouring rain, she stares at me, wide-eyed, and presses her shaking fingers to her lips.

Fuck.

I turn my back on her and take off down the beach before she can respond. That was really fucking stupid. I kidnapped her and now I kissed her.

Jesus. What an asshole.

I shove my hands back to my soaked hair and tug on the ends of it. The pain rippling across my scalp is a momentary distraction from what I just did and what's happening.

I'm only making things worse. And if Cutter and E don't show up with what we were able to get really fucking soon, we are totally fucked.

I only make it a few yards from where Grace still stands on the shore, when the familiar sound of a foghorn splits through the storm. A shape on the water emerges from the driving rain.

The Destiny.

Thank God. They made it back.

It moves slowly through the storm toward the warehouse, and I turn back to see Grace standing there, staring at it, unmoved from the spot where I left her after that brutal kiss.

I run back and snag her hand, jerking her along after me. She stumbles briefly but then follows, hot on my heels, back into the warehouse.

Rion's head snaps up from where he leans over the map with the phone, probably still trying to contact them, and his eyes narrow on us where my hand clasps hers. I let it fall and move away from her as fast as possible.

"E and Cutter are almost here. Get the door open."

He drops the SAT phone and races to the mechanisms

along the wall. He throws open the latch that releases the huge bay door, then presses the button to move the door up.

We stand at the dock as the boat slowly makes its way toward us.

Lightning cracks across the sky and thunder continues to roll around us. This storm system doesn't want to relent. At least it's giving me more time to come up with a plan.

Grace shivers next to me.

Footsteps—human and canine—sound behind me, and Preacher moves up next to me with Milo at his heels. He finally decided to come up for air now that the boys are home.

The Destiny enters the dock, and they toss the lines to me and Rion to secure her. Cutter and E lean over the side and look down at me.

I glare at them. "Where the fuck have you two been?"

Cutter shrugs, and Elijah just gives me a sardonic grin. They both shift their gazes to Grace standing next to me. E raises an eyebrow in question. He's right. She doesn't belong here and shouldn't be hearing any of this.

"Go upstairs, Grace. Take a hot shower and warm up. Take whatever clothes you want from my dresser."

She looks like she's about ready to argue, but Rion turns to her and snaps his teeth. She jumps and races off across the warehouse and up the metal steps.

When I turn back, Cutter is jumping off the rail to a waiting Milo, and E is making his way down the ladder.

I nod at him when he hits the concrete. "I'm glad you guys are here. Because we are truly and epically fucked."

EIGHT

Grace

I reach the top of the stairs with my blood boiling.

What a dick to just order me away like that. After he just kissed me, nonetheless.

But, in a way, I guess it was for my own safety. From him and from myself. I can't even begin to comprehend what that was...what that meant.

Was he just trying to shut me up? And why the hell didn't I push him away?

My hand finds the doorknob but something stops me from turning it.

Voices rise from the warehouse below. Angry voices. Distressed voices.

I need to know what's going on. Whatever is happening impacts me too. I'm still here. And I see no signs of them planning to release me anytime soon.

That means eavesdropping is a necessity, not just me being nosy.

I inch down one step, then another. Warwick's room must've originally been the office for whatever this place was, and if I stand against the side of it but don't go any lower, I can remain hidden around the edge and they won't even know I'm still here.

In theory...

One deep breath fills my lungs. I hold it and lean forward slightly to peer around the edge of the only thing keeping me from being discovered.

The five of them and Milo move to a makeshift table in the center of the open space. Warwick leans over it with his palms flat on the table. The Hulk crosses his arms over his chest and stands on the opposite side. The other three—the tall, lean one who walks with a slight limp, the clean-cut one I only caught a glimpse of on the *Neptune's Daughter*, and the guy with the sunglasses—drop into the chairs on either side of the table and look at Warwick.

He glances back over his shoulder in the direction where I'm hiding.

Shit.

I pull back, cringe, and hold my breath, waiting for his tirade about eavesdropping, but it doesn't come. Either he didn't see me or he did, and for some unknown reason, isn't saying anything. Standing here and listening to them is probably worse than continuing to ask questions, but I have to know what's going on. I have to understand the situation better so I know what I need to do to make it out of here in one piece. With my body, my mind, and my heart intact.

"Where do we stand?"

The question floats up from where they sit at the table. I peer around just long enough to watch the guy in the shades lean forward. That must have been his question.

Why is he wearing those inside anyway?

Their low voices are barely loud enough to hear. I move down one more step and press myself against the side of the office.

There's a pause before anyone responds. My heart thuds wildly.

Warwick's voice finally hits my ears. "I spoke with Arturo before you got here."

"Shit."

I glance around the corner again.

The tall guy shakes his head. "What did that asshole have to say?"

I tuck back to safety.

Warwick lets out a mirthless laugh, and a crack of thunder shakes the building again. "He's not happy."

"Does he know what happened?"

"No. We need time to formulate a plan before we show our hand."

"Do we have a plan?" That question came from The Hulk. I'd know his voice anywhere.

I sure as hell hope there's a plan.

"Not yet. I wanted to see how much we got and go from there."

A scraping sound has me peeking around the corner again. The tall guy rises to his feet. "What about the girl?"

Warwick growls, and I squeeze my eyes shut. I can practically envision those eyes—almost black as night—as he looks over his men. "Arturo gave us twenty-four hours to get the shipment to him. Until we're one hundred percent sure we're out of danger, she stays here."

Shit.

Sounds like these guys are never out of danger, so what does that mean for me?

"Then you're just going to release her and hope she doesn't run straight to the police?" That question came from the guy with the glasses, and the hard edge in his voice sends a chill down my spine.

There's no doubt he would do whatever needs to be done, including eliminating any threats. Mainly me. The man is ice-cold.

"We don't have much of a choice right now other than to

trust her. She didn't rat us out to the Coast Guard when they stopped us because of the threat to her and her crew. We'll send E to Milwaukee to wait for them and keep them in his sights. If they haven't alerted anyone, and we release her safely, she won't say a word, and if she does, I'll deal with it." Warwick's words aren't exactly comforting, but at least he's giving me the benefit of the doubt.

What would I do even if I did manage to get away? What about if they do release me? Do I report it and tell the cops everything? Or do I stay silent, force the crew to do the same, and report the cargo lost in transit due to some issue with the ship?

I need to dislodge the questions from the front of my brain. Listening to them and learning what I can needs to be my focus. The rest, I can deal with later.

"What we gonna do about the fact that we only have half the shipment?" Sunglass guy sounds pissed.

Yeah, what are they gonna do about that?

"Come on, War. You know *Il Padrone* will kill us if we don't deliver everything. No matter how useful we may be to him, he will not accept this type of failure."

A loud slam vibrates up to my ears, followed by Warwick's deep, angry voice. "You think I don't know that?"

I cringe and move up a step.

"We don't have much time before we have to make the delivery, so we need to work on trying to find out where they took the ship and if there's any way for us to get the rest of the cargo. If not, then we need to replace it."

Rion offers a sardonic laugh. "With what? We don't even know what's in the crates."

He's right. If Warwick is correct about the manifest being wrong, then no one knows what's in them, let alone whether it's replaceable.

"We better go look, then."

Chairs scrape against the concrete floor, and I dart up the last couple stairs and into the bedroom. As soon as the door clicks shut behind me, I release a shaky breath and lean back against it.

God, I hope no one saw me.

I rush over to the wall of windows and peer around the edge of the peeling paper on one of them out to the warehouse. Through my limited view, it appears they left the table.

They must've gone on to the ship to check the cargo.

Things are bad. So, so bad. I knew they were involved with something dangerous. Clearly. And the conversation I overheard on the boat earlier hinted at the life-and-death nature of what was happening. This just confirms it. Whoever *Il Padrone* and Arturo are, these guys are dead if they don't deliver whatever they were supposed to take from *Neptune's Daughter* to them in the next day.

But why? How did Warwick get involved in something like this in the first place?

His vague comments about his mom's notes and what I should have figured out hint at the darkness in him, but to lead to this...

What would it take to make someone go this far?

I shiver and look down to my soaked clothes. I need to hop in the shower before he comes up here and realizes I was eavesdropping.

I shuffle across the room and open the only other door. The tiny bathroom barely holds me.

How does Warwick fit in here?

I turn back to the door and flip the lock. Just in case Warwick or one of the other guys decides to check on me. I flip on the shower, and ice-cold water falls from the head. That won't help my situation, so I turn to the cracked and warped mirror while I wait for it to warm up.

The person staring back at me is barely recognizable.

My hair falls limp and wet against my face and over my shoulders, and the remnants of the makeup I put on before this whole fiasco started now runs in dark smears from the rain. Red rings my eyes, and the usually bright green has a dullness I haven't seen before.

Christ, I look like hell.

But I suppose it's to be expected. A hot shower will do me good. Refresh me and give me a little time to think about how to handle this. It's clear I can't just wait for them to let me go. They're sending "E," whichever one that is, to watch the crew, and there's no guarantee they'll get what they need to appease the people they have to answer to.

My only hope is for an opening to present itself to escape. I need to be proactive. Chasing Warwick out into the storm was supposed to help me figure out where we were and how I could get away, but the almost total darkness prevented me from seeing much of anything besides the vastness of Lake Michigan to one side and a wall of trees to the other.

The only clue about where we might be was the lighthouse in the distance. There are almost two dozen along this side of Lake Michigan that are close enough to where the *Neptune's Daughter* was to be our current location, but we are normally so far out from shore and don't see them that often, so I couldn't place it from such a short glance, through driving rain, in the dark.

Not exactly promising.

I struggle out of my wet clothes and let them plop onto the old, cracked tile floor. I step in, and the scalding hot stream of water hits my skin. I sigh. I didn't realize how much I needed this. I drop my head back and wet my hair, letting the water massage the tension from my neck and shoulders.

One thing has become crystal clear after hearing that conversation—it's only a matter of time until things come to a head. A decision will be made soon—one that will ultimately determine what happens to me if I can't figure out a way out of here.

Only staying alert and learning everything I can will possibly save me now.

Warwick's shampoo and soap sit on the small ledge in the shower stall, and I quickly wash and turn off the water. As great as it felt to stand under the hot stream and try to forget where I am, I need to face the harsh, cold reality of where I stand.

Speaking of cold…

The chill in the room when I step from the shower sends goose bumps across my skin. I grab the towel hanging beside the shower and do my best to dry off. My eyes land on the pile of cold, wet clothes on the floor.

Shit. Those are definitely not coming back on.

And of course, I forgot to grab clothes from Warwick's dresser before I came in.

Dumbass.

I push open the door and step into the room. Another shiver rolls through me, but it isn't the cold air that freezes me in my tracks.

It's an almost naked Warwick.

Hard muscle. Swirling ink. That damn V thing again running down below his abs to disappear into his wet, clinging boxer briefs.

Holy hell.

Somehow, I tear my eyes away from the pornographic display to raise them to his face.

The look of pure rage etched across his handsome features gives him a crazed look, and his normally dark eyes are as black as midnight and shimmer with a wrath I haven't seen from him before.

Holy shit…

This is a glimpse of the man he's been warning me about. This man is capable of very bad things.

I take an involuntary step back, pulling the too-small towel tighter around myself. His nostrils flare, and the rigid cord of muscle along the side of his neck bulges.

"I-I'm sorry. I forgot to grab some clothes."

He turns without a word, yanks open the dresser, and tosses me a T-shirt and a pair of boxers. I barely catch them without dropping the towel and back up into the bathroom without taking my eyes off him. For some reason, giving my back to him right now sends more fear skittering through me than anything else that's happened.

Warwick is volatile right now. Even more so than when we were out on the beach.

Something happened. It must have something to do with the crates.

But what could possibly be in them that has him this *upset?*

I tug on the too-large T-shirt and boxers that practically fall off my hips.

I run the towel over my wet hair one last time before I step out into the room. He's fully dressed this time, but the same dark look dominates his face and anger rolls off of him in waves. He fumbles with something behind his back then looks down to secure his belt.

"What's wrong?"

His head snaps back up toward mine, and his lip curls into a sneer. "Are you really going to start asking questions again? Didn't we have this conversation?"

I raise my hands in surrender and step back. "I'm sorry. I just...you're clearly upset about something."

"How is that any of your business?"

He's right. It's not.

But I can't seem to stop myself.

"It's not my business."

"Fuck!" He grinds his teeth together and shoves his hand back through his wet hair. The struggle going on inside him races forward in the tension in his body and shaking hands. "You should know. Especially if you're continuing to do business with these people."

"What people?"

With a sigh, he nods toward the door. "It's easier if I show you."

He wraps his hand around my bicep and practically drags me from the room.

I stumble on the stairs, unable to keep up with his long stride and speed as he powers down them. He leads us barefoot across the dirty, cold concrete floor of the warehouse to where the ship that just came in sits at the dock.

There's no sign of the other guys or Milo, which for some reason has me breathing a sigh of relief.

I may not trust Warwick fully, but the others…I sure as *hell* don't trust any of them even a little.

NINE

War

I thought I knew anger. I thought I had lived with it and let it burn inside me long enough that it was my old friend. I thought I understood it and had accepted its dark, pulsating presence in my life. I was dead wrong.

Because this…what is coursing through me at this very moment, is something far worse than anger. Something far darker, more malicious and malevolent. Something that will bring me to do even those things I never thought I could in my deepest heart.

My grip on Grace's arm is probably too tight as I drag her over to the ladder of *The Destiny*. Still, she doesn't fight it.

Maybe she's finally accepted what I've been trying to convince her is true since the moment we boarded her ship— she doesn't have control here. Just like us, she's become a pawn in the Marconis' game.

A game that just got deadlier.

From the second we opened that first crate and pulled away the top layer of boxes of machine parts, I knew everything had changed. I never questioned what was in the boxes *Il Padrone* had us acquire.

Maybe I did have my head in the sand about what we've

been doing, but I never, in a million years, would have suspected this.

It's just not the M.O. of the Italians. It shouldn't be happening.

I stop at the base of the ladder and shove her in front of me. "Climb." She looks back at me, her green eyes wide like a damn doe about to be shot. I motion upward. "Go."

She hesitates only briefly before she begins her ascent. For someone so petite, her legs sure seem to go for miles as they move inch by inch up in front of my face.

A fraction of my anger recedes, replaced by something far more dangerous. Something I shouldn't be feeling for this woman. Something that could get both of us in a lot of trouble.

Rung by rung, hand over hand, I make my way up behind her, fighting the urge to look up because my boxers are huge on her and do very little to conceal anything.

Knock it off.

She makes it to the top and swings her leg over with some slight difficulty, then stands up and moves to the side so I can get aboard. Once I'm on deck, I grab her arm again and pull her over to where the pallets sit toward the back of the boat.

Three of the six are open, their false contents strewn about with all the real contents in the center of the boxes.

"Look."

Her terrified eyes drift up to meet mine momentarily before she shifts and takes a step forward. She leans over to see inside the opened crates. She gasps and jerks back. "Is that what I think it is?"

A shaky hand snakes out as if she's about to grab one of the packages, but I slap her hand away.

"You want your fingerprints all over that?"

She shakes her head and steps back. "So, it's drugs?"

I scrub at my unshaven jaw, nod, and step away to pace. "Heroin."

"No!" She sucks in a breath. "Holy shit."

Her reaction seems genuine, but I can't shake the niggling feeling in the back of my head that maybe she isn't as innocent as she claims to be.

I don't want to believe she knew. Hell no. She hasn't been acting like she had a clue, but people rarely surprise me anymore with what they're capable of. Especially when they're pushed by something.

"You swear to me you didn't know what was in these crates?"

She whirls around, her eyes darkening and flashing with anger. "Do you really think I would've transported them if I knew what was in them?"

"I've seen crazier things."

People do things when they're desperate.

"Well, I didn't know."

The emotion in her voice is real. She didn't know. She couldn't have known. If she had, she would have run straight to the police. Which doesn't bode well for us when all is said and done.

But just because she's innocent in this doesn't mean everyone is.

"What about your father?"

Her brow furrows, and she narrows her eyes at me. "What about him?"

"Is it possible he knew what was going on? What he was transporting? He was scheduled to make this delivery, right?"

"What? No, of course not. My dad would never...no matter how bad money was, he would never go that far, never allow that. He had morals. He had a backbone."

Ouch. That stung.

She doesn't know everything, so I shouldn't take it personally, but once she does know, that statement already tells me everything I need to know about what she'll think of me and my choices that got us here.

"You said the business was going under. You're almost bankrupt, right?"

A tiny nod is her only response. I can practically see the wheels turning in her head.

"People do a lot of things when they're desperate, that they might not consider otherwise, Grace."

She studies me for a moment, then leans against the crate. "It sounds like you're speaking from experience."

One of her pale red eyebrows rises, and she waits for me to respond.

Fuck.

What does it hurt to tell her at this point? She already knows too much as it is.

What I wouldn't give for a bottle of Jack right now. This would be so much easier with some liquid courage.

Instead, I suck in a deep breath and lean back against the crate next to her. This will fucking hurt, but maybe helping her understand will make her more compliant. If she stops fighting me, stops arguing and asking questions, it will make things easier on all of us.

I can't believe I'm telling her this.

"My mother was the town librarian. She got me reading at a very young age and kept me with my nose in a book as much as possible. I think she thought it would somehow quell some of the less admirable qualities she was seeing in me as a child."

I snort and shake my head at the memory of being dragged into a parent-teacher conference after beating the shit out of Jimmy Ellis in third grade. The little shit deserved it, and Dad knew it. Mom, on the other hand, would have preferred a more diplomatic resolution to the situation.

"My dad owned a commercial fishing company, as you know. He was a drinker, but as long as Mom was around, he kept it pretty much in control. He was never violent or abusive, just a drunk." I suck in another fortifying breath and scrub my hands over my face to fight the burn threatening in my eyes. "Mom died when I was fourteen. Aggressive pancreatic cancer. She was gone within a month of her diagnosis."

I pause and swallow through the lump in my throat.

I can't let this woman see me cry.

Walking will help. I shove off from the crate and pace along the planks of the deck.

"After she died, Dad barely held it together. He started drinking more and one of his captains stepped up and helped with the business when he was too drunk and incapable of handling things. I helped too, as much as I could at that age."

Which wasn't much. I was useless at anything in the office, but I knew how to drive a boat. So, I spent most of my time out on the water, which was my favorite place to be, besides the library. The cool, crisp air. The tangy, fresh smell of the water. The relaxing sounds of the waves slapping against the hull. It was my safe place. A place where nothing and no one could touch me.

And now...it's tainted with everything I've done. Everything that *could* have been had I taken another path.

"My mom had set aside money for me to go to college. It was always her big dream for me to get out of that place, to do something bigger and better, to not end up working on the boats like my dad. She loved our life, and she loved him, but she had dreams for me. Maybe ones that weren't very realistic, but she had them nonetheless."

I chance a glance in Grace's direction to ensure she's still with me. Her red-rimmed eyes follow my every movement, and she hangs on every word.

She's finally getting what she's wanted this entire time. A fucking answer.

"I tried to convince him to let me stay home and help with the business after I graduated from high school, but for being an old drunk, he sure stuck to his guns. He knew it was what Mom really wanted and that she would be rolling over in her grave if she saw me skipping school just to stay home and help him. So, I went to college, and my dad got worse."

Worse is an understatement. It was a shitshow. And at the time, I was happy to be away from it.

Classes, studying, girls, parties…it all took my mind off what I had lost, what I was losing. I shut the rest of the world out and lived in that tiny slice that was campus life. I let myself believe things would be fine when I was done and out. That Dad was fine.

I was so damn wrong.

"Dad's employees kept all the shit together. Until they couldn't anymore."

I pause and stare up at the metal beams of the ceiling. This isn't a memory I want to relive. It's something better locked away in that deep, dark place I store all the shit that brings forth my rage. But it's too late for that anyway. Far too late.

"He OD'd. They found him with a needle in his arm."

Grace's shaky, soft voice floats across the space between us. The woman so full of questions has managed to sit silently until now. "OD'd on what?"

I nod toward the pallet, and she covers her mouth. Tears form in her eyes.

"I came home to discover the business was in far worse shape than they told me. We were essentially bankrupt. He spent the vast majority of the money on booze and drugs and had racked up debts even his crews and office manager weren't aware of. I had no idea it had become that bad, that he had moved on from the booze."

It's my fault for not being there.

I close my eyes and rub at my temples to try to clear the memories away, to try to send the guilt floating off into the cool air. But it still sits heavy on my chest.

"So, then, did you go back to school?"

I sigh and shake my head while I pace.

It's the obvious question, and this time, it doesn't make me mad. Instead, regret forms a lump in my throat.

"No. I probably should have. Just sold what was left of the business to pay off the debts and moved on. But I couldn't. For all of his faults, my father was a good man. The business was his legacy to me, to our family name. It was what I was born into and even though Mom wanted something greater for me, I couldn't let go. Not that easily."

What a fucking colossal mistake.

My weakness. My sentimentality. My need to hang on so desperately to something that was long dead. It all led us here.

"I started looking for a way to try to salvage it."

She nods. She's starting to get a better picture of how we ended up in this mess. But she has no idea what the stakes are.

"An old friend of my dad's told me he knew someone who could help me. He was a *friend* in Chicago. He set up a meeting. I was young and dumb and still reeling from my father's death. His name was Galasso Marconi but everyone just calls him *Il Padrone.*"

I wait for the name to register, but she stares at me blankly.

"He's the head of the Italian mob in Chicago and has been for a long time. I should've known better than to get involved with him, but he seemed so understanding and sympathetic to my plight."

And why wouldn't he be?

It was what he thrived on—finding people who were down and out, weak and willing, people who could offer him something and provide a service. People willing to do anything…

Christ, I was so stupid.

"He offered me five hundred thousand dollars. Enough to pay off all the debts and have some left over for continuing operating expenses. All he wanted in return was for me to transport some cargo for him to work off the debt. It seemed reasonable."

It would be impossible for her not to see where this is

going now. It doesn't take a rocket scientist to figure out how things went south so damn fast.

I just never saw it coming.

Young and naïve. The same things I accused her of being.

"The first couple jobs were just picking things up in Traverse City, Toronto, or Cleveland, and moving them to Chicago. It was easy. I didn't ask questions. Then, after a few runs, he told me the next job was different. That I needed to make sure I had a crew who wasn't afraid to get their hands dirty if need be."

She turns her head back toward the warehouse, searching for the guys. Only an empty space greets her.

Thank God for that.

If they knew I was vomiting my life story to her, they would call me out on being a fucking pussy and probably walk away from this tonight.

"At that point, I was trapped. I couldn't say no. Not if I wanted to stay alive. I couldn't repay that debt any other way. So, I got my guys together, ones I knew had certain skill sets and training, and we did our first *real* job. After that...most of the jobs weren't so easy anymore."

I return to my perch on the side of the crate, and she searches my face for a moment before her eyes dart to the contents. "But you had to suspect what was in these crates. How did you not know?"

I growl and dig my fingers into the rough wood of the crate. "The Italians aren't into drugs. That's one thing they never dealt in historically. There was no reason to think they would be transporting them and bringing them into Chicago."

She snorts and laughs softly. "And you called me naïve."

Rage floods my veins, and I shove to my feet, towering over her. Her ashen face and quivering lip should give me pause, should help me rein in the fire consuming me, but it doesn't. It can't. Nothing can.

Who the hell is she to call me naïve? She doesn't know me, know my life.

Fuck her.

"Fuck you, Grace. Go back to my room and stay there."

I storm past her and jump down onto the dock.

Cutter pushes off the side of the boat not three feet to my left.

Fuck.

He heard everything. Even through his mirrored glasses, the accusation in his stare burns my skin and tells me he didn't miss a word. He must have already been out here, maybe around the back and hidden when we came out.

"Make sure she goes up and stays there."

He doesn't dare argue. Not when I'm like this. And I don't wait for a response. I just blow past him and back toward Preacher's nerd lair.

We need to figure out where to get twenty kilos of heroin. Fast.

TEN

Grace

If I said I slept fifteen minutes last night, that would probably be an exaggeration. Warwick's story and his volatile response to my questions left me more rattled than I want to admit.

I get it now. Why he's doing this. How this all started.

What I don't understand is why he can't get out. There has to be a way to pay off the debt. Warwick doesn't seem like a pushover. So why is he letting *Il Padrone* continue to send him on these jobs? Why does he continue to put his life on the line, and the lives of his men? Why doesn't he just say no?

Il Padrone is dangerous—all these guys are. I'm not so naïve that I don't understand that. But there has to be another way, another agreement that can be made. Maybe he can get a loan from a bank. Maybe it's not too late to sell what's left of the business.

Though, I'm sure he's already thought of that, and probably a hundred other possible ways out. He rejected them for one reason or another.

Who am I to suggest them? It's just his hostage intruding where she isn't wanted or needed again.

My stomach rumbles, and I crawl from the bed into the chilly air of the room. That storm front brought in cold weather I wasn't expecting. And I definitely need to find some food.

I step into the bathroom and pause, my eyes zeroing in on the stack of clothes sitting on the counter. Women's clothes. But not mine.

Where the hell did these come from? Did Warwick bring these in last night…or one of the other guys?

He didn't sleep in here. I didn't even see him after he left me on the boat and the scary dude with the shades brought me up here. He must have slept somewhere else, and the thought that one of the other goons may have been in here during the few minutes I managed to doze off makes my stomach turn and any thought of food evaporate.

I don't want them anywhere near me unless I'm one hundred percent on guard. But Warwick…

Shit.

With him, it's different. Different in a way that's almost as terrifying as being kidnapped. I trust him. Even if I shouldn't. Even though his anger and outbursts scare me.

The way his lips molded to mine, the scrape of several days of growth covering his face against my sensitive skin, the way my heart raced when his arms wrapped around me…it was more than unexpected. It was…ethereal and terrifying.

I haven't been giving myself a chance to think about it, to wonder what it meant, but now, I have to go face him *and* them after his meltdown last night. And I need to figure out how to get them to let me go.

The first step is the pile of clothes. The jeans are slightly too big and the T-shirt slightly too tight, but at least my underwear and bra are dry now.

Thunder rumbles low somewhere in the distance, and the light ping of rain on the roof of the warehouse rings in the tiny room. This storm system is really taking its time moving on.

That will only complicate things for Warwick in dealing with these people in Chicago.

On top of that, I also can't wait much longer to contact the crew or Mom. He said he would release me in forty-eight hours, and we're pushing that, and the twenty-four deadline Arturo gave them, soon. My crew *will* contact the authorities if they don't hear from me.

I need to tell Warwick.

But I shouldn't. I should let them contact the authorities and tell them everything that happened. That's the right thing to do, but deep down, I understand why Warwick is doing this.

He did it to protect his father's legacy and the family name. The same reason I stepped up to captain the ship when Dad died, and I had no fucking business doing it. I should have scraped the money together to hire an experienced captain instead of doing it alone. Warwick was right. I'm no captain. I'm an accountant with a captain's license. Those are two different things.

What he did, what he's doing, goes to another level, but at the heart of it, it's the same. We are the same.

How far would I go to protect Dad's business?

I can't know until I'm there, dangling over the cliff to fall into bankruptcy and failure. We're close, but not quite there yet. My chest aches thinking about losing the business.

And I hope we never get there.

Who am I to judge what Warwick has done?

I slowly pull open the door and cringe as it squeaks on its old rusty hinges. Voices drift up from the warehouse. Excited voices. Angry voices.

Dull light streams in from the high, dirty windows, and thunder rolls again.

Should I stay up here and wait to see what they decide to do with me? Do I go down to confront them and hope it's not my final overstep that pushes them over the edge of their patience with me?

I can't just sit here and wait. I told myself to be proactive, and I need to be.

Warwick's story last night changes nothing as much as it changes everything. The fact that it split my heart in two to hear him talk about his mother and his father and everything he's been through can't be a consideration right now. The fact that I wanted to embrace him, offer him comfort as he told the story and tell him I understood why he did it has to be pushed deep down, deeper than I've ever pushed anything before.

Because if I consider that for one moment, I'll lose my nerve for what I have to do.

I have to get out of here. Away from them.

No matter what it takes.

Slowly, I inch my way down the stairs, and the voices grow louder.

"It's at the Port of Milwaukee."

Someone mumbles a reply.

"We don't know that."

Several voices mix together and something unintelligible gets yelled.

I finally make it to the step where I will no longer have the benefit of hiding behind the office.

Warwick and his crew are all gathered around the table.

The man who has me so completely conflicted stands at the head of the table with his back to me.

His strong, deep voice floats clearly across the space between us. "There's no question what we need to do. We can't get that amount of heroin anywhere else fast enough to save our asses. The only option is going back for the ones we missed."

Shit. They're going back on the ship?

That seems unwise. To say the least.

Even if the crew followed their directions and reported nothing to the Coast Guard or police about me being taken, as soon as they see me, as soon as they know I'm out of danger, they will sound the alarm. And if this pack of goons shows up without me, it will be even worse, because, of course, they will think Warwick and the guys are coming to kill them. And that I'm already dead.

Unless…

I race down the last few steps and onto the concrete floor. "I'm going with you."

Four heads whip around to look at me with wide eyes. Well, at least three sets. I still can't see what's behind the sunglasses. But they're definitely focused in my direction. The fifth guy is MIA, probably the "E" who was sent to watch the crew.

Warwick's dark gaze meets mine. "What?"

Each slow step that brings me closer to them has my heart amping up. "I said, I'm going with you."

The Hulk barks out a laugh and nods in my direction. "Hear that, guys? She thinks we're stupid."

"No." I shake my head and near the table. "I don't think you're stupid. Hear me out."

The tall guy pushes to his feet. "Why the hell would you think we would be stupid enough to waltz you up to the ship we kidnapped you from?"

Fair enough. But they aren't getting it.

Milo wanders around the table from where the guy with the shades sits and makes his way over to me.

I take a calming breath and allow myself a moment to try to steady my voice and remove the shake I'm sure would give away how fucking terrified I am. I bend down and scratch his head before rising.

"It's not stupid. It's really fucking smart. I can walk right up to the ship and scope things out in a way you can't. I can figure out where the crates are and the easiest way to get them without anyone questioning why I am there."

The Hulk snorts and crosses those gigantic arms over his chest. "Yeah, except your crew. And potentially the police and Coast Guard, who are waiting for you to show up or for any signs of you if your guys ratted us out."

I sigh and place my palms against the table to lean over it in the same way Warwick is on the opposite end. The guy has said nothing. "What makes you so sure of that? I may not have been their captain long, but they've all worked for my father for years. They're not going to do anything to put my life in danger. And if that means keeping their mouths shut, we can assume they're going to do it."

"Won't they call the cops as soon as they see you and know you're safe?"

Same thought I had.

I shrug. "Not if I tell them not to."

The guy with the sunglasses crosses his arms over his chest and leans back in his chair. "And why would you do that? Why would you be willing to help us?"

And this is where things get a little awkward. I can't stop my focus from flicking over to Warwick before I answer.

I'm a terrible liar, but I hope to hell I can pull this off and conceal my real intentions.

"I swear, no funny business. I just understand now why you're doing this. Please don't be mad at him, but Warwick told me everything last night about what's happened with *Il Padrone.*"

Their eyes all move to Warwick, and the anger simmering there makes me step back from the table.

The man with the aviators, the only one whose eyes I can't see, and the one has never exhibited even a hint of softness, nods. "I know."

Shit. Did he overhear us last night?

I bite my lip and then take a deep breath. "I understand your lives are at stake here, and you need to make this delivery. I'm not going to lie and say I'm happy about finding out drugs were on my boat in the first place, or about putting them in the hands of people who will distribute them and ruin people's lives."

I glance over at Warwick, who keeps his eyes down on the table, but the tension in his shoulders and clenched jaw tell me everything I need to know. This is way too close to home for him, and he's about ready to fall apart. He needs help. They all need help.

And I can use that to my advantage.

"All I want to do is get you in and out to do what you need to do. Once you're gone, I'll stay with my crew. I won't say anything to anyone. I'll tell my crew you guys abided by the agreement, but I won't give them any more information about you. I'll tell them I don't want to go through the agony of reliving my ordeal by trying to find you and prosecute you. We will pretend this whole thing never happened."

The Hulk snorts again and looks to his buddies. "Are you guys buying this? I sure am not. I don't trust this chick. There has to be another way."

Warwick's head snaps up, and he scowls. "Yeah, what way is that? Give me one good alternative to what she suggested. We can't get our hands on more drugs, and we can't show up with half a fucking shipment either. You know none of us walks out of there alive if we did that. We have to at least try, and we've got nothing at this point."

The tall guy walks around the table to tower over me, and I shift back until my ass hits the edge. I grasp it with my hands, digging into the old, splintering wood.

He glowers at me. "I'm not happy with the situation. I'm not happy that Warwick spilled his fucking guts to you. I'm not happy that you hold our lives in your hands right now. But

Warwick is right." He looks over to The Hulk. "We don't have any other choices. I spent all fucking night looking for another way to get the drugs, talking with some of my old contacts, and it's just not gonna happen. We all know we're not getting more time from Arturo, so that only leaves one option, and that's hers."

Glasses guy frowns and shoves away from the table. "I don't like this. I don't like this one fucking bit."

Warwick rises to his full height and crosses his arms over his chest. "I don't care what you like, Cutter."

Cutter. So…I finally have a name…

Whether it's his real name or not is another question.

"We don't have any options. This is it."

Cutter grunts and mimics Warwick's stance. This close to him, the pale pink-and-red scarring along his right temple and down his cheek and neck are clear. Maybe that's why he wears the glasses.

Scars or not, I don't like the guy. The vibe he puts off is absolutely sinister. The Hulk may be the biggest, but this guy is the coldest. I can see that even from only this short time with him. And he has all of his attention focused on me and my plan right now.

Not good.

Warwick tosses a quick glance at me. "You and I are leaving. I'm going to change. Stay here." He looks at the tall, thin guy. "Go find out what you can about dock security, Coast Guard, police status. Call E and see if anything changed."

The tall guy nods. "There hasn't been anything in any of the reports or scanners about a hijacking or anything about us. Last check-in, E said the crew was at their hotel."

Warwick smacks his hand on the table, and it vibrates through the room. "That doesn't mean anything. You and I both know they could be withholding the information because we have her, trying to keep things on the DL until she's safe. We need to proceed with caution." He turns and strides across the warehouse floor to the staircase, leaving me with Cutter, The Hulk, and the third goon who slowly makes his way down the hallway with a slight limp.

The Hulk snort-laughs and grins at me. "Good luck, little girl. You better not betray us."

Cold dread squeezes tightly around my throat. The threat is direct, and as soon as he makes it, he turns around and disappears back down the same hallway as his buddy…leaving me alone with Cutter. And Milo, who sits at our feet, staring up at us with big, brown eyes.

The inability to see Cutter's eyes unnerves me. My skin heats under his assessment, and I shift where I stand and avert my gaze to the table. He's up next to me so fast, I didn't even know he was moving until he grips my arm and takes my chin in his other hand.

With a quick jerk, he tilts my face up to his.

"Don't double-cross us. If you do, I will fucking kill you."

I gulp and try not to piss myself.

"Warwick may want your pussy and be letting that go to his head, but I sure as fuck don't. You're nothing to me. Nothing but a bargaining chip, and if we lose you, then there's nothing to keep me from killing you and giving you exactly what you deserve for betraying us."

I stare at my own reflection in his glasses, and acid crawls up my throat.

He growls low again and squeezes his fingers into my chin. "Tell me you understand."

I nod as much as possible in his firm grip, and he shoves me backward. "Good."

He stalks away down the hallway with Milo at his heels just as Warwick appears on the top of the stairs.

Thank God…

The malice coming off Cutter in waves has me second-guessing my plan. If I'm caught trying to escape, he *will* kill me. He will find a way.

Is the potential to maybe get away enough to risk my life? Or should I really just help them and let it go like my fake plan suggests?

That's a decision I have to make…and fast.

Warwick descends and approaches me slowly. "Let's go. We have a long fucking day ahead of us."

ELEVEN

War

I don't fucking get it. It would be so easy for her to report us. For her to walk up to literally anyone at the dock and tell them what happened and ask them to call the police.

Deep down, part of me knows that's probably her plan.

But I don't want to believe it.

I want to believe telling her my story, telling her what's at stake and why, was enough to sway her to want to help us... but that's asking a lot. Especially from someone we kidnapped.

I can't blame her for not trusting me. Not trusting us.

Yet, she offered to help, and she follows me out of the warehouse and climbs up into my truck parked behind the building without a word.

I settle into the driver's seat and glance over at the woman who is slowly tearing me apart. Her pale, freckled skin looks almost paler, if that's even possible, and she stares off at the lake while I start the truck.

What are you thinking, Grace?

I'm not sure what Cutter said to her when I was upstairs, but the look on her face when I came back down as he walked away from her was enough to tell me it was something very characteristic of him. Cutter is a "take no prisoners" guy. The kind of guy needed on my team to get the dirty work done. The kind of guy perfect to instill some real fear into a woman like Grace who fights so hard not to show any weakness.

It's times like this, I both appreciate him and maybe fear him a little myself.

With good reason.

The man never cracks, never gives a fucking inch, never shows an ounce of compassion for anyone except maybe me and the guys, and that's only because he knows we have his back as much as he has ours. We're family, the only *real* family any of us has left. The only ones we can rely on.

While I don't think I could ever hurt a woman, he's done just that...more than hurt. Granted, it was in a different world. A different time, under war conditions. He was fighting an enemy who hid behind women and children, who used them to commit absolute atrocities.

Hesitation costs people their lives there. It almost cost Cutter his.

Because someone else hesitated. So, he won't.

Which makes it even more important that Grace understands the consequences, that she understands she better not betray us.

If I were in her shoes, taken hostage, threatened, repeatedly berated by my captors, escape would be at the forefront of my mind, yet, she hasn't tried. The threat against her crew and herself has kept her in line.

But what about when that threat is gone?

Will she really let us walk away with millions of dollars in heroin to keep working for the Marconis, now that she knows what we do for them?

The gravel road dips below us, and dark clouds gather overhead. I lean forward to look up. The forecast was right. This is one hell of a storm system. It keeps circling and hovering above us. Refusing to push off over the lake like weather here normally does. Flooding is already a problem in some parts of the state, and it could become even worse.

Who knows how long the storms may continue?

We don't have much time, and getting the rest of the shit down to Chicago by Arturo's deadline is looking less and less likely. The only way we'll make today at all is if the stuff is still on the *Neptune's Daughter* and we can get to it right away. Even then, we may need a few extra hours to get to Chicago on *The Destiny* in this weather, but we can at least assure him we're on our way. That's better than another call telling him we aren't coming. That might as well be putting a gun to own heads.

This better go well.

I can't take another fuckup or complication. The one sitting next to me is already more than enough to handle.

The small two-lane highway finally appears at the end of the gravel drive from the warehouse, and I turn out onto it and head south toward our fate. Grace relaxes slightly, but the silence in the truck's cab is deafening.

She's always so inquisitive. So full of questions. But after what I told her last night and the way I reacted when she pointed out my idiocy in never questioning what I was doing for the Marconis, I'm not sure what to say.

How does she feel about me after learning everything, after seeing me explode like that?

It can't be good. And I shouldn't care.

It shouldn't matter if my damn hostage likes me or not, if she understands what we're doing and why, if she understands *me*...

But it does.

I wanted to climb up those steps a hundred times last night to talk to her, to...I don't know...apologize for how I acted. I also wanted to stay the fuck away from her—as far away as was humanly possible in the warehouse. So, I slept on the *Calista* alone, with nothing but my conflicting thoughts and stupid fucking conscience eating away at me.

When I told her about Dad and asked her about her father, she made the connection. What I'm doing isn't that far off from what she did in taking over the *Neptune's Daughter* when she's still a newly licensed basically baby captain. Not when you get right down to the nitty-gritty of it.

If she does understand and can sympathize, then maybe her plan isn't just a ruse to escape. Maybe it's a genuine desire to see us safe.

I can't assume anything, though.

I need to make sure she grasps what's at stake here…

I push my foot to the floor, accelerating down the county highway toward the interstate that will take us to Milwaukee. Cutter and Rion will be shoving off on *The Destiny* to make their way to the port any minute now, while Preacher mans his control room and stays in contact with E for updates.

Things are in motion that can't be stopped now. She has to be warned.

"I don't know what Cutter said to you. But I need you to understand that whatever he said, he meant it."

She freezes next to me and turns her head slightly to look at me. I glance at her before returning my attention to the road.

"If you've ever been afraid of me at all during this, understand, he's ten times as ruthless, ten times as unshakable, ten times as dangerous as I could ever be. Anything he promised, he will deliver tenfold. So, don't get any ideas."

She cringes and shrivels back into the seat, making herself as small as possible. "So, he's like the Kraken?"

I jerk my head toward her. "What the hell are you talking about?"

"The way you talk about Cutter…like he's some ruthless, killing machine beast to unleash…like the Kraken."

Jesus. She has no idea how serious this is, does she?

That's exactly what it's like. He's unstoppable once he sets his sights on a target, and right now, his sights are set on *her*… waiting for her to prove she's not trustworthy so he can give her what she deserves.

And her reaction to my warning doesn't bode well.

Where's her outrage? Where's her insistence that she would never betray us? That she intends to follow through with helping us get what we need?

She hasn't said anything like that. That makes my gut twist and my hands tighten on the steering wheel.

"What *did* Cutter say to you?"

I have an idea, but hearing her say it, knowing she comprehends every syllable, is essential to getting a grasp on her state of mind and what we're walking into with her.

She flinches, squeezes her eyes shut, and presses her lips in a tight line. Her hands clench into fists on her lap, and she releases a sigh and looks out the window, away from me. "He said if I betrayed you guys…he'd kill me."

Accurate.

If there's one thing I can always count on with Cutter, it's his ability to put aside personal feelings to get the fucking job done. God knows I've let this woman work her way too far under my skin to act if I needed to now.

A fact I'm finally willing to admit, though reluctantly.

Which leads to the ultimate question…

"Are you planning to betray us?"

She hesitates for a moment and pulls her bottom lip between her teeth.

Christ, why is it so hot?

Those lips under mine in the rain. Her wet body pressed against me. Having her in my arms…

All of it was just…too good. Too much of something I can never have. A few seconds of bliss in an otherwise fucked-up situation of our own making.

Mine for agreeing to do the job in the first place. Hers for turning on that damn beacon, though she couldn't have known what would come of it. None of us could.

I glance over at her.

She releases the lip and clears her throat. "No."

The answer is strong. Unwavering.

But there's something there under the surface.

Fear. Regret.

She's lying.

It's an act. She has every intention of using this opportunity to get away from me, to make sure we end up exactly where she thinks we belong—prison somewhere, rotting away in a cell for all our sins—or at least, the ones she knows about.

Although, at this point, maybe that's the lesser of two evils. Maybe we should just turn ourselves in rather than face the fury of the Marconis if we can't succeed in getting them the rest of the drugs.

They have people inside who would, no doubt, take us out, but at least we would stand a chance with protective custody there. We certainly don't stand one on the outside if we fail. There wouldn't be anywhere we could hide from them. They're too connected. Too powerful. Too unwilling to forgive such a transgression.

We'd never be free. We'd live our lives looking over our shoulders, no matter where we ended up or how much time has passed. That's no way to live either.

There's just no good option here.

We can't fail and run, but putting the drugs in their hands doesn't sit well with me. The anger I felt last night reached Biblical proportions, the kind of wrath that destroys entire worlds. I have to overlook that to do this, to make the delivery.

I'm sacrificing my morals—the very few I have left—to save our asses. The men know what that means for me, and now...so does Grace.

Maybe I have been naïve to assume they were transporting guns or something else, but one thing I always counted on working for them was that they are predictable.

The Marconis have been in the business for a long time, and they have their game down pat. That game never included drugs. Never.

Why the sudden shift to something they wouldn't have touched with a ten-foot pole five years ago?

Maybe it's Arturo's influence.

We all know he's been slowly weaseling his way into more of a management role in the family. He has his eyes set on *Il Padrone's* seat, and it's only a matter of time before the old man croaks and Arturo takes over. The old man has already been taking care of fewer and fewer things personally. The writing is on the wall.

So, a concrete cell and some iron bars may be a better future.

No.

We are not turning ourselves in.

We will finish the job. Even if it means having to release these drugs on the street, which is the last thing I want to do.

And finishing this job requires Grace's help. If she rats us out, we are fucked.

"Let me give you a piece of advice, Grace. Although, I don't know why I'm wasting my time when you haven't taken any of it before." I let out a sigh and stare straight again at the open highway. "Once again, we are not the people you want to double-cross. I told you I'd release you, and I mean it. When we get the drugs safely to Chicago, I will let you go as long as you're going to keep your mouth shut and make sure your crew does too. This is a mutually beneficial endeavor."

She snort-laughs and turns her head to look at me. Those damn eyes shimmer at me and flare with that sassy attitude she's been throwing at me since the moment I stepped onto her bridge and she pulled that damn shotgun on me. "How is this beneficial to me again?"

I would think that would be obvious.

I grit my teeth and shake my head. "You don't die. Your crew doesn't die."

Simple words. True words.

As much as I hate repeating them, that shuts her up.

She sinks back into the seat, and I finally merge onto the interstate to Milwaukee.

We've got more than an hour before we hit town—plenty of time for her to consider what she's going to do when we get there. Plenty of time to reconsider any stupid plan she may have come up with this morning before her little heart-to-heart with Cutter. Plenty of time to change her mind.

Between his threats and my promises, I hope she makes the right decision.

TWELVE

Grace

I'm dead. I am well and truly fucked. So is my opportunity to get away unscathed.

The plan had been to walk around the dock and talk to security and be safely tucked away in the arms of someone with a weapon. Someone who could protect me from these guys. Someone who could ensure the crew wasn't in any danger from that E guy who's watching them before the authorities closed in on Warwick and his guys.

It meant sending them to their potential deaths at the hands of the Marconis if they got away, or sending them to prison if they got caught, but I can't think about what's best for them.

I have to think about what's best for me. Just like Warwick's mom said in the note from *Lord of the Flies*...

The only one looking out for you is you...

Yet Cutter's threat and the chilling words Warwick just said put everything in a whole new light, and the words scrawled in those books by a woman who loved her conflicted and troubled son more than anything in this world ring even more true.

There is no "good" choice...

Choose the lesser of two evils...

What is the lesser of the two evils here? What is the choice I can live with even if no choice is good?

I actually believe Warwick when he says he'll release me once they're safe, and his life, and the lives of his crew, are in very real danger if they don't get what we're after.

The problem is, I'm not so confident they'll get the drugs, let alone deliver them to Chicago. Doing so without raising too much attention—unwanted attention—will be damn near impossible.

Even if the crew is still gone and at the hotel, port security will be there. All my identification is still on board. If I can get near the ship, they'll think it's suspicious to be unloading everything onto *The Destiny* instead of onto the semis or trucks that should've been coming to pick it up later today according to our original schedule—if that hasn't already happened.

I don't even remember where it was supposed to go or who is supposed to come get it. Dad made all the arrangements for this shipment before he died. I should have paid more attention to the details.

There are a lot of things I should have paid more attention to. He hid a lot from me. Despite me doing all the accounting, he racked up all sorts of debts in the name of the business that only came to light when he passed away. Debts we can't possibly hope to repay now. Had I made the delivery, had I been paid for this job...maybe. It would have been a start in the right direction.

But now?

Fucked. Just fucked.

Either I betray them and send them to their deaths or prison, or I help them get drugs to some very bad people who will distribute them.

No good choice.

How the hell did we ever get to this point? How the fuck did I end up with drugs on my ship?

Warwick's words from last night weigh on me. *"What about your father? Is it possible he knew what was going on? What he was transporting? People do a lot of things when they're desperate that they might not consider otherwise, Grace."*

Is it possible Dad knew?

The quiet, soft-spoken man whose lap I sat on during church on Sundays as a child. The one who always taught me right from wrong. The one who taught me it's never right to hurt someone else intentionally. That's the man I don't think could ever do something like this. But I can't forget the man he was in the months leading up to his death either. Haggard. Stressed. So riddled with anxiety he wasn't sleeping. It was all too much for his heart. And maybe it was too much for his resolve as well.

Could you have really done it, Dad? Could you really have taken money to transport this knowing what was in the crates?

I don't want to believe it.

If he did, where's the money?

It isn't in the business accounts or his joint account with Mom. Which means, if he did know, he probably didn't get paid up front, or at least, didn't get much of it. All we had in the account was the normal amount of payment for a shipment like this. So, if he was somehow involved, he was likely getting paid upon delivery. And if these are really the Marconis' drugs, then why wouldn't he be delivering them straight to Chicago? Why would they need Warwick and his guys to hijack the ship at all?

Shit.

There could be a whole other set of problems. Ones I'm sure Warwick has already considered.

"Do we know who shipped the drugs?"

Warwick sighs and runs a hand back through his hair while keeping his attention on the road. "Sort of. Preacher was able to do some research on the holding company attached to the crates."

Preacher?

That must be the tall guy.

Does he even notice he's been dropping their names left and right?

"He wasn't able to trace it to a true owner yet, but he knows it came through the Dominican Republic and originated somewhere either in Central or South America."

I nod and watch the Wisconsin landscape whizz past us on the sides of the highway. Every program I've ever watched about drug smuggling flows through my memory. "Makes sense. That's where the majority of the drug cartels are, right?"

His shoulder rises and falls. "I don't know a lot about the drug trade. No reason to. All I know is that a lot of people end up dead because of it."

I cringe at his words, and my heart aches for him. He lost his mom at such a young, impressionable age and then had a father who couldn't deal. Watching his dad descend into an addiction, even if he wasn't there for the drug part, must have been agonizing. I can sympathize after seeing what happened to Dad recently.

Maybe I shouldn't discount the potential that he did do something stupid. Look how easily Warwick got pulled into this life. While he seems to embrace it, seems to accept it as part of who he is now, I still don't believe this was a choice. Not really.

This man clearly has an intelligence off the charts and the kind of mind that belongs anywhere but on a damn pirate ship in the middle of the Great Lakes. Had he stayed in school, had he been able to finish his degree, where might he be? What might he have been able to accomplish?

Something more than this. That much is sure.

But considering "what ifs" never does any good. The situation is what it is.

"When we get to the docks, this is what's going to happen..." Warwick's low, harsh words leave no room for argument. "We're going to park outside. You'll find out where the boat is docked and come tell me so I can inform the guys. You'll go in and make sure none of your crew is around. If they are, come back out right away and try not to be seen. If the coast is clear, I want you to go check to see if the cargo is still on board. Then you're coming back to let me know."

I nod my understanding. "Sounds like an easy enough plan."

One that shouldn't be hard to fuck up.

Theoretically.

Yet, there are *so* many ways this could go wrong.

"What if I run into security? If my crew alerted anyone, the place is going to be crawling with cops."

His hands tighten on the wheel. "We leave. We regroup. Maybe we come back at night when there will be fewer security officers, maybe a single guard."

He doesn't have to say the words. It's implied what will happen to that single guard if they have to come back to get the drugs later. It won't end well for him.

His dark eyes flick over to me. "You think you can handle it?"

I let out a breath and nod. I'm not sure I can form words right now. My throat is constricting, and it's getting harder and harder to suck air into my lungs.

"Good. Because we don't get a second take on this. One chance to not fuck this up. One chance for you. Don't forget Cutter's warning."

Like I needed the reminder.

I glance at the clock on the dashboard and clear my throat. "Even if we can get what you need from the boat right when we arrive at the port, we're not going to make Arturo's deadline or the one you set for my return."

There's just no way. With the water as churned up as it is right now and storms still rolling in, it will take half a day to get to Chicago. Warwick has to know that.

He nods. "I know. Once we get the lay of the land, I have to call that fucker and update him on what's happening."

"What about my crew? If they're not here, and if you're not releasing me until you get the drugs safely to Arturo, then how do we keep them from calling the cops once that forty-eight hours elapses?"

A muscle tics in his jaw and his knuckles whiten on the wheel. "We'll figure that out when the time comes. Right now, my only focus is finding out if we can get the Marconis' shit. If we can't, none of this will matter anyway."

No. It won't.

Because they'll be facing a death sentence.

And I'll be facing...only God knows.

"Can I call my mom?"

He glances over at me. "Now?"

I nod, and tears burn my eyes. I fight back a sob. "I just... want to let her know I love her and I'm okay. Plus, if the crew did say anything to anyone, she would probably know by now, right?"

He considers my request in silence for a moment then reaches into his pocket and pulls out a cell phone. "Don't tell her anything. Pretend everything's normal."

"Really?"

His fingers brush mine as I take the phone. "Don't make me regret this."

I dial her number with shaking hands and hold the phone to my ear. Rain pelts the windshield and the highway in front of us.

"Hello?"

"Mom?"

"Grace?"

"Yeah, it's me, Mom." I clear my throat and try to put on my best happy voice. "I just wanted to call and let you know we got into Milwaukee okay."

A sigh of relief carries through the line, and I bite back a sob.

"Oh, good. I saw the weather reports and was worried. See, you had nothing to be concerned about. You did great for your first time. Your father would have been so proud."

I doubt that.

"Thanks, Mom."

She doesn't know anything, which means the crew probably didn't report it. Either that, or the authorities didn't alert her because they're setting some sort of trap.

"Are you okay, honey? You sound strange."

I'm sure I do.

"Just tired."

"Well, you get some rest before you have that long haul home. Call me before you leave."

"I will. Love you."

"Love you, too."

I end the call and sit with the phone in my hand, staring at the screen as if it will bring her back on the line.

It's better she doesn't know the truth, doesn't know what's really happening. She just lost Dad. Knowing she could lose me too would kill her.

I hold the phone out toward Warwick.

He doesn't say anything, just takes it from my hand and slips it back into his pocket as the highway sign for "Milwaukee 30 miles" passes us on the right.

Almost there.

Almost time to make the choice from all my shitty options.

THIRTEEN

War

I don't know what I expected to find when I pulled up to the Port of Milwaukee, but it wasn't this.

Through a light rain under an overcast sky, the place is practically deserted. It's usually not busy this time of the week, but still.

Where is everyone?

The dozens of times we've docked here, I can't remember it ever being this empty.

A prickle of apprehension starts at the base of my neck and has my hair standing on end.

Something's not right.

This feels like a setup. Grace's mother didn't seem to know or suspect anything amiss, but that doesn't mean the crew didn't alert the Coast Guard or police when they docked. The authorities could be waiting to see if we do just...if we're stupid enough to return for what we didn't get.

With the Coast Guard building right across the street from the port administration, the chances of getting away if they are waiting for us is slim to none.

I toss the car into park in front of the administration

building and pull out my phone. The guys need to know what's going on. "Cutter, where are you guys?"

"What's wrong?"

I shift in my seat and scan the area down to the right, behind the chain-link fence, where the two huge piers sit. "We're parked in front of the admin building. I don't know, man, it's just quiet. It's making me uneasy."

"Should we abort?"

Probably.

I clench my jaw and glance at Grace who has been silent beside me since she called her mom.

Going in will be a huge risk, but at this point, we don't really have any choice.

"No. We don't have time to mess around with this anymore. Just don't pull into the dock until you hear from me and I give the all clear. We may be coming back later tonight."

He hisses out a curse. "Shit. I sure hope not."

The line goes dead, and I shove my phone back in my pocket.

This is so not where I thought I'd be today. The mysterious cargo should be to Chicago already, and I should be sitting back with a bourbon or a beer with the guys, celebrating another victory and another chunk of my debt repaid.

Things got so fucked-up, so damn fast.

Grace clears her throat. "Do you want me to go in?"

Do I want her to go or does she have to? No, and…

"Yes."

We really don't have any other options. If the police have been alerted, I can't show my face, and there's no way of knowing what the crew said or did when we left with her.

"Just go. Follow the plan. Come back out."

She nods, and her hand shakes as she grasps the handle of the door. It pops open, but she pauses and looks back at me. "I'll be back."

Fuck.

I hate how much I want that to be true. Hate how much my chest aches thinking about her not returning. If she betrays us, betrays me...

Just fuck.

Being surrounded by a swarm of police officers and jail wouldn't be the worst part. It would be knowing it happened because of her, because she lied to us.

I shouldn't expect her loyalty. I've done nothing to deserve it—other than tell her the story of why we're here. Yet, her betrayal would be almost as bad as one of the guys.

And isn't that a fucking bitch.

She steps from the truck with a little bit of difficulty given her height. The door *thunks* shut behind her, and when she reaches the door of the port offices, she pauses and looks back at me.

A tight half-smile tilts up the corners of her lips—those lips I've felt against mine. The lips I shouldn't want. Shouldn't care about.

The door closes behind her.

Shit. Shit. Shit. Shit.

Just sitting waiting in this truck might as well be torture. Having my hands tied right now fucking sucks.

A car pulls in two spots down. My spine stiffens, and I hold my breath.

Two guys climb from it and make their way across the lot to the front door of the admin building.

They barely glance in my direction, and they don't look familiar. Definitely not members of her crew, but I still clench my hands around the wheel and grit my teeth.

Not recognizing them doesn't mean they aren't a threat.

They could be undercover cops.

They could be Coast Guard, or even FBI.

Stop working yourself up, Warwick.

They could be anybody.

They could be fucking fishermen or fucking dockworkers.

But I can't help it.

This is the first time shit has ever gone bad. What happened on *Neptune's Daughter*, that's not something we could have planned for.

Maybe that's my fault for not having some sort of backup plan in case something like that did ever occur, but how could I have ever anticipated it? Especially the drugs.

Good God...the drugs.

I drop my forehead against the steering wheel and release a shaky sigh. "Sorry, Dad. I wouldn't have if I'd known..."

Although, maybe it's not him I should be apologizing to. Maybe it's Mom. Maybe it's the whole fucking world. Maybe it's the people who are in Chicago for bringing this filth into their city, for letting it take their loved ones.

I sure as hell owe an apology to Grace for everything I've already put her through.

But not until I know we're in the clear, until I know she's walking away from this unscathed and so are we.

The minutes tick by agonizingly slowly. I shift and constantly scan the parking lot and what I can see of the dock area for anything suspicious. The actual piers are so far down the road in the port, it's impossible to see much of anything, and there's no way to know what she's doing inside.

Rain continues to fall, increasing from a drizzle to a steady fall.

And I wait...

And I watch...

Nothing.

And no sign of her.

What the fuck is she doing in there?

Calling the police? Asking for help?

Fuck. Fuck. Fuck.

Maybe I should go in after her.

I unbuckle my seatbelt, and my hand wraps around the door handle.

No.

I can't go in. Not if there's a possibility this is a setup.

Though, if it is, wouldn't they have come for me by now? Maybe they're waiting to get eyes on the rest of the guys before taking us down. Or maybe no one has said anything at all.

The front door of the port admin building swings open, and Grace steps out casually. She shivers slightly in the cool, damp air and walks toward the truck.

Relief washes over me, air rushes from my lungs, and I settle back in my seat as she climbs in.

She came back, and there were no police, no Coast Guard, no sign of anyone she might have told what was happening.

"Well?"

Her hooded brows and slight frown have me clenching my fists.

She waves a hand toward the building. "I spoke with someone in the admin office. *Neptune's Daughter* is still docked down by the cargo terminal. It doesn't sound like my crew is there, but I couldn't find out much without telling her who I was. I don't have ID and didn't want to draw any unwanted attention. I think they have security. There were a few guys in uniforms inside talking to someone."

Shit.

"We need to get closer."

The port area is so huge, it's almost a half-mile drive from the admin building down to the piers. If we can get close enough to see the ship and what's around it, we may have a better idea of what's happening.

I start up the truck and turn left out of the lot toward the piers. There's no reason for any vehicles to be down this way unless they're picking up cargo or working. If anyone questions us, we'll have to leave. Fast.

We make our way north down Lincoln Memorial Drive, and the piers come into view on our right.

Grace points. "There she is."

Neptune's Daughter sits right where she should be, but our view is obscured by the support structure for the highway above us and the small buildings and pallets stored under it.

"Shit. I can't see anything from here."

She shakes her head. "Me either. Should we get out and try to get closer?"

"No."

There's too much of a chance of being questioned. We shouldn't be back here, and if she were questioned, we would be in deep shit.

"We'll have to come back tonight."

She gives me a sharp nod. "I think so. Even though it looks dead out here, there are actually some men farther down near the boats working. I can just barely make them out from here."

Shit.

I pull out my cell phone.

It rings while I make a U-turn and head out past the port offices.

"You guys need to drop anchor and hang out for a couple hours. We need to wait until dark to go in."

"Fuck." Cutter groans. "What's the situation like."

"Handful of security now, we think, but who knows once it's dark. Hopefully less. The crew is gone now as far as we can tell, and Grace says they normally stay at a hotel nearby rather than on the ship to get a little taste of luxury for a couple days. So, they may come back, but there's no telling when or for how long. They aren't scheduled to leave for a few more days."

"Well, that's vague and unhelpful."

No shit.

We usually spend days and sometimes weeks planning

jobs, ensuring every scenario and detail is covered. This winging it shit certainly isn't fucking ideal. Even though we had prepared for our raid on *Neptune's Daughter*, it still went wrong. This will be played by ear—something none of us want to do.

But it isn't totally Grace's fault she doesn't know more.

"This was her first time traveling with them so she's not totally sure how things go. She's just going off what her father told her and what the receipts she processes for the books show."

Cutter sighs. "Then, I guess we wait."

"We wait. Call Preacher and update him on what's going on. Try to get an update from E. You and Rion get ready."

"We're not making Arturo's deadline."

I scrub a hand over my face. "I know."

"You need to call him."

"I know, asshole. I am very well aware."

It's the last thing I want to do, but it's necessary all the same. If we don't show, he will send his men after us. There's no doubt. But a call may buy us some time to sort this out.

Might.

I stop just past the entrance to the port and barely catch the look Grace gives me.

"What?"

A tiny smile tugs at the corner of her mouth. "Rion. Is that Hulk's real name?"

"Hulk?" A thick chuckle rumbles from my lips. I still can't believe that's how she's been thinking of him. "Yeah, but I think you should keep calling him Hulk. It fits him a lot better."

Tinkling laughter fills the truck cab and releases some of the tension in my shoulders, but it will just be right back. There's no way we'll get out of this without some bloodshed tonight, and that's the last thing we need.

I sober quickly, and Grace's laugh stops abruptly when she sees my face.

"I need to call Arturo."

She chews on her bottom lip. "What are you going to tell him?"

"I'll think of something."

Fast.

I dial the number and wait.

"Mr. Pike. I hope you're calling to tell me you're almost here with my cargo."

I fucking wish.

My palms sweat, and I wipe one on my jeans, then transfer my phone to the other ear so I can wipe off the second one too.

"We've hit another delay. The weather and the damage to the boat from the storm was worse than I thought. It looks like it will be tomorrow sometime that we'll get down there."

If this goes well and we get what we need. If we don't...

The silence he gives me as a response sends ice flooding my veins. I glance at Grace. Her wide green eyes watch me, and she waits for my reaction to however Arturo responds.

"Mr. Pike, to say I'm disappointed would be an under-statement. It seems my uncle may have misplaced his trust in you—"

"No." I need to end this train of thought. If he thinks this was an intentional betrayal, he'll have his men up here for us in a matter of hours. "Please, I'll have it to you late tomorrow. I promise."

He chuckles, dark, low, and menacing. "Your word means nothing to me, Mr. Pike, but I'll give you one more day because my uncle seems to trust you, and I don't know where you have the cargo. Otherwise, I would send my men up there right now to get it from you."

That's the last thing we need or want.

We've managed to keep the location of the warehouse

private from the Marconis, and that's the only thing saving us right now.

"Tomorrow. I promise."

The line goes dead without another word from Arturo. His non-statement is statement enough.

If we don't get the stuff there, we're fucking dead.

FOURTEEN

Grace

———————

Warwick slides his phone back in his pocket and merges back onto the road.

That call with Arturo didn't sound good, at least, the side of it I could hear didn't.

Which is exactly why I didn't rat out Warwick when I was in the port offices.

I kept picturing the words he wrote in his journal...

He's going to kill me one of these days. Kill us all. As soon as we're of no use to him, we're gone.

I kept hearing the distress in his voice and those of his friends when they spoke about what would happen if they failed...

This is life and death for them as much as it is for me. If they can pull this off, if they can get the rest of the drugs and get them to Chicago, it's the best hope for everyone making it out of this alive.

I couldn't have Warwick's life on my conscience. Not when he's proven to me that he won't hurt me. Not when he's shown me there's something more to him. A man who made a shitty choice for what he thought was a good reason.

Maybe that makes me a sucker, someone who can't help but see the good buried beneath all the bad in someone like him. But what would it make me if I sent him to his death, if I ensured he would end up dead…all because he wanted to save his family business?

Not someone I could live with being.

I just have to trust this will all work out.

He pulls onto the highway.

"Where are we going?"

His dark eyes glance my way. "The hotel your crew is at."

"Why?"

Isn't that the last place we should be going? If they see me, if he lets me go and loses any bargaining chip…it's over.

Warwick doesn't answer for what feels like miles. I squirm in my seat and watch the city fly by.

"I'm letting you go."

I freeze. "What? Why?"

He can't be serious. If he lets me go, and if the crew or I talk, then all of this was for nothing.

"Because the forty-eight hours is almost up, and if the crew hasn't said anything yet, they sure as hell will if you aren't freed." He pauses for a moment, his dark eyes focused on the road ahead, his hands clenched tightly around the wheel. "It's time for you to go, Grace. This has gone on too long."

The burn in my eyes isn't because I'll never see him again. It can't be. It must be because I'm so damn happy this ordeal is over. So damn happy to get back to the crew, and in a few days, back at home in Michigan with Mom and my boring office life.

That *must* be it. The alternative is just fucking crazy Stockholm Syndrome shit.

We pull up outside the hotel, and I stare up at it.

This is really it.

Time to say goodbye.

"I'm sorry, Grace. For everything."

That's it? That's all he's going to say?

I swallow through the lump in my throat and blink away the tears forming my eyes.

The shrill ring of his phone breaks the tension in the truck cab.

Warwick frowns and answers. "What?"

His eyes drift over to me before he looks at the hotel then over his shoulder at something behind us. I glance in the same direction. A red pickup sits across the street, and the guy who must be E stares back at us.

"I'm dropping her off with the crew."

I can't make out the reply, but E's anger is evident even from across the road. I turn back around to face forward.

They don't know he's letting me go, that he's giving their only bargaining chip against the crew revealing what they've done a chance to walk away.

"We'll talk about it later, E. It's my fucking decision." He turns back around and sighs. "I'm heading over to Annie's Diner to eat and kill some time until it's dark enough for us to go in. I'll call you from there. Stay here and watch for any law enforcement or for the crew heading back toward the ship."

Because even though I didn't rat him out at the port, he still doesn't believe I won't alert the police.

It shouldn't bother me, but my chest tightens all the same.

"Goodbye, Warwick. Good luck."

My hand hovers over the door handle. There's so much more that I want to say, that I want to ask, that I need to know. But all the words die on my lips, and I swing the door open and climb down from the truck.

Warwick's dark eyes follow me as I walk around the hood of the truck and toward the doors of the hotel.

Don't look back, Grace.

It won't do any good. For anyone.

If you're doing this, you need to keep your head up and on straight.

I pull the door open and step into the lobby with my heart in my throat and tears in my eyes.

———

Thick black clouds still darken the sky when I step out of the hotel, and a light drizzle falls onto the already wet pavement and road in front of me. The red truck still sits across the street and down half a block.

E is still watching us, waiting to see what we'll do, if anything, to interfere with what they are planning at the port tonight.

I pull the hood on the jacket I grabbed from my luggage the crew brought from the ship up over my head.

The time is now, Grace.

The decision was made an hour ago the moment Darren opened the door to his room and embraced me.

No second-guessing. No regrets.

I wait for a bus to fly past on the street, spraying water up and almost drenching me, then I dash across toward the red truck.

E narrows his eyes on my approach.

I reach the passenger side door and tug on the handle.

Locked.

He glares at me, his blue eyes flashing.

This one is an enigma. I barely saw him on the *Neptune's Daughter*, and then Warwick sent him here to watch the crew. Climbing into his truck and doing what I'm about to isn't wise.

But neither has most of what I've done over the last few days.

"Are you going to unlock it?"

He scowls but the click of the lock opening still sounds, and I tug the door open and climb into the passenger seat.

The hot air blasting from the vents hits me, and I flip my hood down.

"What do you want?" His question is gruff and short.

He doesn't want me here. That's understandable. He's been sitting here waiting for the damn bottom to drop out of this entire thing.

And that's a loaded question. One I can't possibly answer nor do I want to.

"I need you to take me to Annie's."

"And why the hell would I do that?"

"So I can talk to Warwick."

He snaps. "Shouldn't you be talking to the police right about now?"

I probably should be. "No. I didn't call the police and my crew isn't going to either."

A low dark chuckle fills the truck cab. "And I'm just supposed to accept that is the truth? You might have come out here to stall me until they get here."

I raise an eyebrow at him.

"Do you really think I'd climb into a truck with somebody who no doubt has a gun or many guns in here if I was going to have the police show up?"

I've learned my lesson about being taken hostage.

He considers my comment for a moment and shakes his head. "I don't know what game you're playing, little girl, but it's a dangerous one."

"I'm not playing any game. I need to talk to Warwick."

He leans forward, grabs a cell phone off the dash, and holds it out to me. "Call him."

I shake my head. "Not good enough. I have to do this in person."

"You couldn't have done it two hours ago when he dropped you off? When he gave away our only leverage?"

I thought I considered this carefully before coming out here. That all avenues had been analyzed, and this was the best approach.

But maybe I was wrong.

The way E is looking at me like he considers me nothing more than a bargaining chip is a much different situation than I was in sitting in the car with Warwick.

This man has no personal feelings, no sentimental attachment like the one I'm fairly sure is what made Warwick let me go despite the wishes of his men.

"No, it wasn't something I could've told him then because I wasn't sure what I was going to do when I walked into the hotel. Now, I know. Are you going take me to him or do I need to take a cab?"

The cords of his neck strain, and his lips turn down.

He's still wondering if this is somehow a setup.

I can't blame him for that.

But I've known where Warwick would be and what his plan is since the minute I stepped out of his truck. If I had wanted to set them up, the police would've been here by now, a fact he's probably realizing at this moment.

He shoves the phone into his pocket and violently jerks the car into drive.

"If this is just some way to try to get me away from here so your crew can get back to the ship and interfere with what we're doing tonight, it's a pretty fucking stupid move on your part, and you're not gonna like the consequences."

Oh, good…more threats.

These guys sure love making them. I just hope I never have to see what happens if they follow through because something tells me they will…if I ever betray them. If my crew ever gives them up.

E pulls away from the curb and makes a fast U-turn that has me grasping for my seatbelt. I tug it on and watch him out of the corner of my eye as we weave our way through the streets of Milwaukee.

The tension in the cab threatens to crush my resolve. This seemed so right only minutes ago.

When I told Darren and the rest of the crew that my captors had released me unharmed as promised, there were more tears than I thought possible. And, of course…the insistence we alert the police was immediately made.

But before the words were even out of Darren's mouth, I already knew I would reject the suggestion. Because I don't want to see Warwick in prison or worse. I don't give a fuck what happens to the rest of these guys. Warwick, though, he doesn't deserve that.

Not really.

He's a criminal. He's angry and broody and has a temper, but he's not an all bad person. They didn't hurt me. *He* didn't hurt me. When he had plenty of opportunity to do just that. And his willingness to release me now, when their lives are still very much at risk, and they still need to accomplish what could be impossible, shows he wasn't only considering what was best for him and his men—but what was best for *me.*

I couldn't let Darren set the wheels in motion to end Warwick's life—either by having him tossed behind bars or by letting the Marconis end him.

It wasn't easy, but I finally convinced the crew I just wanted to forget the ordeal ever happened and didn't want to have to relive it by pursuing criminal charges and having to testify at a trial. When it came down to it, despite how badly I messed up, I am their captain, and they listened to me and followed my lead by agreeing to return home and list the cargo as missing in transit.

That will create problems for the business. Ones I may not be able to fix, but it's a small price to pay to save someone's life, even someone like Warwick.

E turns a corner and pulls to the curb in front of an old-fashioned fifties-style diner with the name *Annie's* on a sign on the top. He nods toward the door. "Here you go. I'm going back to the hotel to keep an eye on the crew, because I don't fucking trust you. If they make a move toward the port tonight, don't think I will forget this."

Like I ever could.

I unbuckle my seatbelt and climb from the truck without a word to him. I don't need to explain myself to E. The only person who deserves an explanation is Warwick.

The man sitting with his back to me at a booth in the corner. I tug open the door and make my way across the linoleum floor toward him.

Here goes nothing.

I slide into the booth across from him, and his head jerks up. Those cool gray eyes meet mine.

"What the hell are you doing here?" He glances around to make sure no one is within earshot.

"I'm here to help you."

"Go back to the hotel, Grace." His low, hard command cuts at my resolve.

People will say I'm crazy, that I shouldn't be doing this. That he's right…I should go to the hotel, to my crew, and never look back.

They can't understand.

No one can.

I wring my hands together on the table. "I can't do that. You need me to help tonight. E isn't going to leave the crew. He doesn't trust I didn't tell them what's happening tonight. You'll be going in alone."

His hand tightens around a glass in front of him, his knuckles whitening. A muscle in his jaw tics. His heated gaze rakes over me.

I squirm under his assessment.

"You aren't going to take no for an answer, are you?"

I don't bother to fight the laugh that claws its way up my throat. "You've finally figured that out, huh?"

There was never any doubt if they had to go back tonight, there's a good chance somebody's getting very hurt or very dead. And it won't matter who it is—the good guys or the bad guys.

Although, in this case, are Warwick and his crew really the bad guys?

They're doing what they need to in order to protect their asses and save their own lives.

They do enjoy it, though. I saw the looks on their faces when they were on the ship, the way they manhandled the crew. The rush they get from it. These are violent dudes who like to do violent things.

But I don't want to see more tonight.

With me acting as lookout maybe I can help prevent things from getting worse.

Warwick takes a drink from the glass, then focuses his gaze on me. "You're going to stay in the truck."

That's sort of what I had planned and anticipated, but there is another option. "You're sure you don't want me to go in with you? If you do run into trouble with security, maybe I can defuse it. I am the listed captain of *Neptune's Daughter*, and you don't exactly look like a fine, upstanding citizen."

My eyes drift over the tattoos on his neck, in the collar of his T-shirt, on his hands and knuckles.

Every inch of his skin is covered.

He snarls and flexes his tattooed hands. "We'll be fine. This is what we do for a living, and Cutter and Rion have the skills to take care of anything we might encounter."

I chew on my bottom lip and consider the possibilities.

One—they can get in, get everything loaded over to *The Destiny*, and get out without detection.

Two—they get in, get confronted by security, and they have to hurt someone in order to get the drugs out safely.

Three—they get in, get confronted by security, and they kill the security and get away with the drugs.

Four—they get in, something happens, and they don't get the drugs.

Five—they don't get in at all and get no drugs.

The stern set of his lips and hard eyes tell me there's no point in arguing about the matter anymore. I'll be staying in the car…for however long it takes.

He hands me his cell phone.

"Why are you giving me this?"

"We'll park on the road along the front of the port. It gives us the best view of the dock area. You're going to call Cutter if you see *anything*—cops, suspicious vehicles, suspicious persons."

"Suspicious persons? You mean like you guys."

This time, he doesn't laugh, just clamps his jaw together tightly.

It may not be the best time to crack jokes, Grace.

He stares out the window at the darkening night. The cloud cover and constant drizzle will only help cover what we're about to attempt. "Let's go."

FIFTEEN

War

——————

My feet slam into the gravel on the other side of the fence surrounding the port, and I drop into a crouch to wait to make sure nobody saw me climb and jump over.

There's almost no cover here.

Worst possible situation.

Between what Grace and I were able to ascertain earlier and what Preacher found in his online research, there should be only a handful of guards working tonight.

The *Neptune's Daughter* is at the end of one of the massive piers, far back from the road or main building.

Cutter and Rion should be pulling in alongside it any minute.

Get in. Get the stuff. Get out.

This mission is about speed as much as it is about remaining undetected. Realistically, the latter part is probably impossible. *The Destiny* will likely be spotted coming in, but we'll deal with that when it comes.

For right now, it doesn't look like anybody spotted me.

Thank fuck.

And as much as I don't want to admit it, knowing Grace is

acting as a lookout helps dispel one of my major concerns with this mission, but it also creates new ones.

The quiet stillness of the night surrounds me. No signs of security or any alerts anyone has breached the property.

I rise to my feet and hurry along against the side of the main warehouse buildings until there's nowhere left to hide. The only way to get to where *Neptune's Daughter* is anchored is down at the end of the long central pier, which happens to have lights flooding almost every inch of it. Once I step out from the safety of the building shadows, there will be nowhere to conceal myself.

Where the hell is the security?

They should be here.

So, where the fuck are they?

That combined with Grace sitting unattended in the car on the street has unease blossoming in my chest.

Just because she didn't turn us in when she was here earlier or apparently while she was at the hotel doesn't mean she won't do it now or that she didn't make some arrangement with the authorities to try to catch us in the act tonight. Handing over my damn phone to her felt like handing over my own death warrant.

One call.

That's all it would take for her to have the cops swarming here. They would get the drugs and us, and she would be *truly* free.

Of this.

Of Me.

Christ. Why does that make my damn heart hurt so much?

Maybe because I want to believe her. I want to believe she's proven she won't turn us in. But I don't know what happened after I released her. I don't know what she said and what was said to her at the hotel.

I desperately want her to be helping because she *wants to.*

Something I can't examine.

Because

Because if I think about that, or about how leaving her exposed out there in the middle the night where anyone could walk up to her and hurt her has my fists clenching as I race down the dock toward the *Neptune's Daughter*, I would really be fucked.

The moonless night provides zero protection with these fucking lights spaced every few feet.

We should have cut the power...

But that would have drawn more unwanted security attention—or worse.

My lungs burn. My legs ache. A hundred more yards.

Get there. Just a few more seconds.

The Destiny appears slowly out of the dark and slips in alongside the *Neptune's Daughter*.

Thank fuck.

I never thought I'd be so happy to see that damn boat.

A guard steps from the shadows of the building and out into the light on the main stretch a mere twenty yards in front of me.

Fuck. Fuck. Fuck.

His focus centers in on Cutter and Rion pulling in.

Good.

The fucker won't notice me.

Swift, silent steps move me closer. And closer. He reaches for the radio on his hip.

I wrap my forearm around his neck before he has a chance to even react and squeeze. He gurgles and kicks backward at me. Nails claw at my arms.

Tighter.

The pressure on his jugular should have him unconscious within thirty seconds. He struggles and throws his shoulders back at me as much he can but it's no use. I'm much bigger, much stronger, and I caught him unprepared.

He goes limp in my arms, and I drag him to the shadows of the building. *The Destiny* stops in the water.

Hopefully, no one will see him unconscious here.

Cutter and Rion throw the lines down, and I scramble forward and secure them.

Rion leans over the rail and looks down at me. "Any trouble?"

I nod toward the unconscious man tucked in the darkness behind me. "Just him, but there are others around. We need to move fast."

He nods and turns back. I run over and climb up the ladder onto the *Neptune's Daughter*.

It's only been a few days, but it seems like ages ago I last climbed this ladder up onto Grace's ship. It's incredible how much can change so quickly. How fast the world tilts on its axis. All because of one little pixie who won't stop asking questions and sticking her nose into things.

The crates sit out on the deck, waiting to be unloaded and picked up as scheduled tomorrow, just like she thought they would be.

We need at least twenty minutes to move them.

It's too much time exposed, but we don't have a choice.

"Hey! What are you doing up there?" The question rings out in the cool night air.

My stomach clenches along with my fists.

Fuck.

I turn and look over the rail. Another security guard stares up at me.

Shit.

He hasn't seen his buddy yet. If he had, I'd have a weapon pointed at me instead of a flashlight.

"Oh, hi! This is my ship. I just came back because I forgot something."

Lame, but vague is better than trying to concoct an intricate story.

He narrows his eyes on me, focusing in on the tattoos on my hands and neck. "How did you get in?"

I shrug and try to appear nonchalant about it. "Jumped

the fence. Please don't report this. I'll be out of here in a minute."

Without the drugs. DAMMIT.

"Get down here, sir. You keep your hands where I can see them at all times." The guard reaches for a firearm on his hip.

Fuck.

I was hoping it wouldn't come to this, but it looks as though we're fucked. Cutter and Rion better see what's happening and get the hell out of here.

They don't need to get caught up in anything.

But, their lines are still tied. I need to get to them and untie them so they can take off before this guy calls in the cavalry. I make my way down the ladder, my hands tightening on each wrung.

This guy will fuck up everything.

We're dead if we don't get this shit to Arturo.

Fuck.

With only a few feet left, I glance back over my shoulder and gauge where he's standing.

Two feet behind me.

Close enough.

I launch myself backward at him.

It has the desired effect. He's totally unaware, and I land on him, knocking us both back onto the dock.

He scrambles for his weapon, but my fist connects with his cheek before he can get his hand around it. I knock his arm away and land a left on his temple.

His head cracks back against the dock. He winces and swings wildly.

The blow hits me. My head snaps back, pain radiates through my face, and stars dance across my eyelids.

Fuck.

The world spins, and my jaw aches. I shake my head and try to regain my ability to think.

I still hold one of his arms down, but the other is free and reaching on his belt for something.

No way, fucker.

I try to wrap my hand around his wrist, but pain slices through my side.

Fuck. He has a knife!

He slashes at me again, but I block it with my forearm, taking a nice chunk of flesh from it.

Warm blood leaks down my side and my arm and drips onto the dock.

I need to end this.

Before one of us does something we can't undo.

I grab both of his shoulders and slam his upper body back. His head cracks against the pavement, and his eyes roll up and back. The blade falls out of his hand, and I land three or four good blows to his face before he sags slightly under me.

Shit.

I scramble back. He's not moving.

Shit. Shit.

My side and forearm burn, and blood seeps between my fingers where I have my hand pressed against where he slashed my side.

I turn around, and *The Destiny* is already on its way back out to open water. They must have cut the lines from the boat.

At least they got away before any security could call it in, but I need to get the fuck out of here.

I grit my teeth and break out into a run toward the fence line as close to where Grace is parked as possible. The pain splitting my side has me doubling over, and I press against it to stem the flow of blood.

Fuck. This all went so bad.

I should've known.

It looked too easy.

I should've known nothing is ever easy for me.

At least, not lately. Not since I met this woman.

The six-foot fence looms in front of me, and I pause and take several shaky breaths.

Suck it up or you won't get over.

The pain will be unbearable, but I have to do it. There's no other way out of here.

My blood-stained fingers curl into the chain-link. I close my eyes for a brief second, and then, I go.

I block out the pain with thoughts of Grace's soft skin and blazing red hair under my fingertips. Her lips pressed against mine. Her nails scoring my back while I pound into her.

It's probably not the best image to use, and one I shouldn't even consider, but it's there, nonetheless.

Creamy pale skin.

Soft pink flush spreading across it.

A groan slips from my lips—both from the pain and physical exertion as well as the sudden throb in my pants.

I get my leg over the top of the fence and drop on the other side.

Fuck.

My feet don't catch me.

The hard ground is the only thing that breaks my fall. Pain shoots up my arm and through my side and hip.

"Motherfucker!"

I grasp at the fence and pull myself to my feet. Several deep breaths do nothing to clear the red haze of pain clouding my vision.

Shit. I might pass out.

I stagger toward the truck. My toe catches on something, probably my own damn feet, and I lurch forward but put my arm out to catch myself before I face-plant on the sidewalk.

Darkness encroaches the sides of my vision, and another stab of pain shoots in my side.

I stumble again, and this time, there's no stopping my downward momentum.

Striking the pavement feels like running into a brick wall.

My injured arm and shoulder take the brunt of the fall, and a scream that sounds almost inhuman wrenches from my throat.

"Warwick?"

What?

Did someone say my name?

Who the hell knows my name?

"Warwick? Can you hear me?"

Wait…

Grace.

I try to push myself up off the ground with my good arm but barely manage to get up halfway sitting before I fall back over again as the pain shoots through me.

"Oh, my God." Her footsteps pound against the sidewalk, and then she's squatting down in front of me.

In the almost blackness of the poorly lit street area, the concern in her gaze is still evident. She cups my face. Her eyes dart down to where my hand is pressed against my bloody side.

"Oh, my God. You're hurt."

I grunt, and she slides an arm under my armpit. "We have to get you up and to a hospital."

Despite her tiny size, she helps get me to my feet with a lot of difficulty and a lot of cursing and pain so sharp it darkens my vision.

This must be what dying feels like. It must be. Maybe that knife hit something more vital than I thought.

The truck is only a few hundred yards up the road, but it seems to take an eternity to get there. Every agonizing step is more time for the police to get here.

I grit my teeth and move forward, forcing myself to take step after step.

Just keep moving.

Grace tugs the passenger side door open before practically

shoving me inside. It closes, and she's in the driver seat starting the engine.

"We are going to get you to the hospital."

"No."

"What do you mean no?"

I shake my head and wince. "No hospital. Take me back to the warehouse."

She opens her mouth, but I cut her off before she can ask another question.

"No arguments, Grace. Warehouse. I'll direct you on how to get there."

She mumbles something under her breath I can't quite catch, and I drop my head back against the headrest and squeeze my eyes shut.

Fucking shit. Everything is going to hell and taking me with it.

SIXTEEN

Grace

He needs a damn hospital. A doctor. A surgeon. There's so much blood—soaking his shirt, his arm...all over his hands.

And now, all over mine where they curl tightly around the steering wheel.

He looks like death.

Pale as a fucking corpse.

So much like what Dad looked like lying in that hospital bed, taking his last breaths.

Tears pool in my eyes, and I wipe my face with my shirtsleeve.

Breaking down and crying now won't help anything. It won't help him.

I never considered what would happen if Warwick got hurt. We never planned for this. At least, not out loud. At least, not with me. After Warwick called Cutter and Preacher to tell them I would act as lookout, there was very little discussion of what was going to happen. Whether that was intentional to keep me in the dark or to protect me in case anyone showed up and I was questioned, I'm not sure. But we certainly never talked about the possibility of him getting injured.

Shit. Shit. Shit.

When he collapsed onto the sidewalk, I never thought he would get up.

My breath caught in my throat. My heart stopped.

All I could do was scramble from the truck and race to him through the cool, damp night.

And now, he's dying beside me while I drive through the wet streets toward the highway.

This is bad. This is so, so bad.

A shrill ring sounds in the car.

Warwick's phone!

I scramble to get it out of my pocket and glance over at him. His half-lidded eyes meet mine. He gives me a small nod of permission to answer.

Like I wasn't going to.

"Hello?"

"Grace?" Cutter practically snarls my name. "Where are you? Is Warwick with you?"

"We're on the road. He's with me, but he's in bad shape. I think he got stabbed."

His mumbled words have been hard to piece together. All I got was "knife" and "guard."

"Shit." *The Destiny's* engine roars in the background. "It's going to take us a while to get back to the warehouse. Even at top speed. The waters are churned up from the storm, so we have to be careful. I'll call ahead to Preacher and make sure he's ready for you. He has some basic medical training and can help until we're back and Rion can look at him."

What the hell is wrong with these guys?

They act like this is no big deal. It's not a damn paper cut.

"He needs a hospital."

He needs a goddamn doctor, not some haphazard care from these thugs.

"No." Cutter's words are harsh and direct, brokering no argument. "No hospitals. Bring him to the warehouse. If Preacher and Rion can't take care of him, we have other options."

Shit.

I want to scream and rail at him that they won't do what's best for Warwick's health, but this isn't my game to play; it's theirs.

I'm just a pawn—or at least, I was before Warwick released me. Now, I don't know what the hell I am.

An accomplice?

"How far from the warehouse are you?"

I stare at the open road ahead of me. "I have no fucking clue. Warwick, how close are we?"

He groans and flicks his eyes to the road before closing them again. "Forty miles or so."

"He says forty miles."

Cutter releases a sigh. "Okay, good. Just floor it when you get to the county highway. There are never any cops there, so you should be fine."

Fine.

Should be fine…

What the hell does that mean?

It doesn't instill much confidence. I end the call and return my focus to the road. Preacher better be as good as Cutter suggests he is. Otherwise…I can't even think of the possibility.

If Warwick dies now, all of this was for…nothing.

Every bump in the road elicits a groan from Warwick.

My heart amps up another level, thundering against my ribs.

Blood seeps from under his hand where he has it pressed against his side and has already stained his sleeve and trickles down his other arm.

He's losing a lot of blood and fast.

My lack of any medical expertise makes it so much

harder to gauge the situation, but every fiber of my being says to fuck the guys and get him to a damn hospital.

If it were anyone else, that's exactly what I would do.

But this isn't just anyone, and this situation is far from anything else I've ever been a part of.

No.

I have to trust Cutter and Preacher and Rion when they say they can handle it, but the longer we're on the road, the more dire the situation seems.

Why do I care so damn much?

Considering the answer to that question isn't even remotely in the realm of things on my radar right now.

Not the time or place to delve into deep, dark, psychological questions. I've already made so many shitty decisions. Analyzing more of them now would only lead to beating myself up more.

I glance over. His closed eyes, shallow breathing, and the way his temple is pressed against the window don't help the fear seizing my chest.

"Warwick. Wake up."

He jerks up slightly and shakes his head. "Huh?"

"I said wake up. You dozed off again."

Don't let him sleep.

That's what they always say, right? Keep the person awake. Keep them talking.

I can do that. Talk. Ask questions. It usually gets me in trouble. It has been the main source of tension between us since the moment he stepped onto my ship, but now, it might actually be exactly what's needed.

"Just let me sleep for a couple minutes." His mumbled words are barely intelligible.

"No! No!"

He closes his eyes.

Shit.

I can't let him fall asleep. We're close. I just need to keep him awake a little while longer.

"No, you stay awake. Talk to me. Tell me more about your mom."

"My mom?"

"Yeah, tell me about her. You said she was a librarian."

And given what I already know and read in her notes, she understood Warwick better than anyone else ever did or ever could. His two tangled natures, inextricable from one another. One leading him down a dark path. The other shining light where it's least expected.

"Yeah, librarian."

"Did you spend a lot of time there with her?"

He snort-laughs then groans and presses into his side. He tries to shift his weight but flinches, pain taking over his face. "You could say that. Sometimes because I liked spending time with her, but most of the time because I was in detention."

Why does that not surprise me?

Warwick has a good heart. I can see that despite all the ways he tries to hide it and push it down, but there's a darkness there too. One that sends a shiver through me as much as his touch does.

"So, she was the librarian at school?"

He nods again and presses his temple to the window.

"What did you like to read?"

He coughs and clears his throat. "A little bit of everything. She always gave me the classics but pretty much anything I could get my hands on was game."

The notes inside the books in his room fly through my head along with the million questions about the woman who wrote them. For once, he doesn't seem opposed to me asking.

"What about the notes in the books?"

I glance over in time to catch a slight grin pull at his lips. "She started that when I was ten."

The car rolls over a pothole, and he flinches.

Shit. Dammit.

Still a few miles to go.

"What was the first one she ever gave you?"

His eyes open slowly and meet mine when I peek over.

"*To Kill a Mockingbird.*"

One of my all-time favorites.

"Kind of deep for a ten-year-old, isn't it?"

He wheezes out a rattling cough laugh, and I cringe and glance at the clock again, then the odometer. Maybe going eighty-five in this truck isn't the best idea. I don't dare go faster, even though the need to get him there increases with every grimace and cough.

"It seemed fitting at the time."

"How so?"

Just keep him talking...

If he's talking, he's not dying.

"I had gotten into another fight at school. One of many. But this one was different."

"Why?"

He shrugs again and winces. "This one was justified in her eyes. We didn't have a lot of diversity where I grew up. I don't even think I met someone who was black until I was in middle school already. This family moved into town. The dad was black, and the mom was white. The kids couldn't seem to fit in anywhere. Some of the kids were picking on him on the play-ground and I stepped in."

"What did you do?"

He grins. "Let's just say there were a lot of bloody noses and scraped up knuckles and I had a big smile on my face when we were done."

To Kill a Mockingbird.

Of course. His mother's note makes perfect sense now that I know the story.

Defending your beliefs in the face of criticism and

threats of violence takes bravery you must find deep down, but bravery doesn't always mean violence.

Warwick's first response is typically anger and violence. He has to fight to make the right decisions, to be brave in a *different* way. The insight this woman had into him at such a young age is astounding.

"She kept up the tradition after that? Giving you books and writing notes in them."

"Yeah. It was sort of our thing until she died."

The sadness and longing in his pained voice has my chest tightening. The water was always my thing with Dad. The shared love. I swallow through the lump in my throat.

"What was the last one she gave you?"

He looks out into the night whizzing past us. "You ask too many questions, Grace."

Shit.

Too personal. Too much to expect an answer.

He shuts down before my eyes, leans farther into the door, closes his eyes, and drops his head against the window again. "The turn is coming up on the right. It's a gravel road so don't miss it."

It was too good to be true. Him being open with me. Him being honest. Him really telling me something that will help me understand him and what's happening.

His wall is up now.

But at least we're almost there. I don't know if I can keep him talking much longer, and he looks like he's about ready to pass out again.

The hidden entrance to the gravel road that will lead us through the woods to the warehouse on the shore appears on the right, and I slow enough to turn in.

This is going to hurt. The bumps, dips, and gravel will be hell on him, but we don't have a choice right now.

How he's even stayed alert enough to direct me back to the warehouse is a miracle.

Gravel crunches under the tires, and I tighten my grip on the wheel as if that will help absorb each bounce and take some of the pain away from the man next to me.

The lights come into view, and I release a small sigh of relief and lighten my grip on the wheel. I gun it down the road and toward the warehouse.

Please be ready, Preacher.

I don't even know the man, not really, but already, I can't imagine what I would do if something happened to Warwick. If he didn't come out of this okay.

That's fucking terrifying.

Even more so than the mob after me or the fact these men held me captive and I'm willingly returning to them.

Don't worry, Warwick. I have you.

Even if he doesn't want me here. Even if he thinks I should be anywhere else but with him. Even if he's right and I should be.

SEVENTEEN

War

I grit my teeth with the final turn into the warehouse, and when she pulls up outside the door and throws the truck into park, I release a shaky breath.

Fucking gravel road.

Every dip and bump felt like being stabbed again. I wasn't sure if I would puke or pass out or both and had to fight to keep myself from lashing out at her about something that wasn't her fault.

Preacher should be waiting for us. I sure as fuck hope with some pain meds because, Christ, this fucking hurts.

I've been cut before, but this goes above and beyond. If there's any internal damage though, I'm fucked.

Rion is a damn good medic, and he's performed some miracles under worse conditions than what we have here, in fucking war zones being shot at, but he can only do so much. And I'm in Preacher's hands until Cutter and Rion get back. The basic first aid training he received when he was working for the CIA may help in the meantime, but Rion is the real expert, the one who has always handled any of our injuries—though thankfully always minor—in the past.

This doesn't feel minor. Yet, Grace has been so cool and calm through all this.

What's that saying? Grace under pressure?

That's her to a T.

And fuck if it doesn't make me like her even more.

She shouldn't have been there tonight. She should have been at the hotel, with me and everything about this entire fucked-up situation in the past.

But if she hadn't been, I don't think I would have made it to the truck, let alone been able to drive back here. Even waiting for E to be able to get me, if I'd managed to call him, might have been a deadly delay.

As it stands now, it feels like being at death's door.

Grace turns off the engine and throws her door open. The ten seconds it takes for her to race around to my side gives me time to take a steadying breath and to try to hide how much fucking pain I'm in.

My door opens, and she reaches for me. "Come on, big guy."

"Let me help." Preacher's deep, steady voice comes from somewhere behind her. He pushes her out of the way and reaches for me.

"I'm fine."

He scowls as he slides one of his arms under my shoulders and around my back to ease me out of the car. I clench my teeth, and he drags me from the seat.

The wounds on my side and my arm smart like a motherfucker.

He pulls me to my feet outside the truck. "What happened?"

I glance toward Grace.

What does it matter if I say anything in front of her? She literally knows everything now.

"Two guards. The first guy was easy. The second guy was waiting for me once I was already on *Neptune's Daughter*."

Preacher half-drags/half-walks me toward the warehouse. Grace trails behind silently.

"I didn't even get a chance to try to set up the transfer over to *The Destiny*. He ordered me down, and he was armed. I got the jump on him, but he somehow got the knife out and cut my arm and stuck it in my side before I could disarm him."

"Shit." Preacher throws the door open and wrangles me over to the table in the center of the warehouse. "Get up."

Milo whimpers at our feet, his huge brown eyes heavy with concern.

I glower at Preacher. "Like it's that fucking easy."

It's not like I can jump right up there.

I help the best I can to get my ass up on the table. The motion sends pain lancing through my body.

Preacher reaches into a large blue Tupperware tote on one of the chairs and grabs a pair of scissors that he uses to cut away my shirt from my arms and torso. I keep my hand pressed against the wound, holding the material in place.

"Take off your hand so I can look at this."

I let it fall away, and a warm rush of blood flows from the wound.

Motherfucker.

Preacher looks behind him. "Grace, I need your help."

She rushes forward from the foot of the table where she's been standing watching everything with watery, wide green eyes.

"In the blue bin, you'll find rubbing alcohol, a suture kit, and some bottles with different pain medications. Find the Percocet ten milligrams."

I want the damn pain meds. I want them more than I even want to admit, but I need to keep my head. "No meds."

Preacher glares at me. "Don't be an asshole. You're in a lot of pain. You're gonna be in a lot more once I start cleaning and stitching this shit, so take the goddamn medicine."

I gnash my teeth at him.

He presses his hand against the wound, and the world goes black for a split-second.

"Okay, I'll take the pain meds."

The sound of Grace rummaging through the box hits my ears as Preacher pokes and prods at me.

"The good news is, I don't think it hit any vital organs or any arteries. If it had, you'd be bleeding a hell of a lot worse. But, if you just nicked something in there, there's no way to really tell. Maybe we should wait for Rion."

"Just stitch me up."

Preacher and Grace exchange a look, but I'm too exhausted and weak to question it. She hands him the items he asked for and pops open the bottle of pills.

"Open your mouth." She drops two into my mouth and then presses a bottle of water to my lips.

I tilt my head up and down them.

Shit.

I would prefer to stay as alert as possible right now, but Preacher's right. If I go into shock from the pain, it's not helping anyone.

"Sorry, man, this is gonna hurt."

Grace's tiny hand tightens on my shoulder, and Preacher pours the bottle of rubbing alcohol on my side.

"Motherfucker!" I bow up from the table, but Preacher's strong hand against my chest holds me down.

"Lie down."

I grit my teeth and drop back down. He pulls at the wound with his fingers, lifting the skin, and rinses it again.

"Fuck! Can you make that any more painful?"

His hard eyes dart to mine. "I can if you keep bitching."

My teeth are about to crack. Blackness invades the edges of my vision whenever I try to open my eyes. My stomach turns.

Grace's hand tightens on my shoulder again, and I open my eyes to meet hers.

Concern laces their green depths.

Why does she give a shit if I'm in pain?

She should hate me. I fucking kidnapped her and held her here against her will. The last thing she should be looking at me with is concern. She never should have come back.

"There. We're done cleaning it out."

I shift to knock her hand off my shoulder. I can't think straight with Preacher digging around inside me and her leaning over me looking all innocent and worried.

"Let's get you stitched up, and then I can deal with that arm."

Shit.

I close my eyes and drop my head back against the table.

"Here we go, man."

I wrap my hands around the sides of the table and grip tightly as he slides the needle through my skin the first time. My clenched jaw aches, and every muscle in my body burns trying to bite back the scream clawing its way up my throat.

Grace's hand lands back on my shoulder, and she stiffens, almost as if she can feel the pain every time Preacher slides the thread through my skin and tightens it.

I don't know how many stitches he makes or how long it takes, but it feels like a fucking eternity.

"We're done."

A sigh of relief slips from my lips.

Preacher slaps gauze over it and tapes it in place. "We need to watch for infection or any signs you might have internal bleeding. Don't be a fucking cowboy. You have to tell Rion how you feel. He can't help you if he doesn't know what's going on."

Fucking Preacher.

He's just trying to help, but the mothering, I could do

without. I had one of those, and she died. He reaches up and twists my arm toward him. I clench my jaw.

"This one's just a scratch. A couple stitches at most." The rubbing alcohol hits it, and I flinch and gnash my teeth.

He chuckles, and Grace glowers at him and then offers me a soft smile.

Half a dozen stitches later, he bandages me up and piles the garbage at the end of the table. "Go lie down. That Percocet is gonna kick in soon, and you're not gonna want to be vertical."

"No. Arturo only gave us 'til tomorrow. We need to figure out what we're going to do."

Preacher shakes his head. "Christ, you're as stubborn as a fucking mule. I thought some of the guys in Afghanistan were bad, but you're far worse."

Grace eyes him speculatively. She's been slowly collecting information on the guys anytime anyone lets anything slip. I can see her mentally processing the information. She now knows their names—at least their nicknames—and now she knows Preacher was overseas.

If she wants to betray us, she has more than enough to take us down.

But she didn't betray us today, did she?

I let her go, and she came back.

So why can't I put that to bed?

There's too much at stake for me to blindly trust her, no matter how beautiful she is, no matter how accommodating she seems to be, no matter how much I want to believe she sees the necessity of what we're doing.

"Go lie down."

I push myself to a sitting position and groan. "Fuck." With my hand pressed to my side, I swing my legs over the side of the table. My head swims. Darkness encroaches on my vision again, along with something else. The dulling effects of the Percocet are kicking in.

My feet hit the floor, and my legs wobble. I grip the edge of the table for support.

Grace slides her arm around my back to support me.

Funny how the pixie is the one I've been leaning on.

I chuckle to myself, and they both cast me strange looks.

Maybe these meds are kicking in faster than I thought.

I half-stumble and Grace half-drags me across the warehouse floor to the stairs. They might as well be Mount Everest.

How the hell am I getting up those?

I bite back a curse and grab the handrailing.

"You going to make it?" Grace peers up at me with those soft, innocent eyes.

I sneer at her. "I'm fine." I pull my arm from around her shoulder and shift my weight to the railing. Each step sends a jolt of pain to my side but I push forward to the light at the end of the tunnel. Bed.

Grace's little gasps of concern as we move up the stairs make me grit my teeth. Nothing is worse than being weak in front of a woman you're attracted to. Except maybe being attracted to a woman you kidnapped. The woman who should want nothing to do with you, yet she stays around.

She opens the door for me.

"Thank you." I somehow grit out the words before I wobble into the bedroom where the rumpled bed—evidence of where she slept for the last two nights—practically calls my name.

I glance down at myself and groan. Blood soaks my pants and is caked on my side and my hands. I need to clean up before I do anything else, but the thought of walking all the way to the bathroom, starting the shower, stripping, and getting in is just too daunting at the moment.

The room spins slightly, and I grab the dresser for support and close my eyes trying to gather what little strength I have left to fight the pain meds and make it to the bathroom.

A small warm hand lands against my bare shoulder. "We need to get you cleaned up."

I open my eyes just in time to watch her disappear into the bathroom. The water starts, and she reappears.

Her eyes drift down to my side and then up to my arm. She frowns. "We really shouldn't get this wet, but you're filthy. We just can't stay in for long."

We?

The word vaguely registers in my foggy brain before she steps up to me and her hands go to my waist. I catch her wrist.

"What are you doing?"

She sighs. "Helping you get undressed."

"I can do it myself."

"Can you?" Her red eyebrows rise.

I push myself off the dresser in a fit of arrogance and grab for my zipper with a wince. Pain radiates up my arm and through my side. Through the room spinning, soft hands find me and lean me back against the dresser.

"Let me help you."

I'm too dizzy to argue so she unbuttons my pants and shoves them down my legs. My cock stirs. She reaches for the waistband of my boxers.

Down boy. This is absolutely not the time for that.

She pulls them down while averting her eyes, but I don't fail to catch the slight gasp when my semi-hard cock springs free.

I bite back a chuckle as she rises to her feet and slides her arm around my back.

"Let's go."

She manages to wrangle me into the bathroom and help me step into the shower stall.

The hot water stings my chest but I step into the spray and turn my face up to it.

God, it feels good.

I didn't know how badly I needed to get clean until I stepped in here.

The shower curtain rustles. I jerk my head toward it and plant one hand against the wall to keep me upright. I stare at Grace, and she examines me for a moment before quirking one of those damn eyebrows at me.

"Need help?"

Christ, that would be the ultimate embarrassment.

Being unable to take a goddamn shower myself.

Despite how badly everything in me is screaming *yes get her naked in the water with you,* I shake my head. "No. I'm okay."

She sighs and slides the shower curtain shut. "I'm staying right here in case you pass out and kill yourself."

Gee, thanks for that image.

I reach for the shampoo with my free hand. The movement sends a slice of pain through my abdomen and arm, but I bite back the curse.

Show no weakness. She's already seen enough.

I shampoo my head with my good arm and step back into the spray to let it rinse out. Handling the bar of soap proves difficult. It slips from my fingers and clatters to the tile.

"Shit."

"Need help?"

I grunt. "No."

Deep breath. You got this.

I inhale as much as my side will allow and bend down to grab it. The motion sends the world spinning, and I slap my hand against the wall to keep from face-planting into it. I grab the soap and slowly rise again.

Scrubbing away the blood from my body helps release some of the tension from the day. I carefully move the soap around where the bandages cover the stitches.

"We need to change your bandages as soon as you get out."

God, it's like she's psychic or something.

"Are you sure you're okay? I am going to run down to grab some fresh supplies."

"I'm fine." The words come out more growl than speech, and she sighs and leaves the bathroom with some mumbled curses under her breath.

If she wasn't completely fed up with me before, she is now. Maybe that will help keep her at arm's length where she should be.

The soaps rinses from my body under the spray, and I shut the water off. Footsteps in the room alert me to her return. I grab for the shower curtain and pitch forward. The world spins, and my vision goes hazy. I squeeze my eyes shut.

I'm not entirely sure if it's from the drugs or maybe blood loss. Either way, it's not good if I want to stay upright.

My good hand finds the wall, and I take several deep breaths before I reopen my eyes and pull the curtain back. She stands in the doorway with a towel in one hand.

I have to give her credit; her eyes stay locked on mine and don't drift south down my wet, naked body. Were we in different positions, I can't say I would be a gentleman and not look.

She shakes the towel in invitation and holds out her hand. I just stare at it for a minute before the room spins again.

Fuck.

I don't have a choice. If I try to step out of here without some help, I will end up flat on my ass or cracking my head open. I accept her proffered hand, and she helps me climb out of the shower and onto the cracked tile floor of the bathroom.

She quickly wipes my back and legs and then gingerly dries my arm around the wound there.

"I can do that myself."

Her warm breath floats across my damp skin, raising goose bumps. "You can barely stand up. Don't be stupid."

She moves around in front of me, and her green eyes flick

up to meet mine. Delicate hands gingerly brush over my chest and down my side to the wound there.

Every stroke of her hand has my cock stirring a little bit more.

I jerk the towel from her hand and wrap it around my waist, gritting my teeth at the pain that slices through me at the abrupt movement. "I got it."

She rolls her eyes and steps back with her hands raised. "Whatever you say. Now, let me recover those stitches." She turns and steps back into the room, leaving me alone momentarily to consider what a clusterfuck of a situation I've created.

And now, with my ability to think being fogged not only by the drugs but also the touching from and presence of this woman, I'm incapable of seeing a way out of the situation.

At least, not one that ends without me and the guys dead.

"You coming?" Her lilting voice floats in from the bedroom.

I wish.

EIGHTEEN

Grace

He stumbles out of the bathroom with the towel wrapped precariously around his waist. Steam floats around him from the tiny room.

Water still trickles down various parts of his body I missed. I follow one particular rivulet as it courses down from his shoulder, over his tattooed and hard pecs, through the valley of his abs, and disappears into the towel right at that little V thingy.

Heat stirs low in my belly—truly inappropriate given the circumstances, yet there all the same.

Keep your eyes on his face, Grace.

Get to work.

If I can keep myself occupied with other things and other thoughts, this might not be as awkward. I drop down on the bed where the bandages are laid out and wave him over. "We need to replace those bandages."

I need to keep my hands and my mind busy.

His eyes meet mine, pupils pinpointed and barely focused. He grunts, and he shuffles forward until he's standing in front of me. Pale pink blood seeps through the wet bandage on his side, and I pull at the tape holding it in place.

A hand shoots out and grabs my wrist. He squeezes it and shakes his head. "I can do this myself."

Ass.

This man has an attitude unlike anything I've ever dealt with before. He's incapable of admitting he needs help let alone accepting it from me. Agreeing to let me act as lookout must have been agony for him. And now, he stands here weak, high on pain meds, and stitched together, and still can't admit he can't do it alone.

It's like he'd rather die than just let me help him.

"Stop trying to be a fucking macho guy and let me help you. You're about ready to fall over, and we need to get you dried and these re-wrapped before you do."

He freezes.

I wait for the explosion of anger at my words.

It doesn't come.

He slowly releases my hand, his eyes never leaving mine.

He made the right choice…this time.

I pry at the tape holding the bandage in place on his side. It sticks to his skin, despite being wet.

"Fuck!" He grits his teeth.

I pull at another corner.

"Shit. That hurts."

I chuckle and shake my head. "You're such a fucking pussy."

"Pussy?" He raises a dark eyebrow at me. "You think I'm a pussy?"

Before he released me, I might have been afraid of him after saying something like that, but now, like this…

Things are so different.

"You're complaining about a little tape, so yeah, I do."

He shifts slightly, putting his crotch right in front of my face.

Damn.

He's hard.

And very ready.

I half-expect him to tell me he's going to prove he doesn't have a pussy, but I rip off the last piece of tape and expose the stitches Preacher just put in.

Warwick's jaw tics where it's clenched, and I drag my eyes away from his face and to his wound.

The stitches still look good, but I do need to make sure they're dry before I redress them, which means I need him to take off the towel.

I chew my bottom lip.

How does one ask that when the man in question has something very private barely contained under it?

He reaches down and tugs at the knot of the towel at his waist, directly below where the word *LOYALTY* is inked across his skin. It falls away and exposes his full body—hard muscle, tattoos, and...everything else.

"Keep your eyes up here, Grace."

Be a lady. Don't embarrass yourself further by drooling over what's hanging between his legs, Grace.

Mom's voice works into my thoughts, and I shudder, but it doesn't stop me from looking.

It can't.

Holy hell.

His growing erection does not disappoint. I shift to try to dissipate some of the tension building between us.

He clears his throat, and I look up at him. A knowing grin tilts the corner of his lips.

Shit. How long was I staring at him?

He wobbles slightly, and his eyes drift closed.

I'm losing him. I rip the bandage off his arm in one smooth motion.

His eyes fly open, and he winces slightly but doesn't put up the same fuss he did with his side.

Maybe he's trying to avoid any further comments about

his manliness, even though the evidence of it sits right at eye level.

I gently pat dry the wound on his side to a litany of curses coming from him.

"Jesus. Fuck."

I give him a hard look, and he bites his lip and grinds his teeth together.

"For such a big, tough pirate, you sure are a baby about this."

"You try being stabbed."

I snort. "You weren't even stabbed. This is just a graze. You were sliced at best."

I place the last piece of tape and press it tightly against his warm, damp skin.

He hisses and steps back slightly.

It only puts a few more inches between us but it's enough to give me an even better view of his dick, which is now at full attention. His eyes drift down, then he quickly jerks his head up and catches my gaze.

The corner of his mouth twitches.

"Always nice to know that wasn't permanently damaged."

"Clearly not." The words come out a little wispier than I'd like. More breathy. Needy. Totally wrong and inappropriate right now.

"What do you expect? A beautiful woman has her hands all over me."

Beautiful?

Men have called me beautiful and offered me compliments before. Mostly as a way to try to get in my pants. Yet, even though Warwick is very naked and very hard right now, I don't think that's why he said it.

The drugs have loosened his lips and removed any reservations or anything holding him back from speaking the truth. He feels this pull as much as I do. He wants this too, as wrong as it might be, as crazy as it truly is.

Until only hours ago, I was his captive. He was the big, bad pirate who threw me over his shoulder like something out of an old romance novel and carried me away to my fate.

But not anymore. Now, I'm here because I chose to be, because I couldn't walk away knowing what that would mean for him and not knowing what would happen with the drugs and the Marconis.

I rise to my feet slowly and crowd into his space.

Jesus, what are you doing, Grace?

Making really bad decisions.

Before I can give myself any more time to think about how what I'm doing will change everything, I lean in and press my lips to his.

His good arm comes up and wraps around my waist. He tugs me against him with a grunt into my mouth. That had to hurt but it doesn't seem to stop him from claiming me with his lips and tongue.

He kisses me hard, demanding my compliance. I give it right back. All the pent-up aggression that's been building between us unravels. All the heat smoldering there finally sparks.

The heat grows and builds until a fire rages between his naked body and my clothed one. That damn familiar earthy, cool water scent of his swirls around me and invades every breath I take. The beard that's been steadily growing since he took me abrades my soft skin.

God, this is so wrong and so damn right.

This has to be one of the dumbest things I've ever done in my life. Yet, my heart races, and I feel more alive than I ever have, in the arms of the man who could have killed me.

He jerks away, releases me, and shakes his head. His free hand goes back through his wet hair. "What the fuck am I doing?"

Warwick wavers on his feet slightly like he's about to

topple over, and I grab him and spin him around to sit on the edge of the bed. "Lie down."

I'm going to try not to take that "what the fuck am I doing" personally. He wasn't saying that because it was me. It was about the situation. Right? The fact that he just had stitches and narcotics and that his life is in danger with the mob. The fact that I was his hostage…

Shit. When did I become that girl—the one who kisses the bad boy and then wonders why he rejects her?

He grimaces and crawls backward until his head hits the pillow. A relaxed sigh escapes his lips, the ones that just moments ago were pressed against mine. The ones that tasted dark and forbidden.

His eyes drift closed. "Fuck."

The word echoes out into the silence of the room, and I just sit on the edge of the bed and stare at him until his chest rises and falls slowly and rhythmically.

He's asleep.

He's also very naked.

And I shouldn't be staring at him.

I grab the covers and pull them up over him with shaking hands, then kick off my shoes and look down at myself.

I need a shower too.

The clothes I changed into at the hotel are covered in blood, but at least mine from earlier are clean now and sitting on Warwick's desk. They must have a washing machine and dryer somewhere. Maybe Preacher washed them while we were gone.

I grab the pile and take it with me into the bathroom. I crank the water on as hot as it will go, strip while it heats, and climb in.

The hot spray is so damn welcome.

What a last few days.

I'm supposed to be leaving Milwaukee tomorrow and be on my way back home to try to figure out the mess Dad turned our business into. I need to attempt to sort out the books and also keep Mom calm and under control. She has no idea how bad things are, just that I needed to make sure this trip happened. And now, on top of all that shit already festering, I need to file the paperwork on the "lost" cargo and hope it doesn't cause more problems for us. With my luck, it will.

But instead of getting ready to go home, I'm here with Warwick and these guys trying to help them after they robbed me and kidnapped me.

I shampoo my hair and soap my body quickly, letting the scalding water rinse away the remnants of the evening. But it can't erase the feeling of Warwick's arms wrapped around me or his hard body pressed against mine.

How did I end up here?

It all happened so fast.

Is this how those hostages at the bank in Stockholm felt? Did they realize how strange and wrong it was to not want to see their captors in prison or worse?

Because I do know how insane it is…and that doesn't change a damn thing.

I step from the shower and dry off with the only other towel in the bathroom. The clean clothes feel heavenly against my skin. A shower can do wonders. I slowly pull the door open, wincing at the squeaky hinges.

Warwick hasn't moved an inch. He's out cold, and I yawn. I'm finally starting to feel the effects of the day. The adrenaline that's been rushing through my system is dissipating, and I'm crashing hard.

The one place to collapse has been claimed already.

We haven't slept in the same bed together during my time here, but we're short on options, and I'm low on caring about how absurd this all is.

Fuck it.

I climb into bed next to Warwick and pull the covers up over me.

He mumbles something but doesn't move, and I relax back as much as possible knowing I have a very naked, very handsome, very dangerous pirate sleeping next to me tonight.

And that he's more dangerous than ever because of how much I loved his mouth and hands on me.

NINETEEN

War

———

The clank of the dock door opening jerks me awake. Pain shoots through my body.

"Dammit."

The sting in my side and my arm coupled with a soft sigh from beside me sends the entire night rushing back in a hazy fog of broken memories.

Hopping the fence.

The ship.

The security guard.

The knife.

Running.

Falling.

Bleeding.

Grace…

My lips tingle, and my cock stirs at the memory of her kiss last night.

Despite being drugged up and in a fuckload of pain, the feeling of her lips pressed against mine and her body in my arms is crystal clear.

Shit. What the hell was I thinking letting her kiss me? Kissing her back like that?

That's twice now I've let passion overpower reason, and that can't happen if I want to keep all of us alive.

I suck in a deep breath and glance to my left. Her soft, wavy red hair splays across the pillow like a golden amber halo. Her soft pink lips stand out against the paleness of her delicate skin, slightly parted with soft breaths puffing out slowly.

My cock hardens further and brushes against the sheet.

Shit. I'm naked.

The memory of the kiss might be vivid, but what happened after that is a narcotics-induced cloud of darkness.

We didn't. Did we?

I lift back the covers and release a sigh of relief to find her fully clothed.

It appears I've left her virtue intact.

I could've said or done anything to her last night. I was such a fucking mess.

Please, God, don't let me have done or said anything stupid.

The situation is bad enough as it is. We missed our first and second deadlines with Arturo, and we're missing half the drugs. There's no way we can deliver a full shipment today. I don't see how it could possibly be any worse right now.

I push myself up with my good arm and try to bite back the groan so I don't wake her.

Things are worse, because that hurts like a motherfucker. I should just be happy it was a glancing slice and not a full, penetrating stab.

The only time I've been stabbed, it was a mess. Drainage tubes, infections…it was the stuff of nightmares, and I never want to go through that again. And hopefully, I won't have to. Rion will check it today, and if he says I'm good, then I'm good. I trust him with my life.

I gingerly lift up the sheet and shift my way to the edge of the bed. With a grunt and some major effort, I push myself to my feet. A glance back at her assures me she's still asleep.

The dresser across the room holding my clothing looks miles away, but I shuffle over, grab some clothes, and slip out of the room without waking her.

"Jesus, man, do you have to subject us to that this early in the morning?" Cutter leans against the jamb of the kitchen door watching me slowly make my way down the stairs. Milo sits at his feet, tongue lolling to the side while he watches me descend.

"Go to Hell."

He shoves off the jamb and meets me at the bottom of the stairs. Milo whines and stares up at me.

"Sorry, boy, no bending down to pet you this morning." I toss my head back toward my room. "Grace is asleep. I didn't want to wake her up."

Any hint of humor on Cutter's face dissipates in an instant, and even though I can't see his eyes behind the aviator glasses, the glower is visible everywhere else—the set of his jaw, his hard stance, the white knuckles on his clenched fists.

I point a finger at him and make my way over to the table in the center of the warehouse. "Don't say a word. It's not what you think. Nothing happened. She patched me up again after I showered, and then we went to sleep. End of story."

"Well, well, well, Lazarus rises from the grave." Preacher comes strolling in from the back hallway and eyes me up and down.

I set my clothes on the table and grab my boxer briefs. I bend down to step into them and bite back a curse.

No weakness.

Gritting my teeth helps me get through pulling them up, and I do the same with my pants.

Preacher reaches us at the table and eyes me up and down. "How are you feeling this morning?"

I shrug. "As good as could be expected, I guess."

"Let me check these. Rion should be back soon and will

want to look too." He reaches down to my side and rips off the bandage and tape holding it in place.

"Ouch. Shit, man, could you be a little more delicate?"

His eyes move up to my room. "What, like her?"

I glower at him, and he chuckles.

Asshole.

He pushes and pokes at the wound a little. "That hurt?"

"Of course, it fucking hurts. I got stabbed."

"You got grazed. Don't be a baby."

Why is everyone on my case about this? Bunch of jerks.

Preacher rises. "It looks pretty good."

The box of medical supplies still sits on the chair where he left it last night. He grabs an orange bottle, pops it open, shakes out a pill, and hands it to me. "Antibiotic."

He grabs another bottle and turns to me. "Pain medication."

I shake my head. "No narcotics. I'm fine."

"You sure?"

Absolutely.

I nod. "I need to be clear-headed today. We need to come up with a plan."

He grabs another bottle shakes out four pills. "That's going to hurt for a few days. You're going to want to at least take something to help with the swelling and inflammation. And like I said, if you notice anything, you let Rion or me know."

Cutter hands me the cup in his hand, and I down the pills.

"Fuck!" I sputter and gasp as scalding hot coffee burns my throat. "Jesus, man, you could've warned me."

He chuckles. "What fun would that have been?"

Preacher smirks and reaches for my arm. "Let me check your arm, too." He rips off that bandage with zero finesse.

I smack at his hand, and he laughs.

"Where's Rion?" I look to the open dock door and slip where *The Destiny* sits.

"He ran out for some supplies and just got back. He's unloading them."

That means I slept through the door opening the first time when he left.

Jesus, I was really out of it.

"Arm looks good." Preacher grabs the gauze pads and tape and sets them on the table. "I'll let Rion take a look, then we can wrap you back up."

Probably with the same *gentle* touch he's already shown me. *Can't wait.*

"Well, look who finally decided to join us." Rion jumps from *The Destiny* and strolls toward us with the box tucked under his arm. "You look like shit, man."

I grunt and grab my T-shirt from the table. "Can you just check these stitches so I can get dressed?"

He grins, sets down the box on the table, and circles it to stand in front of me. He leans down to look at the wound on my side and then lifts my arm to check that one. "They look good. Preacher did an excellent job. I'm sure he already warned you to let us know if you see any infection or aren't feeling well?"

"Of course, he did." I pull my arm away from him and nod toward the bandages on the table. E steps out from the kitchen with a mug in one hand and a sandwich in another. I wave him over. I hadn't even realized he was back, but there's really no point in having him sit on the crew anymore anyway. "Now, can we get on with this so we can talk about a plan?"

Rion grabs the stuff from the table and not so gently re-covers the stitches. "There."

I tug my shirt on with gritted teeth. "We have a lot to figure out. When I spoke with Arturo last night and told him we weren't going to make the delivery under his deadline, he wasn't very happy. And he sure as hell won't be when we show up with half the shipment today."

They all nod in agreement.

E sits next to Preacher.

Preacher points to the SAT phone. "He's already called three times on the SAT phone this morning. He's definitely not happy."

He probably wants to nail down what time we'll arrive today. I was intentionally vague last night during our call.

Cutter drops down into a chair at the table and sips his coffee with one hand while he pets Milo with the other. "Is there anything else we need to know about last night? Did the guards get a good enough look at you? Did you get caught on any cameras?"

I shake my head and shove my good arm back through my hair. "No. The first guard, I choked him out from behind so he didn't see me at all, and the second one well...his head took a pounding, so I doubt he'll remember much clearly. Plus, he only saw me from up on the boat. It wasn't close, and it was fairly dark."

They all nod.

I point to Preacher. "But keep monitoring the police bands for anything, obviously."

"Of course. There was some radio traffic about a break-in at the port and the guards being taken to the hospital, but nothing about descriptions of perpetrators. So, what are we going to do about Arturo and the missing drugs?"

Good fucking question.

"Well, unless one of you knows where to get twenty kilos of heroin in the next hour, I'd say we're pretty much fucked."

Silence descends over us. The very real threat staring us down weighs heavily on everyone, but especially me.

I'm the leader. I'm the one who roped them into this gig. This is all my doing and all my failure.

"That's what I thought. So, I'm going to go talk to Arturo in person."

Cutter's head snaps up. "What? You can't go down there. It's like walking into the line of fire intentionally."

E nods his agreement. "Walking into the lion's den."

"You think I don't know that? What else can we do? We have to get him half the delivery that we do have, and I'll deal with the fallout of the other missing half."

He snarls. "And by fallout you mean you're going to die? No way. We're all going with you."

I slam my palm on the table. "That won't solve anything. You're all in danger as it is. You don't need to be with me. You'll have time to get out of here or at least be prepared for them coming if I can't save our asses. It's only a matter of time before they find this place and you. Me, all I can do is beg. I don't have anything else to offer."

"What if you did have something to offer?" Grace's soft, hesitant voice floats across the warehouse.

All five of our heads turn her direction.

Fuck.

That's the second or potentially third time she was eavesdropping without us knowing it. This makes me look really fucking bad, like I have even less control than I've managed to fake.

I glare at her. "What the hell are you doing down here? Go back upstairs."

She winces slightly and pauses before continuing toward us. "You said you don't have anything to offer him, but what if you had something to offer him?"

Shock. She's ignoring my order to go back upstairs.

Preacher raises an eyebrow at her. "Like what? We can't get the drugs, and we don't have anywhere near the amount of money it would take to reimburse him for the missing ones. We're talking millions of dollars' worth of heroin."

She nods and takes another hesitant step. "I understand that, and that's not what I'm talking about."

"Then get to the point." Rion's order is sharp and clear. He's reached the end of his patience with Grace, and I'm sure the other guys are close too.

"What if you offered him a ship?"

"A ship?" I look over at the two docked in the warehouse and then back at her. "I'm not following. What the hell is Arturo going to want with our old trawler and the yacht when he already has access to them plus my entire fishing fleet?"

She shakes her head, sending her wild mane of auburn hair flying around her. "Not your ships. My ship."

Cutter sucks in a breath. Rion whistles, E eats his sandwich with an icy calm, and Preacher just stares at her with his arms crossed over his chest.

I don't understand what she's getting at here. "What do you mean, your ship?"

She closes the distance between us and steps up to the table. "What I mean is…he already owns you for all intents and purposes, but what he doesn't have access to is his own cargo ship. We can offer him that. Imagine what he could do if he had unfettered access to a ship like mine plus a crew we hire."

Jesus, she's serious about this.

"Obviously, I'd have to get rid of my current crew. There's no way they'd work with you. We hire people willing to keep their mouths shut for a certain price. People who won't ask questions."

"You have to be fucking kidding me." I hadn't intended that menacing tone, but it's the way it came out.

Grace isn't a criminal, and we've already made her an accomplice by letting her help us last night.

She recoils slightly. "No, I'm serious. Why wouldn't I be?"

"Because why the hell would you want to tangle yourself up anymore with what's happening here? Why would you want to drag your father's business into this world? Why do you want to drag yourself into this? You're free. You can go now. There's nothing more you can do for us. Your crew hasn't reported anything, and you said you're confident they won't, so you're free to just walk out of here and pretend none of this ever happened. Go back to your life, Grace."

Saying those words shatters me, but they need to be said.

She needs to go before she gets even more tangled in this madness.

"I'll have Rion, Cutter, E, or Preacher drive you anywhere you want to go."

Her bottom lip quivers.

Aw, hell. Don't cry.

She sighs and throws her hands up. "This will sound crazy, but I want to help because I like you."

Wow.

She whips around and points to the other guys crowded around the table. "Not these four. These four I don't trust within a damn foot of me. You," she turns back to me, "I do trust you. You've proven to me over the last several days that you would never hurt me. You're only doing what you need to survive, and I can't sit back and let you walk into what might very well be certain death when there's something I can do to help."

Rion's chuckle fills the void of dead air while I contemplate her words. "Well, well, well, Red's got some balls on her."

That she does.

From the moment she pulled that gun on me, I knew she had spunk. And her incessant questions and nosing her way into things that aren't any of her business demonstrated her real tenacity over and over again.

And she's right about Arturo wanting what she's offering. In fact, I'm sure he'd jump at the opportunity to not only get us on the hook for longer to make up for the lost drugs but also to have better access to the waterways and more flexibility with what we can carry and pick up.

But I can't let Grace put herself or her business on the line like this. It's just wrong.

"No."

Cutter leans forward and rests his elbows on the table. "Maybe we should listen to her and consider this more."

"Are you serious?"

Of all of them, Cutter is the last I thought would actually consider this.

He nods. "Do we have any other options right now?"

"Yeah, the original plan. Me going in and beg for our fucking lives and indebt ourselves to them for another ten, or twenty, or thirty years."

Cutter snorts. "Right, because that's a great plan."

"I'm the one who got us into this mess. You four can walk away from it anytime. I'm not about to drag a fifth innocent person into this."

"Am I really innocent anymore?"

Her question has me turning slowly back to her.

She raises her eyebrows. "I mean, I did scout out a robbery for you last night and act as a lookout. Doesn't that make me an accomplice of some sort? Can't I go to jail for that?"

A disgruntled noise rumbles low in my chest. "I would never let that happen. If the police ever found out, we would say we coerced you and threatened you with physical harm or death if you didn't help us. They would never charge you."

There's no way I'd let her go down for anything she's done while in my hands. I forced her here. I forced her to do the things she's done. She was under duress or some misguided Stockholm Syndrome that made her believe she had to help.

She shrugs. "And I could just tell them the truth. That I offered to help."

"Why the hell would you do that?"

"Because it seems like if I don't threaten to do that, you're going to walk into the lion's den with nothing more than a goddamn slingshot to defend yourself."

Rion snorts out a laugh at her biblical analogy. "I think

you're mixing your Bible references, sweetheart. David went up against Goliath with a slingshot, and Daniel went into the lion's den weaponless."

She swats her hand in the air in his direction. "Whatever."

The corners of my mouth turn up at that. She's not intimidated by him in the least.

"I'm just saying when you go in there, have the best ammunition you can—my ship. You wouldn't own it or anything. I maintain the business and everything in my name. My mom has nothing to do with the business, and my brother is deployed overseas and wouldn't want to know what's going on anyway. He's never had any interest, and as far as I know, the business isn't on anybody's radar and is squeaky clean. This is exactly what a family like the Marconis looks for, isn't it?"

Goddamn, she's smart.

And her willingness to walk right down here in the middle of our meeting and lay all of this on the line makes her even fucking sexier than when she had her hands all over me last night kissing me.

Which is exactly why she can't do this.

"No."

TWENTY

Grace

Warwick storms past me after his declaration and toward the kitchen.

Does he really think he can say that and then just walk away from me?

Hell no.

"What do you mean no? Where are you going?" I turn to follow him into the room where we shared our gourmet bowl of Cap'n Crunch only a few days ago.

He growls over his shoulder. "I'm getting some goddamn coffee to hopefully help with a pounding headache you're giving me."

Coffee actually sounds good. The exhaustion—physical and emotional—of the last few days is catching up with me.

I slept more last night than I have since they took me, but it wasn't deep and I kept waking up to check on Warwick. Him sleeping next to me last night might have something to do with my inability to stay asleep, or maybe it was just concern over his wound. Either way, it makes caffeine a necessity this morning.

It's too damn early to be arguing with Warwick. But, yet again, the man won't accept my offer. He can't look past the complicated layers of the situation to see what really needs to happen. This isn't the time to be proud or to reject potential solutions. This is the time to do whatever it takes to save his life and potentially the lives of all those men out there.

I step into the kitchen behind him. "Why did you say no? Why won't you let me help you?"

He walks around the metal island and over to the counter. "Because this is none of your fucking business. Because I don't want to drag you down into the quagmire my life has become. Things with the Marconis are only going to get worse, and you don't need to be involved in this clusterfuck."

His frustration and anger radiate off him, and the tension between us fills the room.

He doesn't get it.

"But that's just it, I am involved. Whether you want to admit it or not, I became involved the second you took me hostage."

He glowers at me and grabs a mug from a cabinet.

Okay, maybe not the best word to use.

Hostage makes it seem so…sinister.

And I guess it was…but like so many things…it's not so black-and-white. Not anymore.

He slams the mug down on the counter, pours coffee into it, and shoves it in my direction then repeats the process before returning the coffee decanter to the machine.

"Still, the answer is no."

His shoulder bumps into mine as he shoves past me and back out into the warehouse.

Asshole.

I'm trying to help, and he's acting like I'm just in the way. I sip at the scalding coffee and follow him.

"Why don't you want my help?"

Rion, Preacher, E, and Cutter all turn to look at us as we make our way back toward them. Milo lifts his head up from Cutter's foot and tilts it sideways, trying to assess the situation.

"It's not that I don't want your help, Grace. It's that your offer of help puts you at risk, and it's one we just can't take."

My heart aches to believe it's because he cares about me, and it's not just about the risk of them being exposed. But that's just stupid.

Isn't it?

It's just another symptom of Stockholm Syndrome—believing your captor gives a shit about you.

But he's not my captor anymore.

That makes this entire thing so much more complicated.

Cutter rises to his feet. His glasses reflect the overhead lights, and he glances between me and Warwick. "I hate to say this, War, but she does have a point."

He steps up to me, putting mere inches between us. Milo leans against my leg at our feet. This dog is so sweet and docile—so different from his owner who seems to constantly be in a state of simmering rage.

I hold my ground. I will not let this guy intimidate me.

He looks down at me, and all I see is my reflection in his glasses and the hard set of his jaw.

"I think her plan will work, but if you betray us, little girl, remember what I told you."

The words are ice cold and cut through all the bravado I'm pushing out while trying to maintain my cool.

Do. Not. Look. Away.

Do. Not. Flinch.

This man feeds on weakness.

Preacher clears his throat. "I agree with Cutter. We don't have any other options. This is the best chance of getting out of this alive."

Cutter finally steps away, back toward the table, and I glance around at all of them.

E nods. "Yep."

Warwick sets his jaw and looks to all the guys before returning his attention to me. "So, it's five against one, huh? It doesn't matter that I'm the boss here, or that this is my debt to pay?"

Rion chuckles. "Apparently not, dude."

Color rises into Warwick's cheeks as anger floods him. He hates being out of control, and he's been nothing *but* out of control since the moment we met.

A woman like me stepping up to him with a plan to actually save them all seems to be a little too much for him to handle.

I don't think it's a sexism thing, though, as much as it may *seem* like it. Warwick is the captain, the one who makes decisions and handles any situation that comes their way. He's the man who carries the burden of caring for his crew, just like I do. He doesn't want someone else stepping into that role, and my idea is just one more opportunity for me to stick my nose where he thinks it doesn't belong.

He scowls at each of his men, staring them down one by one, giving each of them a chance to crack under his assessment and change their minds.

No one speaks. No one moves.

Goose bumps pebble my skin. We wait.

Seconds.

Minutes.

Milo whimpers.

Warwick throws his hands up. "Shit. Since it appears I no longer have any say in anything that goes on around here, I'll offer the Marconis your ship."

I try my damnedest to fight the smile tugging at the corner of my lips, but I know I fail by the glare he shoots my way.

Shit.

I can't help it. Pride swells in my chest. I'm the one who found a way out of this for them.

Maybe with the use of my ship, he'll be able to get out from under his debt to the Marconis faster and leave all this behind.

Stop it, Grace.

That's just stupid, wishful thinking from a naïve girl, and despite what Warwick says, you are not naïve.

They'll never stop doing this. Even if he somehow manages to work off the original debt, plus whatever they claim from the loss of this shipment, what else will Warwick do? Go back to commercial fishing for the rest of his life? What can Preacher, Cutter, E, and Rion do? Though their histories are mysterious at this point, it's obvious something brought them here. Something they're running from. Something they have no plans to go back to.

They're committed to him and are inseparable. They're a team, an alliance, a brotherhood. That won't break just because they're no longer paying off Warwick's debt. And I'd be a fool to believe they'll go on the straight and narrow. Even with all the ways things have gone wrong, they're too good at this to just stop.

But at least he's taking my offer. That gives some hope of things changing down the line. At least it keeps them alive for the time being.

Hopefully.

Preacher grins and looks to each of the guys. "Good, let's get going."

Warwick downs the last of his coffee and slams his mug on the table. "I'm going alone."

Cutter turns to him. "Not this again. There's no way I'm letting you go in there by yourself."

If one of them had been with Warwick last night, things might have turned out differently. They might have gotten the drugs. Warwick might not have gotten hurt.

None of that seems to matter to Warwick, though.

"Like I already said, my battle, my debt."

E shakes his head. "Not happening."

The man doesn't say much, but when he speaks, it's definitive. Not something to argue with.

Rion flexes his hands at his sides. "Man, we wouldn't even be here if it wasn't for you. You expect us to just let you walk away by yourself?"

Warwick sighs. "Yes. That's exactly what I expect."

Something passes between the five men—years of unspoken history. Stories I'll probably never hear. Battles I'll never know about. The things that bind them together as brothers.

I swallow through the lump in my throat. "You're not going alone."

Warwick's head snaps back to me.

I square my shoulders and meet his eyes, holding their dark gaze. "I'm going with you."

He barks a laugh and shakes his head as he turns to walk back toward *The Destiny*. "No, you're not."

"Yes, I am." I slam my coffee cup down on the table and follow him. "Don't you think the Marconis will have a ton of questions about the ship, about the business, about me? Do you really think he's going to let you just tell him you have access to the ship all of a sudden and that's not going to pique his interest? I need to be there in person to explain what will happen, to work out a deal."

Warwick turns around and mumbles something under his breath before he stomps toward the ship.

I turn back to the guys. "Should I follow him?"

Rion chuckles and glances over at his friend. "It depends. Do you have a death wish?"

Preacher laughs. "You better go get on board before he takes off without you."

"Really?"

Preacher nods. E barely reacts, just sips from his mug and watches everything happening.

Cutter scowls and reaches into the holster at his side and pulls out a handgun. "Do you know how to use this?"

I swallow the lump suddenly clogging my throat. "Sort of?

My dad and brother took me out shooting a few times when I was little, but it's been ten years since I handled a gun. Except the shotgun on the ship, of course."

He steps toward me, and I move back. The hostility rolling off him screams for me to keep backing away, but he holds up his empty hand.

"I won't hurt you." He moves up next to me, and I straighten my spine. "This is a Glock. 1911. There's no safety. All you have to do is point-and-shoot."

I eye the gun in his hand. "That easy?"

He gives one curt nod. "That easy."

What Warwick said is true. This man is a cold-blooded killer.

That easy.

"Are you coming or what?" Warwick's words echo across the expanse of the warehouse. He leans over the side of the boat with his hands on the rail staring down at us.

"I better go."

Cutter slips the 1911 into my hand without another word.

What the hell am I supposed to do with this?

My hands shake as I tuck it into my waistband.

Rion nods in my direction, E remains silent, and Preacher offers me a half-smile. Milo whimpers, and I scratch his head gently before I take off across the warehouse.

Every step closer to *The Destiny* I take, the more my legs shake. Warwick turns away and disappears into the wheelhouse.

This will be a long trip to Chicago. A long trip in a small, enclosed space with a man who is very mad at me and kissed me like he couldn't get enough last night.

He was right when he said this was a clusterfuck.

TWENTY-ONE

War

The water churns in front of us, the waves remnants of the angry storm system that's just finally starting to break and move off to the east. The choppiness makes for a slow and bumpy ride.

It will take us almost all day to get to Chicago. That's far too long in the small wheelhouse with Grace sitting in the co-captain's chair, not even a foot from where I stand leaning against the instrument panel.

I don't need to be up here.

The lake is basically deserted because of the storms, and I know this water like the back of my hand. But I can't sit next to her. I can't look at her. I can't be so damn close and have her lilac scent enveloping me without losing my shit completely.

She should not be here. She should not be tangled up in this, and yet, I got outvoted by those four traitors.

I know why they did it, though. They think they're protecting me. They think there's no way I could've talked my way into some sort of agreement with the Marconis without her help.

And boy, does that fucking sting.

There was a time when they trusted me implicitly to do whatever it took to get things done. A time when there was no question I would bring everyone out on the backside unscathed. But it appears in the last five years, things have changed. Maybe I've changed. It feels that way over the last few days. And it's all because of her.

This woman is just...

Beautiful.

Frustrating.

Intelligent.

Infuriating.

Passionate.

Annoying.

Inquisitive.

And positively fucking breathtaking.

The more time I spend with her, the more I'm convinced I made the biggest mistake of my life climbing aboard her ship. Because she and I...we can never happen.

That kiss last night...

That was such a huge mistake. Even more so than the one the first day she arrived when I was so intent on shutting her the fuck up. Because last night's kiss wasn't about stopping something; it was about starting something.

We both knew it. We both wanted it. If it hadn't been for the drugs kicking in, I don't know where that would've gone.

Actually, I do know where it would've gone, and it wouldn't have been good.

Not for me. Not for her. And certainly not for the wound to my side last night.

I wasn't even thinking about that at the time. All I was thinking about was the sweet taste of her lips, the softness of her ass in my hand, the press of her stomach against my hardening cock.

Even now, the memory of the kiss has it straining to life, and I reach down surreptitiously to adjust my jeans.

This may be the longest Grace has gone without talking or asking a question since the moment I met her. Except maybe when she was asleep. After her call to the port and her crew to push back their return home for a few more days, she hasn't said a word. The crew seems to have bought that she needs a few days alone to decompress after what happened before she gets back on *Neptune's Daughter*, so at least it's one less thing to worry about.

But the silence between us is unnerving. There's too much unsaid.

"What did Rion mean back there when he said they wouldn't even be here if it wasn't for you?"

And there she goes again...

I glance over my shoulder at her, sitting with her knees tucked up under her chin, her bright green eyes trained on me. I turn slowly and lean back against the console and kick my legs out.

It was only a matter of time before she asked about the guys and their histories.

"Not my stories to tell, Grace. If they want you to know what brought them here, you have to ask them. They have to be the ones to tell you, not me."

And the chances of any of them opening up to anyone, let alone Grace, about their pasts is slim to none.

If there were ever five guys who consider themselves islands and are incapable of sharing anything, it's us.

Or at least, it was us. Maybe not me so much.

This damn woman.

She chews on her bottom lip and nods. "Fair enough. Please don't be mad at them."

I bite back a laugh. "Why the hell not? They teamed up against me and left me with no other choice."

"I don't know the history between you guys, clearly, but the last few days, what I have seen is that they are one hundred percent devoted to you. Those guys would die for you. They would do anything for you, and they're just doing what they think is the best thing to keep you safe. You can't be mad at them for that." She shrugs. "Well, you can be, but you shouldn't be."

A smile tugs at the corner of my mouth at the way she caught her words there. Because she's right; I am mad and maybe I shouldn't be.

She's also right about their loyalty to me and their loyalties to each other and about their motives for sending her along and agreeing to her plan. But they should know by now, after all these years, after everything we've been through together, that I would not let them come, and I would not drag an innocent woman along for the ride.

Although, I guess I broke that rule when I took her off *Neptune's Daughter* that day.

"Why do you care so much, Grace?" I raise my hands and lower them, the ache in my side reminding me it's almost time to take my meds. "I just don't get it. I know what you told them back there, but now, it's just you and me, so you can be honest. Why are you doing this? Why are you risking everything for us, for me?"

She drops her feet to the floor. I should back away, but there's nowhere to go—just the console behind me.

"Are we really going to play this game, Warwick?"

I really wish she would stop calling me Warwick. Hearing my name from those lips is like a fucking drug I can't get enough of.

"Are we going to pretend you didn't kiss me the other night and again in your bedroom last night? Are we really going to act like even though we're in a really shady situation there isn't some sort of strange pull happening between us?"

There definitely is, but this is far more than a shady situation.

This is life and death.

Why can't she see that?

Cutter gave her a damn gun, for fuck's sake. That alone should have told her this isn't some damn game. I glance over to where I tucked it next to the captain's chair when she showed it to me after she boarded.

The Marconis won't let us near them with weapons, so it's only going to be useful if they come at us while we're still on board, and something tells me Arturo will want to talk with us before he takes us out. Finding his cargo is far too important for him not to.

She moves closer, and my entire body tenses. "I would be helping you even if there wasn't. Because like I said, I don't think you're that person, and I couldn't live with myself if something happens to you or one of the guys and I had it in my power to stop it. But I'd be lying if I didn't say that some of the reason I'm helping is because of you. Because of who you are."

Who I am?

I growl a warning at her. "You don't know me, Grace. You don't know a damn thing about me."

She points backward in the general direction of the warehouse. "I know you did something for those guys that meant enough to them that they're willing to risk their lives for you and they're one hundred percent committed to helping you in this even though, like you said, it's your debt and your problem, not theirs. I know that you loved your parents very deeply, even your father despite him being a flawed man. I know that you're wicked intelligent because of the time and energy your mother put in giving you love of literature. I know that had your father not died, you would be in a very different place right now. A place where you didn't grab me and kidnap me and drag me back to your lair."

Lair?

I have to chuckle at that. "I never heard it referred to as a lair before."

She shrugs. "It's what came to mind. I know that you take

things that aren't yours and you're helping some really bad men. I know you're not a fucking angel, and I'm not as naïve as you think." She takes one more step toward me to within arm's reach. "I know that you'll do everything in your power to talk to the Marconis to make sure that your men walk away from this without targets on their backs, even if it means sacrificing yourself."

Shit.

She's right there.

I don't care what I have to do. I won't put them on the chopping block for me. And I won't let anything happen to Grace either.

If I get even an inkling that things are going south, I will shoot my goddamn way out of there to protect her.

"We're from two different worlds, Grace." I shake my head. "This whatever it is between us is nothing more than forced proximity and sexual tension. Stockholm Syndrome. It will fade."

She stares up at me from under impossibly long lashes. "How can you be so sure?"

Christ, this woman just doesn't let up.

It's time to lay out the cold, hard truth.

"I'm not a good guy Grace. I'm a criminal, and so are they. We would be doing this even if I had no debt to the Marconis because we're fucking good at it. I'm sure because I'm not lucky enough to have something as good as you in my life. I've done nothing to deserve it."

She inches forward, until only a step separates us. My heart beats wildly against my ribs.

"Don't, Grace. Don't put me in the position to fail at turning you down."

Her green eyes flash with need and beg me to change my mind. "What if that's exactly the position I want you in?"

Holy hell.

My cock strains against my jeans, and she presses her tiny, warm body against me.

"You better stop now, little girl."

She grins. "I might be little, but I'm very much a big girl and you know it. I'm a big girl who can make big decisions like who I want to be with. Regardless of the circumstances."

"Did you forget I robbed and kidnapped you? That you're my hostage?"

She pauses for a moment, and a low laugh slips from somewhere deep in her chest. "Not anymore. You set me free, remember?"

True. I did.

"Warwick, you are one very stubborn man."

I chuckle. "And you think you're easy, sweetheart?"

She shakes her head. "No, anything but. Which is why my mother and father always assumed I'd be alone forever. I'm not the kind of woman most men can handle."

"I'll have absolutely no problem handling you."

At least where sex is concerned. In every other area, Grace gives me and my sanity a run for my money.

We both know we shouldn't be doing this, but at this point, it doesn't matter. It's gone on too long, the dancing around each other, the sexual pull and energy brewing between us.

All regret can be saved for later. For this one moment in time, we'll forget the world and just feel whatever we want to. However…we want to.

She pushes up on her tiptoes and presses her lips to mine in a harsh, needy clash that's anything but gentle. For such a tiny woman, she sure knows how to take whatever she wants. And her fumbling hands at my waistband make it pretty clear what that is.

But I can't forget that the boat is still in motion. I need to keep an eye on things even though the radar doesn't show any other boats around and there are no hidden dangers in this area. I push her backward toward the captain's chair then turn so I can lower myself into it.

She pulls away and watches me with hooded eyes. I brush a silky strand of auburn hair off her face and tuck it behind her ear. She leans into my touch, and my resolve breaks.

I tug at my belt buckle, and her hand slides inside my jeans and wraps around my dick.

Holy shit.

It has been way, way too long, and I want to be inside her more than just about anything I've ever wanted in my life before.

I stand and shove my pants down around my ankles, and she reaches for the waistband of her pants. I brush her hands aside and slowly lower the clingy material. She kicks off her shoes and steps out of them.

Tiny panties cover her pussy.

All I want to do is take them off to see what lies beneath. To feel what lies beneath. To touch her. To taste her. To be buried deep inside her.

Her eyes meet mine as she pushes them down her thighs, giving me a full view of what I've so desperately wanted.

This may be wrong in more ways than I can count, but it doesn't matter in the end. We're just two primal creatures searching for something. Contentment. Release. It doesn't matter what it is, we're going to find it together. Or we're going to die trying.

She pushes gently on my chest, and I drop back into the captain's chair and briefly peer over her shoulder to check the water is still clear.

Doing this here and now is fucking stupid.

I catch her face in my palm and grit my teeth against the brush of her hand against my bare thigh. "Are you sure you want to do this, red?"

She nods and settles her thighs on either side of mine, spreading herself wide and exposing herself to me fully.

Sweet mother of God.

My eyes drift down between us to the tiny thatch of red hair between her legs. I slide my hand up her thigh and press my fingers into her wet heat. She moans and drops her hands to my shoulders. I flick and swirl and tug on her clit until she's practically dripping on my hand and ready for me.

She gasps and whimpers when I pull my hand away, but I grasp my cock and run the head through her wetness. She moans and rolls her hips, taking the head of my cock inside her.

Her head drops back, and she slowly impales herself on me, inch by glorious inch, sucking my cock into her body and searing my soul.

This woman owns me.

The grasping of her pussy walls has me gritting my teeth and digging my fingers into her hips. I hold her steady. "Christ, Grace."

Her head falls forward, and her eyes meet mine. Her tongue snakes out across her lips, and I can't resist anymore. I lean forward and capture her mouth with mine, and I drive up the final inch inside her.

White-hot pain from my side spots my vision, but I don't even care. The pleasure coursing through my body quickly overwhelms it as Grace clenches around me and moves up and down, working my length with her tight, wet heat.

"Oh, God, War." She drops her head back again, and I take the open invitation to press my lips against her collarbone and work my way up the exposed column of her neck.

Smooth creamy white skin meets my lips all the way up until I hit that spot behind her ear. I lick and suck, and a little mewl emanates from her parted lips.

"God, yes, just like that. Please don't stop."

Like I could…

TWENTY-TWO

Grace

He's hurting. Every roll of his hips, every thrust, it's agony for him and must be pulling at the stitches holding his side together.

But he doesn't stop, and I'm not going to ask him to.

God no.

Not when I'm so damn close. Not when every damn inch of my body is screaming for him to keep going, begging for him to push me over the edge to the state where none of this exists—no past, no future—just the moment of pure ecstasy.

Our bodies rock in motion with the boat, rolling and dipping with the waves. Wind batters the wheelhouse, rattling the windows and howling through any gaps it can find.

His hands dig into my hips with bruising pressure. His lips are everywhere—my neck, my face, my mouth. The rasp of his beard against my sensitive skin only ratchets me higher.

We breathe each other in, until our separate breaths become one.

I cup his face and gasp into his mouth. One of his hands leaves my hip and snakes between us. His fingers find my clit.

Oh, God.

I jerk and bite my lip.

It's all I need.

A few more seconds, and I'll be gone from this world. All that pent-up tension between us has boiled over and erupted into something combustible. Something toxic and explosive.

Something destructive and beautiful.

I don't know what came over me. Throwing myself at a man like that is so unlike anything I've ever done before.

It was like I was possessed. Out of my mind and body. Watching myself from above. Seeing myself give everything over to the last man who should deserve it.

Warwick took me and my heart hostage.

Who knows what the future holds? Who knows what will happen when we reach Chicago?

But at this moment, we're free to do whatever we want. And what I want is to come, to make him come, for us both to experience the great pleasure we know we can give each other. To forget all the shit swirling around us and just *be*.

I clench around him with each glide up and down. The large head of his cock drags along my G-spot with every movement until finally, with the swirl of his finger on my clit, my world shatters.

Bright lights flash against my lids, and I jerk forward. He grabs my hips and holds me to him as he pumps up into me, dragging out my pleasure while searching for his own release.

"Grace." My name is a prayer. A question. A promise.

Everything I've always wanted to hear.

And then he empties himself inside me.

I still and sag against him, my arms draped around his neck and his face buried in my hair, his cock still seated firmly inside me.

His chest rises and falls rapidly, and his heart thumps against mine.

"You okay?" The whispered words against my neck break the relative silence of the cabin, the only other sounds the engine chugging along and the lap of the waves outside.

I push myself back enough to meet his gaze. Those dark eyes have held so much over the course of the last few days—anger, fear, judgment, resentment, pain—but they flash with something new right now. It sends a shiver through me, not because I fear him but because I fear what I want from him so much.

He cups my cheek, and I nuzzle into it. "I'm fine."

His eyes shift over my shoulder at the water, and I follow his gaze.

"Everything okay?"

He nods. "We're getting close."

It's the last thing I want to hear.

Too soon.

I don't want this time with him to end.

We don't always get what we want in this world, but I've managed to carve out a little slice of it for one brief moment in time.

I slide off his lap, and Warwick stands and adjusts his boxers and pants. I pull my panties and pants back on and turn to him.

"Is your side okay?"

He reaches down and presses against it with a groan. "I'll be fine."

I tug up the edge of the shirt. Fresh blood blooms on the gauze.

"Shit. I hope you didn't rip open the stitches."

His shoulders rise and fall nonchalantly. "There's nothing we can do about it out here. Rion will take a look at it when we get back."

If we get back…

That goes unsaid, but he is thinking it. The way his eyes darken and he stares off at the water tells me it without a word.

It was the first thing that popped into my head too.

Things could go terribly wrong with the Marconis. We

might be taken out before we even get a chance to explain what we have to offer. They might listen but reject our offer outright and put an end to what they perceive as a threat—us.

My hands shake, and I wander over to the side of the console out of his way and stare at the water.

I haven't spent as much time out here as Warwick and his guys but it still feels like home. Or at least it did, until a few days ago.

Being hijacked, being robbed, being taken...I thought all of it might change the way I think about the water. The safety I feel here. But looking out at the rippling lake, all I see is beauty.

But a beauty that can kill you.

Churning waves and the remnants of dark clouds still drifting off to the east remind me this water can be deadly. It can kill, just as easily as the man standing next to me, the man I just gave myself to.

"Shit." I drop my face in my hands.

Warwick steps up beside me. "What's wrong?"

I shove my hand back through my hair and shake my head. "We didn't use a condom."

Warwick watches me for a moment.

"I'm clean, Grace. I just renewed my captain's license and got checked a month ago, and I haven't been with anyone since."

That's some minor relief.

But it's not what my curse was about.

"I'm clean too. I haven't been with anybody in almost two years, and I was tested shortly after but..."

His eyes soften and he raises his hand to brush a thumb over my cheek. "But...but what?"

I inhale slowly and try to steady myself before unleashing this on him. This could pull his focus away from where it should be—on convincing the Marconis to accept our offer. This could change everything—for both of us.

"I haven't taken my birth control the last three days because I've been here with you."

There it is. The daunting truth. One neither of us even considered before we gave in to what was building between us.

His eyes widen slightly, but he otherwise maintains his stoic expression.

This is a big deal. A situation I've never let myself get in before. The last thing either of us should be worrying about right now with what we're facing just down the shoreline.

He offers me a tight smile—one that's probably supposed to be reassuring. "When we're done with the Marconis, we'll go to a pharmacy…if that's what you want."

If that's what I want.

I don't know what the hell I want…

Other than I know I want him.

How fucking stupid is that?

Despite our terrible meeting, despite barely knowing each other, despite being on our way somewhere where our lives are at risk, I still want Warwick Pike.

But a baby with him?

Jesus Christ.

I'm not ready to be a mother. It wasn't even remotely on my horizon or within my realm of consideration before two minutes ago when I realized what we'd done. Having a baby is life changing. Having one with the man who kidnapped you… that's just…inexplicable.

I've made a lot of dumb decisions in my life, but this may be at the top of the list. Not sleeping with Warwick. That, I could never regret. It was everything I needed and everything I thought it would be and more. But not paying more attention…

That was very stupid.

"I'm sorry, Grace." He takes my hands in his. "It was really irresponsible of me not to think about using a condom."

"No, don't apologize. I'm just as much at fault."

If not more.

Something squawks on the console, and Warwick releases me and turns toward it. "We're almost there."

I nod and then wander back to the captain's chair. I climb onto it and tuck my knees under me. "What should I expect?"

Other than the few things I've picked up from overhearing the guys talking, I have no idea what we're walking into. I probably should prepare myself, but I didn't want to face the reality of what's to come just yet.

He sighs and shrugs. "You know that opening scene of *The Godfather*? Where people are coming to Don Corleone and asking for favors on his daughter's wedding day?"

I nod.

Who doesn't know that scene?

"Well, it's a lot like that only with more guns and more threats. *Il Padrone* is a harsh man, but he's not unreasonable. It's his nephew you need to worry about."

"Arturo?"

He nods again. "It's been clear he's been trying to establish himself firmly as the heir apparent the last couple years, and that includes taking a much harsher stance on some things."

"So, that's what he was doing calling you?"

He shrugs. "Sort of. *Il Padrone* doesn't get his hands dirty. The only times I've ever spoken with him in person was our initial meeting and when he advised me that my role was changing. Otherwise, Arturo is essentially the one in the family who does all the face-to-faces and issues all the threats."

"It really is like something out of a movie, isn't it?"

Warwick snorts. "Yeah, except in the movies, the people are getting shot with fake guns and walk off screen as soon as they cut. If they don't like what we have to say during this meeting, no one's ever going to hear from us again."

I shudder and wrap my arms more tightly around my legs. "Do you think they're going to like what we have to say?"

A suffocating silence answers me as he stares out at the water. Light rain pelts the panes of glass of the wheelhouse, and the northern suburbs of Chicago inch by on our right. Still, he doesn't answer.

He doesn't think this will work. He thinks we're doomed and floating to our deaths.

A chill spreads through my body, and I wrap my arms around myself and shudder.

Finally, he turns, drops down onto his knees in front of me, and captures my face between his hands. "You've given us our best shot. I'm sorry about the way I reacted before. It's just…"

"I get it, Warwick. You're the captain. You're their *Padrone*. You're the one who should be making the decisions and coming up with the plans. I'm just some girl you kidnapped who's trying to insert herself in the business that isn't hers and won't stop asking questions."

He smiles—the first true, genuine, complete smile I've seen from him—and the darkness in his eyes dissipates for a split second. "You're not just some girl I kidnapped. You're so much more than that."

And just like that, I fall even further down the rabbit hole that is Warwick Pike.

He's an enigma. A man made of everything unknown, mysterious, and contradictory. A man capable of thoughtless, selfish actions just as easily as selfless ones. A man who earned the love, respect, and loyalty of the men back at the warehouse and someone who managed to worm his way into my heart despite his best efforts to convince me to stay away.

A man who has the power to destroy me.

TWENTY-THREE

War

"Well, Mr. Pike, how lovely of you to finally join us."
The unease that's been creeping up my spine since the moment we pulled in to the docks, and increased after Marconis' goons shoved us in the black SUVs the moment we set foot on dry land, finally reaches my throat.

I swallow past it as best I can and grab Grace by the arm to lead her to one of the chairs in front of *Il Padrone's* desk.

The man sitting behind isn't the one I'd hoped for. Instead of *Il Padrone*, whose immense presence—both physically and psychologically—would fill this room but at least give us a chance to talk, is not here and Arturo occupies the spot of honor. In his typical crisp black suit and perfectly straight tie, he looks very much the mobster and every bit as lethal as he really is. His hard eyes leave no debate about how this meeting will go.

Not well…for us.

I slip my hand down from Grace's arm to twine my fingers with hers. A gentle squeeze is the only reassurance I can offer her right now.

"Please sit." He waves toward the chairs, and I release her hand so we can both sit.

225

Arturo watches us with his hands steepled in front of his mouth. Assessing us. Measuring us and giving us time to squirm.

I glance around the room. "Where's *Il Padrone*?"

The large room is empty save for two of Arturo's goons—one near the door and one standing behind his boss—and us, but all the photos on the walls and desk still contain *Il Padrone*. This is still his domain. His empire to run.

Arturo sneers. "You really aren't in a position to be asking any questions now, are you, Mr. Pike? My uncle is indisposed. You'll be dealing with me today. And luckily so, because he's very displeased with the situation."

No shit.

The moment we got off the boat, one of Arturo's men boarded to examine the cargo, and when he emerged a few moments later, his phone was pressed to his ear and he was barking something very angry to whoever was on the other side of the call.

We knew we were in deep shit. Nothing in the angry set of Arturo's jaw gives me any hope we're somehow out of it, either.

"It seems we have a problem, Mr. Pike. Actually, many problems, the least of which is the fact that you disappeared for several days with our product. But then you show up, and half the product is mysteriously missing. You can see how this looks. Can't you?"

I know exactly how it looks—like we spent the last three days selling off half his heroin and pocketing the money for ourselves. Like we betrayed him in the worst way possible.

It looks really fucking bad.

"It's not what you think, Arturo."

He releases a low, menacing chuckle and waves his hand. "Of course not. Because you would have to have a death wish to steal from me."

"Don't you mean steal from *Il Padrone*?"

Something dark flashes in Arturo's eyes.

Holy shit.

That's why I'm not meeting with *Il Padrone*. He has no idea Arturo is bringing in drugs. This is Arturo's side game.

It's never made sense to me, since the moment we opened those boxes, that *Il Padrone* would all of a sudden be delving into the world of drugs, let alone stealing them from someone else. If he were to do it, there are a dozen avenues he could have pursued to set up a supply chain that wouldn't require sending us to take it from someone else. It didn't make sense *Il Padrone* would be involved with heroin. That's because he isn't.

He probably has no idea what's going on or what Arturo has been up to. He's stepped back so much, handed over so many of the everyday duties and dirty work to his nephew, he's in the dark and doesn't even know it.

That little bit of information could come in handy in the future.

If I make it out of here alive.

"So, Mr. Pike, regale us with the harrowing tale of what truly happened to my product."

I glance over at Grace who sits shoulders slumped forward slightly, her eyes averted from Arturo.

"I assume it has something to do with this lovely woman you brought here today since we normally don't allow anyone into our private meetings."

And believe me, I would rather she wasn't here. Exposing her to this type of snake feels like the worst thing I've done to her. Considering what's already happened, that's saying a lot.

I nod and place my hand on her arm. "This is Grace Albright. She was the one who was the captain of the ship that was hauling the cargo."

Arturo's eyes narrow on her. "Her?"

"As unlikely as it seems." I nod and give her arm a gentle squeeze. "Yes. Her father passed away, and she was forced to take the shipment herself."

He scoffs. "Well then, I can't imagine your problem stems from anything that happened on the ship."

Ouch.

That one stings a little.

"Actually, Ms. Albright managed to turn on the emergency beacon as we were boarding. We didn't have enough time to unload everything because the Coast Guard was on its way out, and we had to leave with what we are able to get on board *The Destiny*."

Arturo frowns and nods slowly. "So, when I spoke to you the other evening, you only had half my product and you knew that, yet you did not tell me."

I cringe, and his dark eyes bore into me. "Yes. I was telling you the truth about the storm, though. It was far too dangerous for us to try to come down here, and we had repairs to do on the ship, but I was also stalling to try to figure out a way to get the rest of the product."

"The fact that you showed up without it tells me you failed with whatever plan you managed to cobble together."

Fail is an understatement.

I clear my throat and nod again. "Yes. We tried to get back on the ship at the dock to get the rest of the boxes last night after I spoke with you, but we couldn't get past security."

"So, what happened to my boxes?"

"They're still sitting on the ship, or they were discovered by the authorities investigating the break-in at the port, or they were picked up by whoever you were trying to steal them from."

He glowers at me over the top of his fingers.

That's right. I figured you out, motherfucker.

The drugs were never his. There wouldn't have been any need to steal them off the ship if he had paid for them and arranged for the shipment. He's taking them from someone else, and by the looks of the size of the shipment and the amount of money we're talking, we're not dealing with pissant street-corner drug dealers here. He's ripping off someone big. Someone who is probably just as dangerous as him, if not more so.

It's not the brightest way to try to get into the drug game.

But I bite back that comment because God knows I don't need this man any angrier at me than he is right now.

"Now, Mr. Pike, this is quite the dilemma. You see, I am in need of the items you were paid to procure for me. Now, I no longer have them, and I have individuals waiting for their delivery."

I nod but keep my mouth shut. I don't have an answer to that problem. Grace shifts uncomfortably in her chair. She knows we don't too.

"How do you suggest we remedy the situation, Mr. Pike?"

"Well…" I run my hand back through my hair. "We have an offer for you. A proposition, really."

He opens his hands. "A proposition from the pirates. I can't wait to hear this."

Asshole.

"Grace is now in sole control of her family shipping business. Her father is dead, and her mother is uninvolved. Her only sibling is out of the country. The ship is hers to do with as she pleases."

Arturo's dark eyes start to warm. He can see where I'm going with this.

"She has offered the use of her ship to you to make up for any losses incurred. If you can arrange another shipment…"

Or should I say, arrange a shipment in the first place, but I bite that back.

"Perhaps we can replace what was lost. We will ensure it gets here."

He drops his hands to his lap. "It's an interesting proposition, Mr. Pike and Ms. Albright, but that doesn't help the angry clients I have right now who want their product immediately."

"I know it doesn't." I shake my head. "Unfortunately, all I can say is you have to use your very impressive negotiating skills to work that out with them. What I'm offering you can not only make up for this incident, but it will also benefit you greatly in the future."

His eyebrows shoot up. "You mean Ms. Albright intends to allow this to continue even after her debt is repaid?"

She shifts forward in her seat, and her eyes flick over to mine before she nods. "Yes. I want Warwick's debt worked off as quickly as possible. This should help move things along."

Arturo's eyes dart back and forth between us. "And why, Ms. Albright, are you putting your neck on the line for the guy who apparently robbed your ship."

That's the million-dollar question.

I hold my breath and wait for a response to him.

"Because Warwick doesn't deserve to be stuck under the thumb of a piece of shit like you."

Oh fuck.

Arturo's men gasp, and his eyes widen.

You can't say something like that to Arturo Marconi and expect to walk out of here alive. I jump to my feet and put myself between Grace and Arturo. I hold up my arm. "I'm sorry. She didn't mean…"

But instead of the gunfire I'm anticipating, the sound of laughter fills the room, and Arturo drops his head back.

What the fuck is going on?

He presses his hand against his chest and chuckles. "Oh, Ms. Albright, you gave me a much-needed laugh. While I appreciate your honesty and your desire to stand up for your," he looks me up and down, "friend, you can certainly see my concerns with you offering me something like this out of the blue. I don't know you. I don't know your business. I don't know anything about this proposal. And yet you expect me to just accept it and let you walk out of here as if you haven't cost me millions of dollars."

I relax my stance and shift so Arturo can see her again.

She gives him a hard smile. "I would never expect you not to do your due diligence. You're a businessman, and I've been doing the accounting for my father's business for a very long time. I'm aware of how important it is to know everything you can about who you're getting into business with. We will stay here until you've made your decision."

He flashes a grin at her and then directs his attention to me. "Mr. Pike, it seems you found a very excellent business partner. When you came in here begging my uncle for help all those years ago, had you had someone like her at your side then, you may be in a very different position now."

Don't I know it.

Arturo pushes to his feet and reaches across his desk, extending a hand. "Give me a little while to look into this and make a decision. In the meantime, I'll provide you accommodations."

I take his hand warily, and Grace rises and holds hers out. He leans in and presses a kiss against the back of her hand.

My blood boils.

His fucking lips on her.

I want to leap across the desk and throttle him, but instead, I reach for her hand and tug her toward me and away from him.

"This way." One of the goons motions toward the door, and I turn and follow him, dragging Grace behind me.

She leans into me so he won't be able to hear her. "What just happened back there?"

I press my lips to her temple. "We got a momentary reprieve."

TWENTY-FOUR

Grace

"Stay here. We'll bring in food, and there's clothing in the closet and dressers." Arturo's goon turns and slams the door shut behind, leaving me and Warwick alone in the surprisingly opulent prison cage.

It's more like a spa resort room, actually, but there's no doubt it's a prison all the same. Just like the cabin on the *Calista*, this room appears to offer no way out except the door we just entered through.

I didn't know what to expect when Arturo said we had to stay, but it wasn't this.

A large four-poster bed and heavy oak furniture fill the room. All we know is they had brought us to some sort of house. We were shoved into an SUV and blindfolded. Something I never want to experience again. But Warwick held my hand and stroked it softly with his thumb, reassuring me that we would be fine, that we'd offered Arturo a good deal and he wouldn't do anything rash.

Yeah, right.

I would like to believe him, but I don't know the man, and from what I've seen and heard, I don't exactly hold out much hope we're getting out of this unscathed.

Being brought here raises my hopes slightly.

If he were planning to kill us, why bring us somewhere so beautiful and opulent? Why not just end it now?

"What is this place?"

Warwick drops my hand and tries the door handle. "It's locked." He ventures farther into the room. "I'm not sure where we are, but I think it might be Arturo's house or maybe a safe house of some sort?"

That was my guess too. "And we're stuck here until Arturo makes a decision."

He turns back to me and frowns. "It appears that way."

My stomach clenches the farther I move into the room. Captive again—this time at the hands of a true madman.

I pause at the foot of the bed. "I guess there are worse places to be."

Warwick's hard black eyes have softened to a steely gray, and his shoulders slump a little bit. "You mean like being held hostage in that shithole warehouse I live in?"

I don't answer because I'm not entirely sure what will come out of my mouth if I try to speak. Things have changed so much in the last few days. I've changed so much. I'm not the girl he pulled off that ship. I'm someone else and something else. Something stronger. Someone with my eyes truly open to the real world for the first time in a long time. Someone who can see him for what and who he truly is, even if he can't.

But it doesn't change how we met. It doesn't change what he did. It doesn't change that he will always be the man who took me hostage, even if he does have good buried inside him, hidden under the wall of tattoos and short-tempered anger.

Where does that leave us? What kind of future can we have?

I can imagine how that conversation would go...

"How did you two meet?"

"Oh, he kidnapped me."

I chuckle to myself, and he narrows his eyes on me.

"Grace, are you okay?"

Tears finally well in my eyes for the first time in a long time. I shake my head and try to swallow through a dry throat.

Am I okay?

"Is this about what happened before?"

I know what he is referring to—the elephant in the room. The fact that we did something incredibly irresponsible.

But it isn't even about that.

I'll deal with the fallout of that later if it comes.

This is about everything.

His quick, determined steps close the distance between us, and he takes my face in his hands. "I'm so sorry about everything, Grace. If I could go back, if I could do it all over again I..."

"No." I shake my head and press my hands against his. "There's no point in having regrets about this. What's done is done. Like I said, you didn't have much of a choice in all of this. You made a decision years ago that sent you down this path. You couldn't have known it would intersect with mine."

"Would it make me a huge asshole if I said I'm glad that it did?" A tiny grin plays on his lips despite everything. "I'm glad our worlds collided. I'm just so, so sorry I had to pull you into all of this."

He leans down and presses a gentle kiss to my lips. This one is slow. Determined, yet not the least bit harsh. So incredibly different from every other kiss we've shared, yet so much more meaningful.

One hand slips up and tangles in my hair to angle my mouth to where he wants it. His lips move with mine—soft, delicate, almost lovingly.

I sigh into his mouth and lean against his chest.

I need this now. I need *him* now, no matter how crazy that sounds.

I just do...

His hands slide down to cup my ass, and he lifts me with

ease to wrap my legs around his waist. I slide my tongue along his lips, and he opens for me. He moans into my mouth, and our tongues tangle slowly, languidly, tasting each other, devouring each other, learning what we can with what little time we may have.

The tempest of emotions I have about Warwick and our situation floats away on a wave of need and lust.

He lowers me to the king-sized mattress and sinks down on top of me. His mouth leaves mine, and he pulls back and brushes his thumb across my lips.

"You're so goddamn beautiful."

His eyes say more, but he reaches for the hem of my shirt without another word. He tugs it up and off and tosses it over his shoulder in one smooth motion.

If he's feeling the wound on his side or arm now, he isn't showing it. Maybe the adrenaline and hormones rushing through his body are masking the pain. He may regret this later, when the pain comes raging back, but for right now, I'm not reminding him of the consequences if we keep going.

My core aches for him as his hand slides down across the expanse of my stomach to the waistband of my pants. He pulls them off along with my panties, slowly letting the tips of his fingers brush along my thighs, sending goose bumps skittering in their wake.

I shift up and unhook my bra and let it slide from my shoulders.

He stands at the edge of the bed fully clothed while I'm naked and exposed to him in the full light of the bedroom that is our prison.

But it's a prison of my own making.

I chose to be here. I chose to be here with him.

I don't regret that decision. I can't. Not when his dark eyes are looking at me like this. Not when my body throbs and heats for his touch.

He unzips his jeans, slides them off, and kicks them to the

side. His shirt goes next, exposing the blood-soaked bandage at his side and on his arm.

My eyes go straight to it. "Shit. Your stitches."

He glances down and waves me off. "I'm fine. I will deal with it later. You're all I'm worried about right now."

Well, shit.

My heart flutters, and my hands itch to touch his smooth, hard, tan skin. I want to learn every line of his tattoos, drag my fingertips and tongue across them. I want to lick and taste every inch of him.

But he has other things in mind.

He grabs my ankles, tugs me to the edge of the bed, and drops to his knees between my legs.

Oh, God.

Warwick's tongue on me.

Jesus Christ.

Warm lips press against the inside of my thighs. Slow kisses spread across my heated skin, working their way closer to where I need them the most.

His tongue snakes out and glides through my wetness. An approving groan slips from his lips, mingling with my moan, and I bury my fingers in his hair and clutch him tighter against me. His hands shift up and slide under my ass cheeks, squeezing tightly and angling me exactly how he wants me.

Every touch of his lips and flick of his tongue send me higher and higher, driving me toward the brink of release or insanity.

I don't know which.

His dark eyes meet mine. They burn with a desire unlike anything I've ever seen, and like a moth to a flame, I'm drawn into it and give myself over to him with one more flick of his talented tongue, even knowing I'll get burned.

My orgasm crashes over me like a tidal wave without warning. This tsunami of pleasure rolling through every fiber of my being, stealing my breath and any words I could use to describe it. Drowning out reality and all the what-ifs and concerns it carries with it.

I clutch at his head, pulling him tighter against me, and he draws my clit between his lips and sucks hard to drag out my pleasure.

It's too much and not enough all at once.

"Oh, God…War!"

I push him away, and he slides back with a satisfied grin on his face. This is a totally different Warwick than the one who's been with me the last few days. This one isn't worrying about what's going on around us. This one is concentrating one hundred percent on what's happening in this room.

His hard cock juts out from between his legs, and he reaches down and wraps a hand around the base.

I shift back across the bed and drop my head back on the huge, soft pillows resting against the headboard. He climbs onto the bed and prowls toward me, a look of absolute devotion and determination in his dark eyes.

This man is on a mission to give us something we've never experienced before. A shudder of anticipation rolls through me, and I squeeze my legs together to quell the throb between them.

He settles over me and spreads my thighs with his, opening me to him.

Warm lips press scorching kisses to my breasts, across my collarbone, up the length of my neck until they finally meet mine. He glides the head of his cock through my slickness and pushes into me, catching my gasp in his mouth.

"God, Grace, you feel so fucking incredible."

He nips at my bottom lip and rolls his hips, driving himself even deeper inside me. I clench around him, and he stills with his lips pressed against mine. He groans into my mouth.

His eyes spark with the flame of need, and he pulls his hips back and drives into me. I arch my hips up to meet his thrusts, and he shifts his hands up to capture my wrists and hold them together above my head.

He takes control, setting an easy, deliberate pace designed to build us up slowly to release.

The kind that steals your breath and any conscious thoughts.

Every snap and roll of his hips ratchet me higher, coil me tighter. Heat blooms where our bodies connect, and every time his cock plunges deep into me, he grinds his pelvis against my clit, sending lightning bolts of pleasure vibrating through every fiber of my being.

"Warwick...please..."

I don't know what I'm begging for...

Release.

Apology.

Forgiveness.

Absolution.

Maybe all of it.

All I know is he is the man to give it to me at this moment.

I score my nails down his shoulder blades and dig my heels into his lower back, urging him forward harder and faster.

He grunts low near my ear and nips at the lobe as he hammers into me with deep, powerful strokes.

"Fuck, yes. Like that."

He clenches his jaw and rolls his hips.

The world explodes around me, and an ocean of rapture threatens to drown me in it.

Warwick continues to drive into me. He holds my hands over my head and makes love to me like the world may end tomorrow.

And I guess it might.

My orgasm drags on and on, a never-ending barrage of pleasure that only quells when he groans out my name and buries himself deep inside me for the final time with his release.

He collapses on top of me and rolls to the side, bringing me with him. His hands capture my face, and he leans in and presses a reverent kiss against my shaking lips.

"I'm sorry, Grace."

The words seep deep into my soul. He's said them before, but not like this. Here, wrapped in his arms, lost to the entire world, the whispered apology erases all the pain the last few days have caused. This Warwick is the one I always knew was there. The one I always knew would be a danger.

TWENTY-FIVE

War

TWO DAYS LATER

Grace arches back into me and moans. The sound vibrates through her body and against my chest, and I pump into her even harder...force myself even deeper.

That sound.

Every sound she makes when I'm inside her...

It drives me absolutely insane.

Any control I may have had disappears when I grasp her left leg and drag it up and back over my thigh, spreading her even farther open. My right hand clutches her against me, and I kiss the back of her neck and make my way across to her ear.

The taste and feel of her warm skin against my lips sends my heart racing.

This woman is everything...

And I need all of her.

I suck her earlobe between my lips and bite down gently. She bucks on my cock and digs her fingernails into my forearm where it's wrapped around her waist.

"Oh, God, War!"

"You like that?"

She nods and whimpers as she rolls her hips back to meet every thrust.

This. Being her with her here like this, wrapped up completely in each other, buried inside her, is the only thing good to come of this entire mess of the last week. The only thing that has kept me from losing my shit while we've been in here waiting for word from Arturo. Her. Nothing but her.

She clenches around my cock, and I groan into her ear. I snake my hand down to find her clit and roll it between my fingers. She mewls and tightens around me even harder.

"God, I'm going to come."

God yes…

There isn't a single sound in the world I'd rather hear than Grace coming. Knowing I gave her that release, that I caused that bliss…it's pure ecstasy for the male ego.

"Yes, come for me." I thrust into her half a dozen more times, rolling and snapping my hips with every drive forward and twisting her clit between my fingers.

She comes hard and beautifully. Her pussy ripples and squeezes my cock and drags my orgasm from me. I shoot my load into her, fighting the urge to bite down on her shoulder to mark her as mine, then she sags back against me.

Both of us pant, out of breath, and I kiss my way across her cheek and turn her head so I can get to her mouth. She moans into mine, and her tongue snakes out and tangles with my own.

"That was incredible." The words are whispered against her lips, just for the two of us, but I want to scream from the goddamn rooftops.

What I've managed to find with Grace over the last few days is something I never thought existed, something I never thought I could find, something that only appeared in fairy tale children's books, cheesy romance novels Mom used to read, and in the movies.

Something I don't deserve yet crave all the same.

I nuzzle against her, breathing in her lilac scent.

The door flies open.

What the fuck?

I scramble to pull the covers up over myself and Grace. She leans into me, and I wrap my arm around her, sheltering her from whatever's coming through that door.

Shit. What now?

It's been two days with no word from Arturo. That doesn't bode well.

Forty-eight hours of waiting for the worst. Forty-eight hours of waiting to die. Forty-eight hours of living like it's our last. That's been the only positive in all this—that I've been with Grace through it all.

But instead of Arturo storming in gun's blazing, a tall, beautiful dark-haired woman enters in a crisp, immaculately tailored black suit.

She doesn't bother to hide the weapons in the holsters at her sides. Shrewd hazel eyes scan the room before she turns back to the hallway. *"Tutto a posto."*

Who the hell is this? What did she say?

It sounded like Italian.

Over the years, I've seen most, if not all, of the Marconi goons, and not a single one has tits, or a presence like this. This bitch means business.

I can't imagine Arturo would let a woman protect him. He's far too misogynistic for that.

The man who enters isn't Arturo.

Il Padrone appears at least twenty pounds heavier than the last time I saw him and struggling a little bit more with each step. Despite that, he still demands the attention of everyone in the room and enters with clear purpose.

His eyes roam over us, and he offers a cordial smile, so different than the one Arturo gave us. This one holds hints of warmth absent from his nephew's.

"Mr. Pike. Ms. Albright." He holds his hands out. "My

apologies for not coming to see you sooner. My nephew failed to mention you were visiting. My nephew has failed to mention a lot to me lately."

Bingo.

Just like I thought. Arturo is up to something. Something *Il Padrone* is not on board with.

"I do hope your stay here has not been too difficult. Had I known, I would've released you two days ago, when you arrived."

I nod and tug the comforter up tighter against my chest. "Thank you, sir. We're fine."

For the most part.

"Excellent. I understand my nephew sent you to intercept some cargo that was not his to take."

Is this a trick?

If this is a test about my loyalty to the family, the wrong answer could cost me dearly. But something tells me *Il Padrone* isn't happy with Arturo and is only looking for the truth.

"Yes, sir."

He nods and crosses his hands behind his back to pace at the foot of the bed. "My nephew has been quite vocal about his desire to take the family business in a different direction." He looks over his shoulder at the tall mysterious beauty stationed by the door. "I have other things in mind."

What is he talking about?

He waves his hand. "But that is none of your concern. You're free to go. Whatever deal Arturo made with you is null and void. He was not speaking on behalf of the family. I'm the only one who speaks for us. The only terms you need to abide by are those of our original agreement which will remain intact until your debt is repaid. You will be dealing solely with me from now on. Arturo has to learn his place. And it's not behind my desk."

Holy shit.

It's a pretty strong statement about the man who, for all

intents and purposes, is his heir apparent. Things are definitely brewing in the Marconi house, things that will no doubt be affecting us all in the future.

"So, I'm free to go too?" Grace's voice is soft and wavers slightly.

I squeeze my arm wrapped around her shoulder, and she leans into me farther.

Il Padrone nods. "You are, Ms. Albright. Return to your business as if none of this ever happened."

As if none of this ever happened?

That's easy for him to say. Not so easy for me or Grace.

"One of my men will get you back to your ship as soon as you're ready." He offers a broad smile, and his thin skin crinkles around his eyes, giving him a warm, friendly vibe, almost like a grandfather instead of the deadly Mafia Don. "And again...my apologies that you had to endure this. I hope it does not reflect negatively on your feelings for me and my family."

He turns and leaves the room; the woman trailing behind him with only a quick glance back at us. The door clicks closed, but no sound of the lock engaging hits us.

Grace turns to look at me, her eyes wide. "So that was *Il Padrone?*"

I nod and run my fingers through her hair. "Yeah, that was him."

"And the woman?"

"I have no idea."

But she's clearly someone important to be at his side like that. Just another mystery that won't be solved.

"We're free, at least from the new deal..."

I nod and climb from the bed. I make my way to where my freshly laundered clothes sit. "It appears so."

"That's good then, isn't it?"

I nod again. "Yeah."

It is good, especially for Grace. It didn't really matter one way or another who I was working for. Arturo would've had me doing more drug runs no doubt, something I would prefer to keep my hands out of, but it wouldn't have been much different than anything I've been doing for the last five years.

For Grace…this means she's free. Not just from the Marconis, but from me and everything it would have meant to her and to her business to be tangled up with us and these goons.

She can go home. She can pretend none of this ever happened. As long as…

As long as she's not pregnant.

We won't know that for a while, and there's no point in speculating and worrying about something that may never come to fruition. What is important now is she's free.

And I won't be the one who forces her to stay.

I tug on my clothes, and she climbs from the bed.

"You're quiet."

My chest tightens. "Just thinking."

"About what?"

I sigh and wave my hand. "About what all this means."

"What all what means?"

"This…what just happened over the last few days."

Her brow furrows. "With the Marconis?"

"The Marconis and us."

She leans against the post of the bed, and her eyes narrow on me. "What about us?"

Christ, this will hurt.

But there's really nothing else to do but pull the damn Band-aid off.

"I never meant for any of this to happen, Grace—the kidnapping, you and me, any of it, especially not you and me."

Her bottom lip quivers, and I catch her hand before she can move away from me.

"I don't mean it like that. I don't regret a moment we've

spent together like this. Except that I wish every time could have been somewhere romantic and full of champagne and flowers and everything you deserve instead of on a shitty old boat on Lake Michigan or in a goddamn lavish prison cell."

I wish that so damn much, but it's nothing more than a dream.

"Grace, all of this...us...it's all just an illusion. We're not some fucking fairy tale. I'm not your knight in shining armor and you're not a damsel in distress. You never were. From the moment I met you, you had a goddamn gun pointed at me. You managed to do something no one else has in five years. You got the drop on us. You got a call out to the Coast Guard and a weapon on me."

It was pretty impressive and brilliant.

The look of determination on her face. The skittering of my heart when I saw that barrel pointed at me.

"What are you saying, Warwick?"

"What I'm saying is...you're free. Not just from the Marconis. From me, too. It's time for you to go home. To your business. Back to the life you had before we set foot on your ship. Back to a time when you didn't know me. The time when I didn't exist in your world."

A tear trickles down her cheek, and I swipe at it with my thumb. My eyes drift down to her flat stomach, and I swallow through the sudden tightness and dryness my throat.

"And if you're pregnant....it's your decision. I'm in no place to tell you what's best for your life, what's best for you. So, I won't stand here and tell you what to do. Only you know that. But if you are pregnant and you want to keep it, I'll take care of you. Both of you. But we can't be together. This life, my life is not anything I want you or a child tied up in."

No fucking way.

This isn't a world for love or children or family. The only family I'll ever have is the four men back in that warehouse waiting to see if I come back alive.

"It's why I didn't want to agree to your plan in the first place. I don't want you living your life looking over your shoulder wondering if something I did or the guys did is going to come back to hurt you. It's not any way to live a life. And I would know; I've been doing it for five years. You can hate me all you want, but I'm right about this."

Her tears flow in earnest now, and she chokes back a sob and presses her hand over her mouth. She shakes her head slightly. "I want to hate you so much right now, Warwick. But I can't. Because I know you're right. Your life is dirty and dangerous, and we're not the fairy-tale couple who gets the happily ever after. We can't be."

She pushes up onto her toes and presses her lips against mine.

The kiss says a thousand different things even though we don't say a single word. We fall into each other's arms.

Everything we can never say is all there wrapped up together in the slide of our tongues, the press of our bodies, and the shared breaths.

It's all we will ever have.

TWENTY-SIX

Grace

SIX WEEKS LATER

I press the phone to my ear and scan the numbers on my spreadsheet again. "I really appreciate your willingness to work with us on this, Mr. Matlock."

"I'm looking forward to it, Ms. Albright. Your father always had big plans, so I'm happy to see you stepping up and pushing forward after his death."

"I'm sure as hell trying."

God knows, it hasn't been easy. Finding a new crew was the first hurdle.

I didn't want to let my crew go and paid them a hefty severance the business really couldn't afford to keep them quiet and from asking any more questions.

They did everything right when Warwick and the guys came on board, but after everything Warwick and I shared, after everything that happened, I didn't want to spend my days hearing them talk about the pirate attack and how awful it was because...they really weren't that awful at all.

Cutter was an ass, E was angry, and Rion could be a real jerk. Preacher was just quiet. And Warwick...there's nothing to say there. No words that can sum that up.

But all in all, after everything I saw when I was with them, they weren't all bad guys, just guys who do bad things.

"I'll be in touch, Mr. Matlock."

"I look forward to it."

I set the phone down in the cradle and lean back in the big leather office chair that once belonged to Dad. I spent so many years on his lap here while he shuffled around paperwork and made phone calls. Yet, I had no idea what went into running this business.

Even when I was doing the accounting and handling the office, that only gave me a glimpse into what it really took. I can understand now how the stress got to him and why his heart finally gave out.

It could kill the strongest of people, but I'm not letting it kill me, and I won't let the business die.

Just like Warwick with his father's fishing company, something deep inside is telling me how important it is to keep it up and running.

I rest my hand against my stomach.

Maybe for future generations…

Not knowing is killing me.

I look at the clock and take a deep breath. He'll be here soon.

The set time and date we made before we parted ways that day. He's making that drive from their warehouse to Traverse City today to get the answer to the question we've both undoubtedly been asking all these weeks.

I have my suspicion what the test will say. I haven't exactly felt right lately, and I'm late. Only a few days, but stress can do weird things to the body, and there's no denying what I went through could fuck up anyone's system.

My stomach rolls.

Nausea because I'm pregnant or because I'm nervous about seeing him?

I haven't mentally prepared myself for having him walk

through that door yet. I don't know if it *is* possible to mentally prepare myself. Not after everything that happened.

It feels like some movie I watched long ago that just keeps replaying in my head over and over. Some cheesy old-time pirate flick with swashbuckling bad guys and a damsel in distress screaming for help who then gets swept away and falls in love with the captain.

I chuckle to myself. Warwick with long, flowing black hair and a cutlass is about as comical as me in a corseted dress.

I'd much rather dream about the real thing—inked, and hard, and passionate.

A car door slams outside, and heavy steps move up the sidewalk. My chest tightens around my racing heart, and my fingers tug on the pendant of my necklace so hard, I might snap it.

I didn't think I'd be so nervous to see him again, but the flipping of my stomach and the acid crawling up my throat has me wishing I'd taken a Xanax or something before he got here.

The door opens, and his massive frame blocks the bright afternoon light behind him. He steps forward and lets the door close behind him.

Warwick Pike in all his glory.

His black hair is a little longer and unrulier than I remember, and the beard that had grown in during the week we spent together is now full-blown, but the same dark gray eyes stare back at me and the same mouth that created so much turmoil and also gave me so much pleasure quirks up on one side.

I swallow through the lump in my throat. "Hey."

"Hey." His deep voice rumbles through me and releases some of the tension I've been holding.

God, I've missed him.

How is that even possible?

We only had a couple days together. Less than a week. It

was nothing. The blink of an eye in the grand scheme of things. Yet, he left an indelible mark on me, on my heart.

Silence fills the room between us, and he shifts his weight from foot to foot without taking his eyes from me. I wipe my sweaty palms on my jeans and rise from the chair.

"Well, let's do this."

He's here for a reason, and it's not for us to stare at each other.

I turn toward the hallway. A hand on my shoulder stops me.

He tugs on it, forcing me to face him and stare up at the man I've dreamt about every night since we parted. "Wait. There's something I need to tell you before we go in there."

My stomach clenches, and a cold sweat breaks out across my skin. "Is it the Marconis? Is everything okay?"

I'd be lying if I say I haven't worried and thought about it every single day. I've had the cold pit of dread sitting in my stomach wondering if Arturo or even *Il Padrone* set something in motion that could hurt Warwick or the guys or come back to bite me.

He lays his palm against my cheek. Without even thinking, I lean into it, and he brushes his thumb along my skin lightly.

"No. Something more important than that. Something I should've come to tell you sooner, but I was too fucking scared of what you'd say, about how you'd react. I was too fucking afraid of dragging you back into this."

Into what? What the hell is he talking about?

He leans forward and presses his lips to mine gently, then pulls back. "Us. What we so hastily started under the worst of circumstances. I know I told you I'm not your white knight, and this isn't the fairy tale. That's still true, and I still don't want you involved in this life, don't want to expose you to it, but I'm a fucking selfish man, and all I've dreamt about for the last six weeks was you in my bed when I fell asleep and in my arms when I woke up in the morning. You beneath me and on top of me. You asking all your annoying questions that make me want to scream and punch something. It's just you."

No.

I shake my head. "You don't mean that…"

He grasps my chin and forces me to look up at him. "I do. Every single day, every single hour, every single minute since you left has been agony for me. I never thought I'd find anyone I wanted to be with, who I wanted to give myself to so badly. And then you come along—quite possibly in the most complicated fashion in the history of two people meeting— and you changed everything for me."

For me too.

But he can't mean this.

Can he?

"We are tied into this deal with the Marconis, but now that my eyes are open to everything that's going on, now that you opened my eyes, I know it's time we need to try to get out."

"But how?"

His jaw tics, and he shakes his head. "I'm working on that. The point is, it's all because of you. Because you kept asking questions, because you kept pushing me even when I was a total asshole and didn't want to examine the things you so easily saw."

"You were an asshole. A lot."

He grins and brushes some of my hair behind my ear. "I know, and I probably always will be. It's that asshole part of me that isn't willing to let you go. That isn't willing to live without you."

Tears burn my eyes.

This is what I've wanted to hear, isn't it?

So why doesn't it feel real?

Because there's too much that has happened between us…

Because this can't possibly work.

"But this has to be your decision. The decision that you make free from any pressure on my part. I'm laying it out there for you, but you're the one who has to do something with it. If you decide you don't want to risk putting yourself in the line of fire again, I completely understand. If you decide I'm just too much of an asshole, I more than understand. And…"

His eyes drift down to my stomach

I lay my hand against it.

"If it turns out you're pregnant and you don't want my baby within ten feet of me, within a hundred feet of me, I more than understand that too. I won't do anything to put you or that baby in danger. It needs to be your decision to be with me, and if you want that, then I'll do everything in my power to make sure you and the baby are safe. If there is a baby…"

If there is a baby…

I wasn't prepared for any of this. I thought he was coming in to take care of the baby business and move on.

Of course, I've considered what a life with Warwick would look like.

Despite the danger, despite the unknowns, if I am pregnant, I have no doubt in my mind Warwick will protect me and the baby with his life. And so will the other guys.

We may never be a hundred percent safe…

But who is? Nobody.

And what's life if you can't live it with the person you want to be with, the person you are meant to be with.

Am I meant to be with Warwick?

All of this happened for a reason, and while anyone who knows the whole story on the outside may not be able to understand it, may not be able to comprehend how two people who met the way that we did could possibly ever be together, could possibly ever make it work, in the end, it shouldn't matter what anyone else thinks.

All that matters is what we feel and what we can make happen.

Warwick Pike appeared like a squall line on the horizon—

unexpected and ominous on an otherwise perfect day. Dark. Powerful. Menacing. He battered everything in his path and left behind the irreparable damage.

I never thought I could love a storm so much.

But I can't risk my heart to this man if there are any doubts on his part.

"You're sure this is what you want?"

He nods, and I blink away another rush of tears.

"More sure than I've been about anything in a really long fucking time. My life is all about uncertainties. But not you. You are never an uncertainty, not anymore."

Those are the words I didn't even know I needed to hear all these weeks. The ones that immediately fill the void in my chest that's been there since we said goodbye.

"Oh, Warwick. I've missed you." I throw my arms around his neck and bury my face against his warm skin.

He kisses my temple and squeezes me tightly.

I let him hold me for a moment, just savoring the feeling of his strong arms wrapped around me, his warm, steady breath against my ear, that rhythmic thud of his heart against mine.

I finally pull back because we can't delay any longer. "Let's go do this."

He nods and kisses me gently before I take his hand and lead him down the hallway to the bathroom.

He stares at the door and shifts awkwardly. "Do you want me to come in with you?"

I laugh and shake my head as I release his hand. "I think I can handle that part by myself."

"Oh, right."

Warwick nervous has to be about the cutest thing I've ever seen. The man is always so dark and broody, so intent on maintaining a stern, authoritative air. Seeing him like this, all discombobulated and unsure of himself, really is something I need to cherish because I know it won't happen very often in our future.

I pull the door shut behind me and turn to face the tiny bathroom and the pink box I left sitting on the counter for his arrival.

My heart has never beat faster than it does at this very moment. Not even with Warwick's gun pointed at me. Not even in front of Arturo or *Il Padrone*.

The next five minutes can change everything.

I suck in a deep breath.

Don't think about it. Just pee on the damn stick.

If I let myself think about it too much, I may have a panic attack, and that's the last thing we need right now.

What we need is an answer.

I get my business done, set the test on the counter, and wash my hands.

There. It's done.

Now, we just wait.

I open the door and lean against the jamb. Warwick hasn't moved from his position propped up against the wall just outside the door. His eyes meet mine. One corner of his mouth curves up.

"How long do we wait?"

"Five minutes."

His warm eyes darken slightly, and he opens his arms to me. "This is going to be the longest five minutes of our lives."

I chuckle and push off the jamb. I offer him a grin, and he cocoons me in his hold. "Probably."

Epilogue

WAR

R ion, Cutter, E, and Preacher stare back at me from where they sit around the table. I lean over the monstrosity, my palms flat against the harsh wooden surface.

They're waiting for me to say something.

Since I'm the one who called this little meeting, I better get straight to the point. There's no reason to beat around the bush.

This has gone on for far too long—the danger, the uncertainty, the inability to live for ourselves and decide our own fates.

It doesn't need to be this way.

Not anymore.

"It's time we did something about the Marconis."

A dark grin spreads across Cutter's lips underneath the reflective sunglasses. "About damn time."

Rion, E, and Preacher all nod.

I couldn't agree more.

I hope you enjoyed reading *Squall Line*, the first book in The Inland Seas Series. Book two, *Rogue Wave*, is available now at all retailers.

CUTTER

Complete the mission.
It's what I was trained to do—no matter what.
But when things go to shit right in front of me, my objective gets compromised by a set of fathomless amber eyes.
This isn't a woman's world.
Yet, Valentina refuses to see how dangerous the course she's plotted really is.
How dangerous *I* am.

VALENTINA

The man who saved my life is just as lethal as the one trying to take it.
Maybe even more.
While he may have rescued me, in the end, Cutter is my enemy.
The one intent on destroying everything I've strived for.
But the scars of his past draw me closer even though I know I should move away.

Cutter and Valentina.
Anger and desire.
Fight and surrender.
This wave may drag them both under...

AVAILABLE NOW: books2read.com/RogueWave
Sign up for Gwyn's newsletter to stay up to date on releases and other news: www.gwynmcnamee.com/newsletter

About the Author

Gwyn McNamee is an attorney, writer, wife, and mother (to one human baby and two fur babies). Originally from the Midwest, Gwyn relocated to her husband's home town of Las Vegas in 2015 and is enjoying her respite from the cold and snow. Gwyn has been writing down her crazy stories and ideas for years and finally decided to share them with the world. She loves to write stories with a bit of suspense and action mingled with romance and heat.

When she isn't either writing or voraciously devouring any books she can get her hands on, Gwyn is busy adding to her tattoo collection, golfing, and stirring up trouble with her perfect mix of sweetness and sarcasm (usually while wearing heels).

Gwyn loves to hear from her readers.
Here is where you can find her:
Facebook:
https://www.facebook.com/AuthorGwynMcNamee/
Twitter:
https://twitter.com/GwynMcNamee
Instagram:
https://www.instagram.com/gwynmcnamee
Bookbub:
https://www.bookbub.com/authors/gwyn-mcnamee
FB Reader Group:

https://www.facebook.com/groups/1667380963540655/

Website:
https://www.gwynmcnamee.com

OTHER WORKS BY GWYN MCNAMEE

The Inland Seas Series (Romantic Suspense)
Squall Line (Book One)

WAR

Out on the water, I'm in control.

I don't make mistakes.

But the fiery redhead destroyed my plans and

left me no choice.

I had to take her.

Now I'm fighting for my life while battling my growing attraction for my hostage.

Grace may have started my downfall, but she could also be my salvation.

GRACE

The moment he stepped foot on my ship, I knew he was trouble.

He took me, and now, my life is in his hands.

But things aren't what they seem, and Warwick isn't

who he appears.

The man who holds me hostage is slowly working his way into my heart even as greater dangers loom on the horizon.

War and Grace.

Dark and light.

Love and hate.

This storm may destroy them both...

Rogue Wave (Book Two)

CUTTER

Complete the mission.

It's what I was trained to do—no matter what.

But when things go to shit right in front of me, my objective gets compromised by a set of fathomless amber eyes.

This isn't a woman's world.

Yet, Valentina refuses to see how dangerous the course she's plotted really is.

How dangerous I am.

VALENTINA

The man who saved my life is just as lethal as the one trying to take it.

Maybe even more.

While he may have rescued me, in the end,

Cutter is my enemy.

The one intent on destroying everything I've striven for.

But the scars of his past draw me closer even though I know I should move away.

Cutter and Valentina.

Anger and desire.

Fight and surrender.

This wave may drag them both under…

Safe Harbor (Book Three)

PREACHER

When it comes to firewalls, no one gets

through my defenses.

For the past five years, protecting this band of f-ed up brothers has been my mission.

But Everly pulls me from my cave and does the one thing no one else ever has...

She makes me believe there's a life outside the world

on my screens.

Too bad actions have consequences, ones that threaten everything and everyone around me.

Including the beautiful tattoo artist who has managed to etch herself onto my heart.

EVERLY

The emotional upheaval of the last six months would be enough to break anyone.

And I can already feel myself cracking.

A tall, sexy, tattooed bad boy is the last thing I need thrown into the mix.

All I want is to keep my head down and pour my pain

into my art.

But Preacher walks into my life and offers me safety in a world where I thought there was none.

Until our pasts finally catch up with us…

Preacher and Everly.

Fear and loss.

Hope and heartbreak.

This harbor may be their salvation.

AVAILABLE AT ALL RETAILERS:

books2read.com/SafeHarbor

Anchor Point (Book Four)

ELIJAH

Life outside the walls of my prison cell is far harder than the time I did inside.

There, I had my misery to keep me company.

Out here, I'm forced to face the reality of

everything I've lost.

Nothing can repair the gaping hole in my chest.

Yet, a broken woman wrapped in chains threatens to unravel the tangle of excuses I use to keep everyone

at arm's length.

But letting Evangeline into my world means exposing her to the real threat.

Me.

And all the terrible things that come along with that.

EVANGELINE

Taken.

Enslaved.

To be sold to the highest bidder.

The monsters who stole me away from my life

have no conscience.

I'm not so sure the man who rescues me is any different.

He's an ex-con and a pirate— not to be trusted.

But the dark veil of anguish that shrouds him can't hide the truth of
who he is at his core.

Elijah isn't the enemy.

He may be broken and tormented…

And exactly what I need.

Elijah and Evangeline.

Agony and regret.

Faith and acceptance.

This anchor may pull them both down…

AVAILABLE AT ALL RETAILERS:

books2read.com/AnchorPoint

Dark Tide (Book Five)

RION

There is no black and white in this life.

The line between right and wrong blurs.

I'm constantly crossing it.

Saving a life is just as easy as taking one.

And I'm damn good at both.

Finding a woman who can survive in this world was never on the
radar.

But Gabriella pulls me from the bottom of a bottle and touches me in a way no one else can.

Too bad secrets and lies have a way of catching up with everyone.

GABRIELLA

How did I end up here, slinging drinks at a dive bar in the middle of nowhere?

The choices that brought me to this were never even a glimmer of possibility only a few years ago.

How things can change so fast…

And now, my path puts me on a collision course

with Orion Gates.

His bigger-than-life size and personality should

be a warning.

The profession he's chosen should be the ultimate

final straw.

But instead, I find myself unable to resist his pull.

A decision that could lead to the end of all of us.

Rion and Gabriella.

Lust and lies.

Betrayal and ruin.

This tide may drown everyone…

AVAILABLE AT ALL RETAILERS:

books2read.com/DarkTide

The Hawke Family Series

Savage Collision **(The Hawke Family - Book One)**

He's everything she didn't know she wanted. She's everything he thought he could never have.

The last thing I expect when I walk into The Hawkeye Club is to fall head over heels in lust. It's supposed to be a rescue mission. I have to get my baby sister off the pole, into some clothes, and out of the grasp of the pussy peddler who somehow manipulated her into stripping. But the moment I see Savage Hawke and verbally spar with him, my ability to remain rational flies out the window and my libido takes center stage. I've never wanted a relationship—my time is better spent focusing on taking down the scum running this city— but what I want and what I need are apparently two different things.

Danika Eriksson storms into my office in her high heels and on her high horse. Her holier-than-thou attitude and accusations should offend me, but instead, I can't get her out of my head or my heart. Her incomparable drive, take-no prisoners attitude, and blatant honesty captivate me and hold me prisoner. I should steer clear, but my self-preservation instinct is apparently dead—which is exactly what our relationship will be once she knows everything. It's only a matter of time.

The truth doesn't always set you free. Sometimes, it just royally screws you.

AVAILABLE AT ALL RETAILERS:

books2read.com/SavageCollision

Tortured Skye (The Hawke Family - Book Two)

She's always been off-limits. He's always just out of reach.

Falling in love with Gabe Anderson was as easy as breathing. Fighting my feelings for my brother's best friend was agonizingly hard. I never imagined giving in to my desire for him would cause such a destructive ripple effect. That kiss was my grasp at a lifeline —something, anything to hold me steady in my crumbling life. Now,

I have to suffer with the fallout while trying to convince him it's all worth the consequences.

Guilt overwhelms me—over what I've done, the lives I've taken, and more than anything, over my feelings for Skye Hawke. Craving my best friend's little sister is insanely self-destructive. It never should have happened, but since the moment she kissed me, I haven't been able to get her out of my mind. If I take what I want, I risk losing everything. If I don't, I'll lose her and a piece of myself. The raging storm threatening to rain down on the city is nothing compared to the one that will come from my decision.

Love can be torture, but sometimes, love is the only thing that can save you.

AVAILABLE AT ALL RETAILERS:

Books2read.com/Tortured-Skye

Stone Sober (The Hawke Family - Book Three)

She's innocent and sweet. He's dark and depraved.

Stone Hawke is precisely the kind of man women are warned about — handsome, intelligent, arrogant, and intricately entangled with some dangerous people. I should stay away, but he manages to strip my soul bare with just a look and dominates my thoughts. Bad decisions are in my past. My life is (mostly) on track, even if it is no longer the one to medical school. I can't allow myself to cave to the fierce pull and ardent attraction I feel toward the youngest Hawke.

Nora Eriksson is off-limits, and not just because she's my brother's employee and sister-in-law. Despite the fact she's stripping at The Hawkeye Club, she has an innocent and pure heart. Normally, the only thing that appeals to me about innocence is the opportunity to taint it. But not when it comes to Nora. I can't expose her to the filth permeating my life. There are too many things I can't control, things completely out of my hands. She doesn't deserve any of it, but the power she holds over me is stronger than any addiction.

The hardest battles we fight are often with ourselves, but only through defeating our own demons can we find true peace.

AVAILABLE AT ALL RETAILERS:

books2read.com/StoneSober

Building Storm (The Hawke Family - Book Four)

She hasn't been living. He's looking for a way to forget it all.

My life went up in flames. All I'm left with is my daughter and ashes. The simple act of breathing is so excruciating, there are days I wish I could stop altogether. So I have no business being at the party, and I definitely shouldn't be in the arms of the handsome stranger. When his lips meet mine, he breathes life into me for the first time since the day the inferno disintegrated my world. But loving again isn't in the cards, and there are even greater dangers to face than trying to keep Landon McCabe out of my heart.

Running is my only option. I have to get away from Chicago and the betrayal that shattered my world. I need a new life-one without attachments. The vibrancy of New Orleans convinces me it's possible to start over. Yet in all the excitement of a new city, it's Storm Hawke's dark, sad beauty that draws me in. She isn't looking for love, and we both need a hot, sweaty release without feelings getting involved. But even the best laid plans fail, and life can leave you burned.

Love can build, and love can destroy. But in the end, love is what raises you from the ashes.

AVAILABLE AT ALL RETAILERS:

books2read.com/BuildingStorm

Tainted Saint (The Hawke Family - Book Five)

He's searching for absolution. She wants her happily ever after.

Solomon Clarke goes by Saint, though he's anything but. After lusting for him from afar, the masquerade party affords me the anonymity to pursue that attraction without worrying about the fall-out of hooking-up with the bouncer from the Hawkeye Club. From the second he lays his eyes and hands on me, I'm helpless to resist him. Even burying myself in a dangerous investigation can't erase the memory of our combustible connection and one night together. The only problem… he has no idea who I am.

Caroline Brooks thinks I don't see her watching me, the way her eyes rake over me with appreciation. But I've noticed, and the party is the perfect opportunity to unleash the desire I've kept reined in for so damn long. It also sets off a series of events no one sees coming. Events that leave those I love hurting because of my failures. While the guilt eats away at my soul, Caroline continues to weigh on my heart. That woman may be the death of me, but oh, what a way to go.

Life isn't always clean, and sometimes, it takes a saint to do the dirty work.

AVAILABLE AT ALL RETAILERS:

books2read.com/TaintedSaint

Steele Resolve (The Hawke Family - Book Six)

For one man, power is king. For the other, loyalty reigns.

Mob boss Luca "Steele" Abello isn't just dangerous—he's lethal. A master manipulator, liar, and user, no one should trust a word that comes out of his mouth. Yet, I can't get him out of my head. The time we spent together before I knew his true identity is seared into my brain. His touch. His voice. They haunt my every waking hour and occupy my dreams. So does my guilt. I'm literally sleeping with the enemy and betraying the only family I've ever had. When I come clean, it will be the end of me.

Byron Harris is a distraction I can't afford. I never should have let it go beyond that first night, but I couldn't stay away. Even when I learned who he was, when the *only* option was to end things, I kept going back, risking his life and mine to continue our indiscretion. The truth of what I am could get us both killed, but being with the man who's such an integral part of the Hawke family is even more terrifying. The only people I've ever cared about are on opposing sides, and I'm the rift that could end their friendship forever.

Love is a battlefield isn't just a saying. For some, it's a reality.

AVAILABLE AT ALL RETAILERS:

books2read.com/SteeleResolve

The Deadliest Sin Series (Dark Romance)

WRATH (Book One)

All I see is red.

Blood.

Pain.

Rage.

It consumes me.

The moment he took her, wrath invaded my soul.

I only have one purpose.

End him and take back what's mine.

Love isn't always clean, and wrath is the deadliest sin.

AFTER WRATH (Book Two)

They took something from me.

Something that can never be replaced.

They destroyed something.

Something that can never be repaired.

Only one thing can appease the burning rage in my soul.

Unleashing my wrath on those responsible.

The Dragon will rise.

Death will reign.

Because wrath is the deadliest sin.

SURVIVING WRATH (Book Three)

I fled into the night and didn't look back.

I grieved.

I loved.

Then he appears.

Dark.

Dangerous.

I never thought wrath would find me again.

But you can't run from it.

Not when wrath is the deadliest sin

The Slip Series (Romantic Comedy)

Dickslip (A Scandalous Slip Story #1)

One wardrobe malfunction. Two lives forever changed.

Playing in a star-studded charity basketball game should be fun, and it is, until I literally go balls out to show up my arch nemesis. When I dive for the basketball and my junk slips out of my gym shorts, I know my life and career are over. There's no way the network can keep my kids' show on the air after I've exposed myself to millions of people. I don't know how Andy, the new CEO, can go to bat for me with such passion. I also never anticipate how hot she looks in a pair of high heels.

Rafe's dickslip has made my new job even more stressful. It's hard enough being a woman in a man's world without dealing with sex organs being publicly displayed when someone is representing the company. But he's an asset to the network, not to mention hot as hell. I can barely keep my eyes off him or his crotch during our meetings. Defending him to the board puts my ass on the line as much as his, but it's worth it. So is risking my job to fulfill the fantasies I've had about him since he first set foot in my office.

Things may have started out bad, but… some accidents have happy endings.

AVAILABLE AT ALL RETAILERS:

www.Books2read.com/Dickslip

Nipslip (A Scandalous Slip Story #2)

One nipple. A world of problems.

I own the runway. Until my nipple pops out of my dress during New York Fashion Week and it suddenly owns me. Being called a worthless gutter slut by a fuming designer is the least of my problems. My career is swirling around the toilet like the other models' lunches. Until smoking hot Tate Decker steps in with a crazy idea about how his magazine can maybe salvage my livelihood.

It's less than two feet in front of me. Perfect and perky and pink. And the woman it's attached to looks absolutely horrified. I need to help her, and not just because she's beautiful and has a perfect rack. Using my position in the industry to expose the volatile nature of our business puts my career in jeopardy in an attempt to save Riley's. I'm willing to risk that, but falling for her isn't part of the plan.

When love and tits are involved... Things can get slippery.

AVAILABLE AT ALL RETAILERS:

www.Books2read.com/Nipslip

Beaver Blunder (A Scandalous Slip Story #3)

One brief mistake. A world of hurt.

No panties. No problem. At least until I slip on the wet floor and go heels over head in front of my colleagues and half the courthouse. Returning to consciousness can't be more awkward, until I find out who my sexy, argumentative, and bossy knight in shining armor really is. My career may not survive my beaver blunder, and my heart might not survive Owen Grant.

Madeline Ryan tumbles into my life on a wave of perfume and public embarrassment. She falls and exposes herself in front of me, and I find myself falling for her despite the fact she fights me every chance she gets. Being a woman in a good ol' boy profession demands a certain brashness, but it definitely has me thinking, maybe litigators shouldn't be lovers.

With stressful jobs and big attitudes, going commando has never been so freeing.

www.ingramcontent.com/pod-product-compliance
Lightning Source LLC
Chambersburg PA
CBHW060305260626
47160CB00007B/2507